Cloud 9 minus one

Cloud 9 minus one

SANGEETA MALL

HarperCollins *Publishers* India
a joint venture with

New Delhi

First published in India in 2009 by
HarperCollins *Publishers* India
a joint venture with
The India Today Group

ISBN: 978-81-7223-851-3

2 4 6 8 10 9 7 5 3 1

HarperCollins *Publishers*
A-53, Sector 57, NOIDA, Uttar Pradesh – 201301, India
77-85 Fulham Palace Road, London W6 8JB, United Kingdom
Hazelton Lanes, 55 Avenue Road, Suite 2900, Toronto, Ontario M5R 3L2
and 1995 Markham Road, Scarborough, Ontario M1B 5M8, Canada
25 Ryde Road, Pymble, Sydney, NSW 2073, Australia
31 View Road, Glenfield, Auckland 10, New Zealand
10 East 53rd Street, New York NY 10022, USA

Typeset in 10/13 Garamond Premier Pro
Jojy Philip New Delhi 110015

Printed and bound at
Thomson Press (India) Ltd.

This book is for...

My father, Raimohan Pal, for having a dream.
My husband, Damodar Mall, for having a vision.

Just a Story

While writing this book, I have taken many liberties with facts. The description of the IIM, Bangalore campus is only slightly accurate. And unlike the characters portrayed here, my professors were some of the sharpest minds in the industry. IIM purists might quibble with some of the descriptions and settings that I have created. To them I say, this is fiction, and facts are always incidental to a good story. People might ask why I chose the IIM, if I didn't want to be true to its layout. I chose it because, like all bad students but good loyalists, it is in my blood, and I wanted it to figure in my first novel. So if you don't like the way I've fooled around with the 'real' IIM, ignore that part and enjoy the rest of the book.

A Special Debt

While I was giving the final touches to this book, my husband Damodar fell critically ill. My heart said he would survive, but my brain, receiving daily medical inputs, said otherwise. It was a shattering experience, made bearable only by the generosity of hundreds of friends who gave of their time and almost boundless sympathy.

In any relationship there are people who give when asked to give, and there are others who just give without ever being asked. But there are very few people who step forward for no good reason than that it's their chosen role in life, to reach out to people in need with all their resources, including money. Without ever meeting anyone like this, I described such a person in this novel, Priya. And then, just on the eve of its publishing, I actually met, not one, but two such people.

It just so happens that Kishore and Sangita Biyani are married to each other. Both of them, individually, have taken on the task of nurturing wounded birds only because the birds need it. They care about people in need, and Damodar and I were two such people. So they cared about us and for us.

I count myself fortunate that I needed their care. It has shown me what real generosity is. Thank you, Kishoreji and Sangitaji. You brought our very rocky vessel ashore with grace and dignity. And proved that real goodness can exist outside the pages of fiction.

1

'Are you sure?' the man at the desk asks sternly. He has a sour face, as though his task is repulsive, even unnatural.

'Of course I'm sure! *We* are sure,' says the bride, looking at her husband-to-be with a smile that spreads all the way across the room. The groom smiles back, and the rest of the bridal party seems to take a step back, as though it doesn't wish to intrude upon so much love.

A few words, a couple of signatures, a small form filled by the registrar, and it's all over. The newlyweds look dazed. I can't blame them. To enter a new life with the stroke of a pen is a shattering experience. The lack of ceremony only enhances the sense of unreality. In that noisy, shabby place, with its mixture of stinking paper and dust, nobody is given the right to feel married, to feel loved and wanted. The registrar's office of Bangalore, like registrar offices all over the country, registers everything – lease agreements, property sale agreements, marriage, whatever. Of course, the registrar can't favour marriage. Why should he? It has nothing to do with him, two people affirming their vows. He's just there to ensure that the mandatory forms are filled in, the necessary witnesses are present and, of course, the required fees are paid. If it were two trees getting married, there still wouldn't be a problem in that place if all these conditions were met.

We almost stampede out of the ten by ten feet room, glad to breathe some air, even if it is only to breathe the carbon monoxide laden fumes of Bangalore city. There is traffic everywhere on M. G. Road, on the road and on the sidewalk, but everyone seems to know that we belong to a marriage party and the traffic automatically skirts around us. We step away from the newlyweds, but they want none of that. The bride links her arm through mine while her husband is instantly surrounded by friends and family and I know that in some ways, this is still a conventional Indian wedding.

While we mill around on the sidewalk in a bemused state of limbo, I do what all married women do when they attend a wedding – think about my own. Eighteen years ago, I was the shy bride, impatiently awaiting the moment when I could finally be alone with Kailash and for once forget that there was a world outside that was perpetually intruding into my consciousness, demanding, demanding, demanding. The memory impels me to usher all the people hovering around the couple into the waiting taxis taking us to the next part of the event. I push forward with all that stuff, stuff that will get the bride and groom alone quickly, so that they, too, can forget the world.

✍

Rewind to four months ago.

'We write to confirm your participation in the seminar on "Theatre and Semiotics" that is going to be held from _ to _ June 2008 at __ Conference Centre. The organizers will arrange for your stay and travel from Philadelphia to New Delhi and back for this period. You will be a speaker in the panel discussion "Theatre: Moving across Boundaries". The detailed programme is attached.

Please send us your travel details so that we can make the necessary arrangements for meeting you at the airport.'

The email stared at me. I was sitting in my office, and this was the fourth mail I had opened. Kailash had forwarded the mail to me without any subject, and it came as a knockout blow. I vaguely remembered Kailash mentioning something about an invitation and laughing that for a change he was being paid to do what he loved doing anyway, i.e. going to India. But I hadn't been paying any attention then. The past year had been insanely frantic at work. I felt as though I was doing the job of ten people, and wondering why I should bother with such slavery, for isn't that what it was? I envied Kailash his easygoing existence, promptly forgetting the long hours he put in at home, assessing student papers, and the myriad other tasks that an associate professor of theatre was expected to perform at the University of Pennsylvania.

The invitation to the symposium was, in a way, a reward for his brilliance. It wasn't the first invitation he had received, but usually they were from somewhere closer, like New York City. Even San Francisco was too far for him to be invited. But obviously, the Indian organizers didn't think so.

Of course, I was proud of my husband. It was an honour to be invited to speak at such a prestigious event. And if I was a tad jealous of his fame, well, I brushed aside my jealousy. I might not be as well-known as him but I was making great strides in my own career, even though it didn't feel like it sometimes, when I was calling the plumber to fix a pipe in one of the cottages, for instance. Or when I waited for hours at the airport to pick up a guest, since the hospitality associate had quit for a job as an investment banker and I hadn't found a replacement.

'How come I don't get an invite to a fancy do at Ooty or someplace?' I asked Kailash that evening. 'Don't they need writers' colonies there? I'm sure there are enough writers in that country now.'

'I guess they don't need them as much as they need theatre directors,' said Kailash, his eyes gleaming mischievously.

'Theatre!' I snorted. 'Who needs theatre? It's such a bourgeois activity! Too expensive for one, and far too snobbish. And all that politics is so damn outdated!'

'Order, order!' said Kailash, tapping the table with his spoon. 'There are young kids here. Mind your language!'

The kids giggled as though on cue, and I glared at my husband. 'Leave the children out of this.'

'Of course! We can continue this discussion after dinner.'

I knew what that meant. Most of our discussions ended up on the rug in front of the fireplace. But this time I was going to stand firm. 'So how come theatre guys in India have become so rich?' I continued. 'How can they afford an international symposium?'

'Does it matter? I don't care where they get their money from, so long as they pay for my expenses. The point is, do you guys want to come along?'

For a moment there was complete silence. Even the children stopped eating. Come along? To India? Just as though he were asking us to go for a morning stroll with him! I hadn't been home in three years, and the children in five. There was never an appropriate time to go. If my mother hadn't died, I wouldn't even have gone three years ago. And after that, there was no real reason to return.

I swallowed my heart, which had suddenly leapt into my throat at Kailash's bombshell, and said, 'You want us to go with you?'

'Hmm!' he replied, as he tried to prise some lobster out of its shell, seemingly unaware of the silent shrapnel of doubts and questions flying around. 'Might as well. We can have a holiday together. See the Taj and so forth. I'm sure we have enough saved up to do that. The children will enjoy it, won't you guys?'

Isha and Rohan were too bemused to answer this casual query. For them, India was a forgotten dream. Isha was five when we left India, certainly too young to retain any memories, while Rohan, two years older, would also have just the haziest of recollections.

'But what will we do there?'

'Shruti, what does one do on vacation?' asked Kailash patiently. 'Especially in India? One sees some places, one meets some people, one eats some food. Come to think of it, that's so *unusual*, right?'

'We were thinking of going to Spain this year,' I continued, ignoring his sarcasm.

'So we'll go to Spain next year. Spain isn't running off anywhere, not for another year at least. Let's do India this year.'

'In the summer?'

'Is it very hot there in the summer?' asked Isha.

'Very,' Kailash and I said in unison. 'But what's a little heat when we're together, huh?' continued Kailash. 'You can be in the pool all day long.'

Isha smiled, the swimmer that she is, and I knew we were going. Isha and Kailash, they were the ones who always took the decisions in the family. Rohan just nodded when I asked him what he wanted to do and I knew that while I could only propose, it was my daughter and husband who disposed.

There is a difference between prescience and foresight, and I am the first to admit that I have neither. I had certainly not anticipated this day when I had deleted that email from my inbox ten months ago.

'Hey guys, twenty years are almost over. How about getting together where we first met, getting drunk, getting stoned, getting friendly once again. And not to mention, getting our families.'

The alliteration had just added to my irritation. I hadn't seen my classmates, any of them, for twenty years, and suddenly I was being asked, in such a fearfully cheerful tone, to meet them. Why should I? In Bangalore, of all places. In the summer, of all times. My instinctive response had been, no way! What if Priya was there?

Of course, I hadn't told Kailash about any of this. Why should I? He and I, we were after and beyond my IIM days, and I was happy to let things remain that way. In books, chapters were connected, but life, I knew, wasn't a book of chapters. It was a set of rooms, and as one moved forward, one shut the doors behind. And I had shut the IIM door a long time ago. There was really no need to open it now. Kailash, I knew, didn't expect it either.

But though I was reluctant to go to India at that particular time, I still decided to check with Xenia the next day about my doubts, without telling her what the main one was. Xenia Jones is a co-worker of sorts. She is co, but I'm not so sure about worker. She told me once that she was with me only because I needed help. I had let the statement pass. One always took Xenia with a sense of humour.

That day she looked the way she always looks. Xenia has turned fashion into a bizarre statement of protest in the form of mutating current styles to suit her personality. That morning she wore a pencil skirt that had a flounce just at the hem, making her look like a ridiculous, uptight hen. Xenia is anything but uptight, as the blouse she was wearing with the skirt proved. It was fuchsia and flouncy, and the skirt and blouse were merrily clashing with each other under the guidance of the chef's hat that perched, two sizes too small and azure blue, on the woman's pink curls. Xenia looked like tropical foliage gone wild, and the twinkle in her eye said she knew it.

Xenia is the cook at the Big Creek Writers' Colony. I am the manager. The colony is a set of twenty five cottages situated on a twenty-five-acre plot of land outside Philadelphia, each cottage containing two independent dwelling units, so that the occupants do not need to see each other if they don't have to, though once one writer said to me over breakfast, 'Fucking writers! Always pee at three in the morning. I'm not complaining about the peeing. It's the flushing that's annoying. Why can't they leave it alone till morning?'

My job is to listen to such absurdities and decide what is worth paying attention to. Xenia is the resident chef, and her job is to rustle up three dollar breakfasts and five dollar lunches, which is all our budget allows, and to make them look like French creations. I'm the one who's guilty of making her a part of the colony. She can't cook to save her dying mother, but she wears the ghastliest shirts, and I had to find out where she got them. Over the years she has learned to cook, but only a little. However, her coffee is the best you can find on the East Coast, and that is enough compensation for our visitors. But not, interestingly, for Xenia. She is going to quit this hole, she has told me several times, as soon as she has got her novel workshopped by the writers. Unfortunately, no writer stays long enough to go through the entire novel, and the suggestions each one offers are vastly different so that ultimately, Xenia is where she always was, which is nowhere. Once, I asked her what the novel was about.

'It's about the meaning of life, all life, starting from the smallest amoeba to George W. Bush, the most powerful man in the world.'

God bless Xenia. It is statements such as these that keep our friendship going; these and the shirts. Xenia is smart, and some day she's going to move on, but for the moment, luckily for me, she has settled at Big Creek for reasons best known to her alone. I can't imagine a better friend. She is passionate but has the ability to calm me down when I fly into one of my infrequent rages. Not only does she cook, though some would question the assumption that what she serves is food, but she talks to the writers, listens to them and warns me if she senses something is amiss. I could easily get another cook but I couldn't get another friend like her.

'So why do I not want to go to India?' I asked my head chef.

'Menopause?' she said, rummaging around in the pantry for something which had apparently gone to the moon, judging by the extensiveness of the search.

'Hey! I'm not that old!' I shot back indignantly.

'You're not?' grinned Xenia. 'No, I guess not. Look, what's the big deal? India's home for you guys, right? And you ought to go home.'

'Ye-es,' I said doubtfully. 'But we never go home in summer. It's insanity.'

'Come on, Tee, you know you're the most insane person in this place.'

My name is Shruti. Xenia butchered it, turned it into Ratty, till I protested, and then simply shortened it to Tee. Much better.

'You mean I'm as insane as you. That cake is never going to rise,' I pointed out, momentarily diverted.

'Of course it will, you retard!' retorted the fashion goddess.

'You haven't added the eggs.'

'Fuck! Tee, you're a genius! I guess this goes into the trash then. I'll have to start over.'

'Hey!' I protested. 'That's money you're throwing! Couldn't you have made something else from that batter?'

'Like what?'

'I don't know. Cookies? Pastry shells? Something?'

'Nope. And you should go,' said Xenia, scraping twenty dollars' worth of cake batter into the bin.

'Are you sure?'

'Of course not! You'll probably all die of one of those tropical diseases – you know, yellow fever or something. But hey, what's life without a little risk?'

If I didn't know that my friend is far more educated than she sounds I might have protested that there is no yellow fever in India. But I knew Xenia was just trying to rile me. Fortunately, I avoided the trap.

It was easy for her to say I should go, I told Xenia

peevishly, but India was no longer worth going to. It was becoming just like America.

'You mean you don't like it because it is like the greatest country on earth? I don't think I understand but I'm sure you have a point,' she said.

'I don't mean that. It's like, everything is becoming McDonaldised. Rent-a-car, fast food, conference calls....'

'And that's bad?' Xenia's tone dripped incredulity.

'Noooo....'

'Tee, just go. Don't eat the fast food, don't rent a car if you don't want to, and don't call me, not even on conference. Go in a horse-cart, if that's what they did in the good old days.'

'Of course not,' I said haughtily. 'We had a car.'

'Look, I don't get it. Do you want to go or not?'

Xenia's exasperation was partly to do with the fact that I was holding up her work. After the first cake disaster, she needed all her concentration to get on with things, and I was most certainly in her way. I returned to my office to brood over why I shouldn't go to India, and I couldn't think of one sound reason but intuition. And intuition, these days, counts for very little.

Xenia walked into my office while I was on the intercom with Russell Banes, the latest sensation to hit the literary circuit. A sensational pain in the butt, is all I could say about him. I considered him a one-book wonder, but maybe that was the result of an argument we had had about the tab he had run up after a week of drinking. The prices were extortionate, he claimed. They were below market price, I said, counting to five before I replied. Who the fuck cares about the damn market price? Lady, you'd better watch out. I can spread the word and not a single writer will come to the Big Creek. It was a three-minute walk from my office to Banes' cottage. I contemplated walking up while he was still squawking on the phone, and giving him one where it hurt. But he was a writer and I wasn't, and by virtue of this fact, he was deserving of respect, and I ground my teeth and said I would look into it.

He had been paid a million bucks for his book, the drinks tab was seventy-six dollars, and the phone call lasted for twenty minutes. Disgust didn't even begin to describe it.

'What do you want now?'

'Can you get me a few shirts? I've seen some pretty ones at the World Market. Something like that.'

Xenia's taste in shirts is terrible. I wasn't sure if I could bring myself to buy those garish, sequinned tops from Janpath for her, that were meant, I always thought, exclusively for tourists.

'You're assuming I'm going,' I said coldly.

''Course you're going. Lash wants you to, doesn't he?'

I ground my teeth. 'He's not my boss.'

'No?'

'No. And I'm still undecided about the trip.'

And that is how we found ourselves at the Indira Gandhi International Airport in Delhi on a blazing midnight in June, getting hugged by people whom I had last met three years ago.

As for the visit to the IIM, I stuck to my refusal. In my mind, that is. Since I hadn't shared the invitation with anyone, there was no discussion about my going there. And with family? Strictly no! I wasn't going to have my family meet those weirdos I had once called friends. And no, I wasn't one myself. A weirdo, that is. Those days were gone, thank god. And I was sensible now.

'Jump!' I shrieked, as I sailed over the last three steps in my old house in Greater Kailash. Isha and Rohan looked at me as though I had sprung horns. Kailash wasn't there to witness my insanity. We had just come down from the terrace, where we had played hopscotch in the hot midday sun. As I passed the hallway, I caught my reflection in the ornate brass mirror that had been my mother's most prized decoration piece. I couldn't believe what I saw in it. My face had become at least two shades darker, my hair was streaming down my neck, cheeks, ears, eyes, to form a ghastly waterfall, my lips were chapped, and copious amounts of sweat had discoloured my white shirt which had sprung loose from the waistband of my shorts. The day I caught Isha looking like that, I gave it to her in no uncertain terms. But it was vacation time, right? I could look like this, all the time if I chose to.

Our plans were ready, and I was to call on the travel agent that day to do the bookings for Agra and Jaipur. These would be easy, we were told, since nobody visited these places in the summer.

'Kabhi bhi,' the agent had said breezily. 'There's no hurry.'

One week of meeting relatives and eating delicious food, one week for Kailash's conference and buying Xenia's ridiculous shirts, and one week of touring and we were going to return to Philadelphia, tanned and refreshed. That was the plan.

'Isha! Rohan! Get ready! We have to go to the travel agent. Hurry up!'

'What about the letters?' asked Rohan.

'We'll sort them out later. Come on, there's no time now.' I grabbed the bunch of mail that had been lying in the doorway and stuffed it in my handbag. The Indian Postal Service was by and large reliable. My instructions to have all my mail forwarded to my aunt's house were followed most of the time. But once in a while stray letters continued to come to my parents' place, bills and leaflets and things.

It was late evening by the time we returned to our hotel. Our bookings were all done. Kailash's conference had three more days to go, and after that it was the weekend, when we were going to head to Agra. Two days for Agra, another two for Jaipur, one more for Delhi for doing some necessary stuff at my old home. That's how the countdown was. One reason why I didn't want to come to India was because I didn't want to see my parents' old house in such a sorry state. And yet I didn't have the heart to sell it. Some decisions just can't be taken in a hurry.

We were having dinner when Rohan reminded me about the letters. He is my conscience-keeper, a serious-faced young man who keeps me in line. I believe he laughs at me sometimes, but perhaps it's when I'm not looking.

'You said you'd check the mail later,' he said between mouthfuls of butter chicken, the children's favourite Indian food.

'What mail?' asked Kailash.

'Bills and so forth,' I replied vaguely. 'I'll go through them later.'

'Later-shater nahin, yaar,' he said, mimicking my absent Punjabi accent. He took every opportunity to remind me that I was from hardy frontier stock. Six generations of living in a city didn't dilute that, according to my husband. 'Do it now. No procrastination.'

So, after dinner I opened my bag to take out the crumpled bundle of envelopes and papers, nestling beneath our tickets. The children had switched on the television, Kailash was sorting through the conference papers, and I started discarding the letters one by one. The tenacity of some of the direct marketers amazed me. There were at least six inserts from one of them. I was about halfway through the disposal when I came upon the envelope with the Indian Institute of Management logo on it. I momentarily contemplated throwing it without opening it. What could my alma mater require from me after all these years? After a moment's hesitation, I opened the letter.

'Dear Shruti,

You must have seen the email inviting you to the twenty year reunion of the PGP 1986-88 batch. We are in the process of making reservations at the Institute Guest

House. Please let us know your plans. We have already
received confirmations from a number of your classmates.
The reunion weekend promises to be an exciting event
with plenty to do for the whole family while, of course,
giving you an opportunity to meet your long lost friends.
Rooms can be reserved from Friday, _ June to Monday, _
June. Check out will be before 12 noon. A vehicle will be
arranged to pick you up from the airport. You can inform
us by email or post.

    With regards,
    Vijay Srinivasan'

The letter was dated a month ago. I gave a mental shrug in
preparation for trashing the missive. My plans for the rest
of the trip were made and, though Mr Srinivasan didn't
know it, they didn't include a weekend in Bangalore.

    I balled up the expensive letterhead and aimed at the
dustbin.

    'What's that?' asked Kailash.

    'What?'

    'That. It doesn't look like a flier.'

    Wasn't he looking through some other papers? Why
was he so interested in what I was doing?

    'It's not,' I said shortly.

    'So?'

    Kailash wasn't about to let go so easily. 'All right, it's
an invitation from the IIM. There's a twenty year reunion
this weekend.'

'Twenty year reunion and they tell you now?'

'No, of course not. They sent me an email a year ago, actually.'

Kailash stared at me expressionlessly. 'And you didn't tell me about it?'

I could sense a row brewing, even as Rohan's eyes turned in my direction curiously. I'm not the only one sensitive to bad vibes. I tried to placate Kailash. 'There didn't seem any point. We weren't going to come all the way for that, were we?'

'We weren't?'

'I mean, we haven't really talked about that time.'

And whose fault is that, his eyes asked me. 'So?'

'So why should we go?'

'Why not?'

'What's the big deal? Why should we visit a place we are so unfamiliar with? For heaven's sake, it was all so long ago! I feel old just thinking about it! Besides, we're going to Agra in case you'd forgotten,' I said.

'I hadn't.'

'So why should we change our plans like this? It costs money! Cancellation and all that. Why should we change?'

From his initial anger, my husband's eyes were now reflecting laughter at my floundering. 'Because you studied there, because they are your friends, because I want to see what one of the most premier institutions of learning in India looks like, and because the kids haven't seen Bangalore,' he said, counting off on his fingers.

I knew how to counter all those reasons. For once, I was

as smart as Kailash. I held up my own fingers and started counting. 'Firstly, so what if I studied there? Secondly, they're not my friends, well, most of them aren't. Thirdly, you're too old to either study or teach at the Indian Institute of Management so forget idle curiosity. Fourthly, the kids haven't seen anything of India apart from Bombay and Delhi, and Bangalore isn't that special. So scratch.'

'I get it!'

'Get what?'

'You're scared.'

'Scared? Of what?' I asked scornfully.

'I don't know. How about you tell me?'

With Kailash, I have been nothing but honest. It has led us into tricky waters sometimes, but anything else would be truly dangerous. Now was not the time to start lying. 'Honestly, I'm not scared.' It wasn't a lie, not exactly. Just a small misinterpretation. Those are allowed. 'I don't see what's in it for us. A bunch of middle-aged people who I'm never going to meet again, strangers all. I mean, what's the point?'

Kailash didn't reply but I knew I hadn't won this round, not yet. I wonder if I'll ever fully understand my husband. His easygoing visage hides thoughts and ideas that I can only guess. Perhaps that's why I'm still in love with him. The enigma is so fascinating, especially when the mystery is solved. But at that moment there was nothing that I found attractive about my spouse, except the thought of strangling him and his enigmatic behaviour. Why on earth was he so keen to go to Bangalore?

As for me, I chided myself, what was wrong with meeting old friends? Why should the thought be so abhorrent? A couple of lunches and dinners, some casual backslapping, a few photo-ops, and we would be clear and through. Harmless, innocent fun, not too different from a visit to the park. So there were memories there. There were memories everywhere. One didn't stop visiting them. There was Priya. And others, reminded my inner voice sneakily. I swatted the inner voice away but called another one.

'And in any case, we're going to Agra,' I told Xenia at the end of my recital. The phone call must have cost the better part of my gratuity, but needs must.

'Tee, didn't you do the Taj bookings?' asked my listener.

'Yes. So?'

'And you knew that this reunion was scheduled for the same weekend?'

'Well, umm....'

'You knew. So now you'll simply have to cancel them.'

'Cancel what?'

Xenia sighed in exasperation. 'The bookings, darling. You'll just have to go to this place, this bang-bang....'

'Bangalore,' I supplied helpfully.

'Yeah, there.'

'I can't do that!' I sounded and felt horrified.

'Why not?'

'Xenia, it'll cost an arm and a leg to cancel the bookings now!'

'But you said you'd done only the flight, not the hotel. So that's not going to cost much is it?'

I wondered why I had even called this annoying woman. She was no help at all.

'So go to bang-bang.'

'It's not bang-bang, okay?' I said with irritation. 'It's the Indian Institute of Management, Bangalore.'

'Right. That one. Tee, go and knock their brains out with your sexy self.'

'Shut up, you freak! I have two kids, in case you've forgotten. And a husband.'

'Yeah, yeah! Christ! I'm not telling you to make out with anyone, just lay on the old oil on the ex.'

'Xenia, can you hear me? Loud and clear? Good! I don't have an ex, all right? My past, present and future are all Kailash.'

'Nix!' replied the chef. Xenia's phone was on speaker and I could hear her banging away at pots and pans, probably deep in the middle of another culinary disaster. 'Of course you had an ex. Weren't there any handsome roosters there, my friend?'

'Several,' I replied, haughtily. 'In fact, there were practically only men there, ninety-eight of them, if I'm not mistaken, and only five females.'

'Wow! Don't women go to college in India?'

Xenia isn't as ignorant as she may appear sometimes.

'College is different,' I replied. 'And the Institute, IIM for all of us, is *very* different.'

There was only the sound of the banging for a while,

and I was annoyed that Xenia's attention was wholly on her terrible cooking rather than on my whole existentialist question of how advisable it was to return to my roots, or rather, my shoots.

'So, who was your ex?' she said after a few minutes.

'Xenia, didn't you hear me? I don't have an ex.'

Xenia sighed at this pronouncement.

'Carlita!' Xenia called out to her assistant, another kitchen genius who doesn't know one end of the spoon from another, but who needs to live in the US and earn money to send home to her spastic son and brilliant daughter in Mexico and then bring them over one day, god and Xenia willing, and who had had the good fortune to sit next to Xenia on a Greyhound from New York to Philadelphia and confess to her that she had no business being in that country. But Xenia had made it her business, and now the kitchen, for which I, as manager, was wholly responsible, was the site of fearsome culinary battles, some resulting in ignominious defeats.

Carlita's English is better than my Spanish, but barely. I understand one word, 'si'; she understands five English words, I think, including 'si'.

'Carlita, get this. There are ninety-eight hunks and five nubile, sexy, smart chicitas in one place, living in each other's pockets for I don't know how long. What are the chances that interesting games were being played in those sexy college dorms? I would say about 9.99 out of 10. What do you say?'

'Si,' replied the sous chef, presumably doing bad things to pastry dough.

'See? It's just not possible, amigo, to go without nookie in that hothouse,' said Xenia.

'Oh, all right, all right. There was someone.'

'Ah!' Xenia exclaimed triumphantly.

'But not in the way you mean,' I tried to defend myself.

'I don't mean any way, darling. There's only one way, and that is bump and grind.'

Really, obscenity is Xenia's middle name and I wonder how she has ended up being my best friend.

'Oh god, Xenia, just leave it alone, will you? It was nowhere as dirty as you think.' Why was I justifying myself to Xenia? Why couldn't I simply go along with whatever she was insinuating, even though it was true only in parts?

'But if it had been clean, you would have bathed in it, now wouldn't you?'

She had me there. I honestly didn't know. And I didn't want to find out. And so I didn't want to go, Jaggu or no Jaggu, Priya or no Priya. And I couldn't tell Kailash why I was so reluctant.

Xenia ignored my grouchiness. 'Go to Bangalore, show this ex what he's missed, leave him slurping like a hot dog and come back. How's that for a great fantasy?'

'He is not an ex. And his name is Jaggu. All right? Jaggu. Try saying that, as in jug with an ooh!'

'Sounds good,' said my friend dismissively. 'So you're booking the tickets, right?'

—✳︎—

'So what did you do today?' Kailash looked up from the game of Scrabble he was playing with Rohan. He wasn't winning, I noted with vicious satisfaction. I was none too pleased with my husband at the moment. In the morning he had instructed me to ensure that the tickets were changed for Bangalore. *Instructed* me! I don't like instructions.

'Umm, nothing much. I bought Xenia's tops from that Tibetan shop on Janpath, and Rohan got his ears cleaned from an ear-cleaner in Chandni Chowk, and we went to Parathewaali Gali. Oh, and I called up Chitra Masi, and she was there! She usually lives in Calcutta, I mean, Kolkata, but she's in Delhi for some time, and we're going across tomorrow. Of course, you're invited, but she's out when your conference ends and....'

My babble tapered off when I saw Kailash's expression. It wasn't an expression as such. More a clear warning, the loud siren of an impending missile attack, and the one who didn't heed it got annihilated. It had taken several annihilations for me to understand this.

'Shruti, did you change the tickets?' he asked politely.

'Umm, actually, umm, no, I didn't. I couldn't get to the agent before they closed.'

'Then please do it tomorrow,' he said in his best head boy manner.

And so I did it the next day.

—✠—

The flight is exhausting. Three people bombarding me with questions about what to expect. Flattering it is. For a change, I'm the centre of attraction.

'How big is it?' asks Rohan, who is fast on the way to believing he has the key to the world.

'The campus?'

'Bangalore.'

'Not very large. Let's see. It isn't as big as Delhi, but it's lovely. It was called the City of Gardens, with reason. It's got beautiful roads, nice shops, huge gardens, delicious food and wonderful coffee. You'll love it.' Wikipedia has its uses.

There's a man sitting next to us on the plane. Through the two hour journey from Delhi to Bangalore, he has been working constantly on his laptop. Now he looks at me and smiles. 'Going back after a long time?' he asks.

It is Rohan who replies. 'Yes, after twenty years.'

'Ah,' says the man.

I wonder what that means. But striking up conversations with strangers on a plane is right up there on my list of things-I-don't-do. But it's not on Rohan's, apparently.

'We're going to IIM,' he volunteers. 'Mom studied there.'

The man gives me the look that everyone gives at the mention of the IIM. It's a look that carries a certain mixture of awe, fear and curiosity.

'I tried getting admission there,' he confides in me,

though I've given no indication that I'm listening to him. 'Thrice, as a matter of fact. But no go.'

'It's getting harder all the time,' I say vaguely. This is not a conversation I want to have. In Philadelphia, nobody cares about the IIM. Nobody asks me about it. I am what I am, and the IIM has nothing to do with it. I deal with writers who, for the most part, except for super jerks like Mr Banes, treat me with respect, even love. I know I've earned it. I can't say the same about this particular badge of respect, Ms Ex-IIM.

The man offers his hand for me to shake. I'm not sure if he wouldn't like my autograph. 'Welcome to Bangalore,' he says with a smile. 'And India.'

Is my foreignness that obvious?

'Ramamurthy. I work at Infosys. Call me if you need anything – tour guide, taxi, medical service, anything.'

A business card materialises in his hand, and is transferred to mine. We're disembarking now, and Mr Ramamurthy is lost in the melee that disembarking from planes in India involves. My sense of humour is restored. Welcome to India indeed! Why, I could teach Mr Ramamurthy a thing or two about India. I'm not completely a foreigner, though the bewildering arrival lounge doesn't fill me with any confidence.

'Wow, Mum! That was so neat! You impressed that man, you know that?'

'Yes, well, Rohan, let's not talk about that.'

'Why not?'

'Because it's complicated,' both of us say together, and

then laugh. Rohan knows me too well, I believe. I wonder if that's a good thing.

'Welcome to India,' I tell Kailash, moving in step with him.

'What?'

'You, foreigner, welcome to India.'

'Shruti, do me a favour, start the jokes only after we reach IIM, all right? Let's find a cab first.'

There's no need for that. The Jet Airways plane carried roughly two hundred passengers. There are about five hundred people waiting on a narrow strip of landing to meet these two hundred people. The odds of the right people connecting with each other can be calculated. They are enormous. Taxi drivers, hotel courtesy cars, relatives, personal chauffeurs, and everyone who thinks going to the airport to receive people in India is exciting, all jostle with each other to be the first to meet the arriving party. The noise is deafening. The four of us and our two trolley carts, with our aura of foreignness, all attract a bevy of taxi drivers, each one more polite and glutinous than the other, till I discover I'm brushing them aside like flies, as is Kailash. But before we get completely sucked into the crowd, Isha points to a large banner.

'Mom! Dad! Look! Over there!'

Sure enough, there's a large banner held aloft, above the heads of the assembled crowd, carrying the legend, 'IIM Bangalore welcomes PGP 86-88'. Isha has seen the IIM part, though the rest is a mystery to her.

The string of initials has meaning only for an insider.

'PGP stands for Post Graduate Diploma Program, and my class was the batch of 1986 to 1988,' I explain to my mystified family as we make our way towards the banner, and to the two young men holding it aloft. I had informed 'Vijay Srinivasan' about our flight details, but hadn't expected a pickup. It had all been so last minute. Now I am relieved to see the banner.

'Hi,' I say to them chattily. 'That's me.'

'Hello, ma'am,' replies one of the bespectacled men politely, and I'm promptly put in my place. For a moment there, I had forgotten that there's a huge gap between PGP 86-88 and PGP 2007-2009. But these are just numbers, I tell myself. I am a 'PGP' and so are these young men, and that is all that matters. Of course it's a foolish thought. Just being connected to the IIM in some way doesn't really make me a part of a family, does it? But the sense of ownership and possession remain.

A voice hails from behind us, 'Ruts?'

For a moment, I ignore it. Ruts! I've almost forgotten that name. The last time it was used was in 1988. And then I buried it, just as I buried everything associated with that name. The voice repeats again. 'Hey, Ruts! Hey! Remember me?'

I turn to see a greying man clad in the uniform of a middle-aged-corporate-executive-being-casual – designer T-shirt, branded jeans and expensive loafers on his feet. 'Jaggu?' I ask, unsure if I'm making a mistake. There's no mistake.

It's the voice that I remember and recognize, not the

face, not the arms that wrap themselves tightly around me,
binding me to someone who should by rights be a total
stranger, considering I have spent ten times the time without
him than with him. For a minute Shruti is completely
forgotten as Ruts takes over, threatening to sweep away the
former in the torrents of the past. We disengage eventually,
and I take a good look at my old friend. I barely know this
grey-haired man. I've made a mistake. Oh, it is Jaggu, all
right. But not the Jaggu I once knew.

I know my mouth is agape and I'm staring. I know
what I look like when I stare, like a boneless fish. I recall
Xenia's words. 'Show this ex what he's missed, leave him
slurping like a hot dog.' Yeah, right! Slurping at what? At
this ugly specimen? But wait a minute, I tell myself. What
do you care about the slurping? This man is practically a
stranger now, and you are a married woman in love with
your husband. Oh, all right, if you say so, says the voice in
my head grouchily. But at least hitch up your jaw. I do so,
and assume a polite smile.

There is a broad grin on Jaggu's face as he stares back at
me. 'I can't believe it's you. In flesh and blood! The great
Ruts Malhotra!'

I once did a course in Photoshop. There's a feature in
it where one can erase the background of a picture, and
keep just the people in it. Something similar seems to be
happening here, only now it isn't a picture. For a moment,
Kailash, the children, the woman hovering behind Jaggu,
even the banner boys, all vanish, as the two of us stare at
each other. My mind is a blank. It has been a long time,

almost half a lifetime. Twenty years, one month, three weeks and four days, to be precise. Shut up, Shruti!

I hear a throat being cleared noisily. Kailash looks a little bemused, and there's a crooked smile on his lips. I've often told Kailash he should have been a witch, and perhaps someone would have burnt him at the stake. Since the day we met, all those years ago, my husband has had the ability to divine everything that goes through my mind. I can see that now, too, he can see through to my utter confusion.

In a haze, I find myself being introduced to Jaggu's wife, Vijay. 'My better half,' says Jaggu and I hurriedly pull Kailash forward as well. The children have bewildered looks on their faces.

'Jaggu, meet my two heroes, Isha and Rohan. They keep me in line whenever I stray. Don't you, guys?'

It's more than a hint, its a plea. I want them to be polite, to present their own personalities, to show the world why I love them so much.

'Why did you hug Mom and call her Ruts?' asks Isha.

Jaggu grins. 'It's a long story. I'll tell you later. Come on, let's get out of here.'

Jaggu hasn't lost his habit of teasing a smile out of every girl he meets. Isha has agreed to place her hand in his as we are led out of the airport terminal to the waiting bus. Do I envy her?

Kailash and I lag behind. Kailash holds out his hand, his eyes glinting with mischief. 'That was an interesting encounter.'

'Yes, wasn't it?' I say, unwilling to enter into discussion about Jaggu right now. But Kailash is nothing if not tenacious.

'So, is this the old flame, the lost affair, the could-have-been-but-wasn't man?'

'Your eloquence is marvellous,' I reply as we settle down into our seats. Isha has entered into an intense conversation with her new acquaintance, while his daughter is making polite overtures towards Rohan. We all seem to be playing 'happy families', and I wonder if I am the only one to feel the undercurrents of tension.

The new airport at Bangalore has recently opened and it glitters, its haughty demeanour a deterrent to any pretensions to familiarity. The children are impressed, as indeed I am as well. No wonder that man on the plane treated me like an alien. I *am* one in this transformed landscape. This Bangalore has nothing to do with the city where I spent two years of my life. I think I'll just change the name. Perhaps that will help me deal with this change. We are driving down a road that goes on forever, villages dotting either side of the highway. But eventually we enter what is clearly the city. I am shocked. Crowds and squalor surround us. Now then, what should I call this place? How about Urbs Horribilis? Or, in short, Yucky? As these thoughts pass through my mind, Isha exclaims, 'Look! Mom! Dad! I just saw a hen and her chicks. We almost ran over them!'

To my relief, my daughter is fascinated by the sight. I, on the other hand, feel a surge of irritation at being forced to slow down because of some livestock that probably shouldn't be there in the first place.

'They must have escaped from their coop,' I try to justify.

'I think they came out of the house,' says Jaggu wickedly, and I shoot a dagger at him with my eyes.

I've already anticipated the next question. 'Hens inside a house?' asks Rohan.

Jaggu supresses a smile, while I am left floundering for an answer. Kailash steps in at just the right moment. 'Rohan, you've forgotten this is India. People can't afford to have separate enclosures for their animals.'

Kailash's tone forces Jaggu also to adopt a more serious tone of conversation. 'It's the same old story, Rohan, and as you grow older, you'll learn economics like the rest of us, though, if I remember correctly, your mom was pretty poor at it. You'll learn about poverty and how a necessity in one place becomes a complete luxury in another.'

Jaggu's wife, Vijay, who has been silently observing everything all this while, enters the conversation now. 'It isn't true that there aren't separate enclosures for animals. Of course there are. But sometimes, people are forced to keep their animals with them, especially if there's no way to protect them otherwise. It's rare but it happens.'

'India is a strange country,' I offer weakly to my children.

Both Kailash and Jaggu burst out laughing at this, and Vijay too joins them. 'I think I like India,' says Isha, and I am truly astonished. What can she possibly like about this country, I wonder.

'I think I can make more friends here,' she explains.

Out of the mouths of babes and sucklings!

'Wow! Thanks for the certificate, dude,' says Jaggu, pumping Isha's hand vigorously and making her blush.

The Jaggu brand of charm is intact. At one time it had worked its magic on me. Now my daughter is becoming a victim. Seriously, I'm not jealous of my daughter. Seriously. I'm not insane. But this has to stop.

'I still don't know what you do,' I ask Jaggu.

'Do you want the long or the short version?' asks Jaggu, winking at my daughter. My god! That's shameless! Isha is actually laughing!

'Are the two different?' asks Kailash, joining the fun.

'No!' replies our resident comedian. By now both Kailash and Vijay are laughing with him, and I find my sense of humour restored. What's wrong with me? Why am I so uptight?

'So what *do* you do?' asks Kailash.

'I'm an engineer. I build automobiles. Or rather, I work in a company that makes automobiles.' He names a multinational automobile corporation.

'That's interesting,' says Kailash politely.

'Is it? To me it is. But I'm not one of those five-star IIM achievers who become chief executives at the age of forty, with millions in salaries and billions in stockholdings. Finance and computers, both bore me. I'm just a regular guy who likes cars.'

Jaggu and regular! Since when?

'There was a man on the plane who thought Mom was really cool when she said she studied at IIM,' says Rohan.

'Yes, buddy, it's all in the name. Out here in India, at least. What did your mom say to the man?'

'Mom! What did you say?'

'It's all just silliness, Rohan. We should be proud of who we are, not where we went to college.'

'Then why do you tell me to study hard so that I can go to a good college?' asks my pert son.

'Touché!' says Jaggu with a grin.

―✵―

While we are having this conversation we have been making steady progress towards the IIM facility on Bannerghatta Road on the outskirts of Bangalore. I wait for the approach of the fields that once indicated that we were near the campus. The bus halts in front of a large gate in the middle of a crowded road, and I realize with a shock that we have arrived. Bannerghatta Road is no longer in the deep suburbs of Bangalore, surrounded on all sides by farms and villages. It is now in the heart of a city that appears like a patch of water spilt on the floor, spreading on all sides shapelessly.

Not for the first time, I get the feeling that I've come to a completely new place, and I wonder why I've bothered to make my way to this urban sprawl that has nothing to distinguish it. I grope around in my mind for some memories of this place, and there are none. What memories I do have relate to another time, to almost another era. I know twenty years mean a lot of changes, but surely something of the past must remain? How can everything get erased? Do people also get erased over time? Suddenly, I miss home, and it occurs to me that home is no longer India. Home has become Philadelphia, and the urge to call Xenia then and there becomes almost too hard to suppress.

2

'Xenia, it's me!' I whisper into my mobile.

'Tee! Hey! What's up? Are you all right?'

'Yeah! Yeah! I'm fine.'

'Speak up. I can't hear you. Hey, what's that racket?'

'There's a party going on, with a live band! You know, for all the ex-classmates.'

'A party? With a band? And dancing?'

'Not too much dancing, no,' I clarify somewhat defensively.

'But enough, I'm guessing. Wow! You guys really live it up, huh?'

'Never mind all that! How are things there? All well?'

'Babe, we spoke yesterday. Not much can go wrong in one day, can it? And don't worry so! Everything's just fine! Russell Banes did pay his liquor tab. Finally. So you can rest easy. But we're not inviting him again, not even if he's the next J. K. Rowling. So, you tell me. How's the ex? What did he say when he saw you? Did you knock him over? Is Lash jealous? I wish I were there. It's so fucking exciting, man!'

'Well, if all's well then I guess that's it. Congrats on

getting that chap to pay. You're marvellous, dude. I'll call you again later.'

'Hey come on, Tee! Speak to me. What's wrong?'

'Nothing. Everything. I don't know. Oh, Xenia, I miss you. Things are so different from what I expected. I don't recognize a thing!'

'What about the ex? Did you recognize him?'

'Of course!'

'There you are then. You've got the most important part sorted out. Now just relax, and go with the flow. Flutter those sexy eyelashes a little. Let him see what he's missed. And eat that yummy chicken by the pound. Keep smiling, babe.'

Xenia, the chronic loser, giving therapy to Shruti, her boss and a far more successful woman in the career stakes. It makes me smile.

'Xenia, you're an ace! Now go back to the baking, and don't forget the eggs.'

The game that I call 'Remember me?' is in full progress when I return to the party in the lawns behind the main campus building, the one that houses the administrative block and the classrooms. In one corner, there is a band playing old seventies' numbers. There are Chinese lanterns strung upon the trees. Soft laughter can be heard from the various groups of people talking. Children let out the occasional shriek, and are quickly silenced by their parents. There are about forty people assembled in the lawn, roughly twelve families. The game consists of a coy question, 'Who am I?' And then the answer comes,

'Bugger! You look different! What's happened to your hair/ belly/ teeth?'

Almost everyone is playing this game, all the classmates, I mean. I'm not a part of the game. Nobody has trouble placing me. There were so few of us girls. Kailash, I notice, plays along with the game, though he isn't an alumnus. But that's Kailash for you, always willing to go along with whatever is going on in his presence. He listens to all the dialogue, he claims. It helps him with his playwriting.

We are all creatures of memory. It is what grounds us, makes us feel connected. Only by looking back can we relate to the now. An amnesiac would probably have no moral issues at all. He would never be able to decide right from wrong, having no memory of the matter. And how we treat a memory decides what we become. But I shall not revisit memories, I tell myself, even though I have been chatting with Jaggu for the past half an hour. If Jaggu isn't a memory, I don't know what he is. Half of me wants to talk to him, and the other half wishes either he or I were at least ten thousand miles away from this place.

'Why did you come here?' I ask him.

'Curiosity,' he replies with a crooked smile. 'What about you?'

Because I was railroaded into it against my will by my husband. 'The same reason,' I say, hoping my smile is suitably bright. I don't ask, curiosity about what? I don't think this conversation is going anywhere.

'And what do you think?'

'What do you think?' I parry. 'I mean, it's changed a lot,

hasn't it? Almost unrecognizable, I think. I don't know if that's a good thing. Like, umm....'

'You haven't changed. Not one bit, Ruts. You're just as I remember you.'

And that nicely shuts me up. God, where the hell is Kailash? Why is he never around when I need him? I look around to see if there's anyone keen to talk to me, but everyone is engrossed in their own chatter, and no one comes to my rescue. To be honest, I had expected *something* to happen. I mean with all that history, the weekend wasn't going to be totally harmless. But this soon!

'Remember the first day that you came to this place?' asks Jaggu. '*Hi, I'm Shruti,*' he mimics.

I laugh a little too heartily. Of course I remember that awful day. Something more than merely joining the IIM happened that day. On that day, I grew up. Just like that. There are people who become adults gradually, and there are people who don't become adults ever. And then there was me, Shruti Malhotra, who at 9.59 on the morning of _ July 1986 was a child, an adolescent, and at 10.00 a.m., as her feet stepped into the dining room of the IIM, Bangalore hostel became an adult. Snap! It was like being born. One moment a foetus, the next, a bawling baby.

'I'm going to do it,' I declared to Lalita. It was October and the weather in Delhi had started turning pleasant. We were sitting in the college canteen nursing a cup of tea over two hours, while the desultory ceiling fans turned noisily and gave a modicum of comfort. Lalita and I had been best friends since primary school. We were together all the time. But not for much longer.

'Do what?' asked my friend, absentmindedly. Term exams were due in just four weeks time, and books had sort of become part of our bodies. Lalita's nose was stuck in a thick volume as I spoke.

'Appear for CAT,' I said.

'Hmm.'

'The Common Admission Test,' I elaborated.

'Hmm.'

'Lals, listen to me!'

'What?'

'You're not listening!'

'You're not talking! What do you want?'

'I said I'm going to appear for CAT. I've decided!'

'Well, bully for you! I thought you wanted to be a writer or economist or something. How is CAT going to help?'

'It won't, of course. But I still want to go for it.'

'So you want to be a manager?'

'I guess so.'

'And not a writer?'

'I guess not.'

'And you're sure about this?'

'I guess so.'

'You don't sound too sure!'

'I guess not.'

'Shruti! What's wrong with you? Do you or do you not want to enter the corporate world?'

'Yes, yes I do. I want to be a business manager.'

'So, I guess this means your ambition to teach at D School ends right here. We were supposed to go there together. And now are you going to ditch me?'

D School, for the uninitiated, refers to the Delhi School of Economics.

'Hey Lals! Stop being so senti! Just because I want to appear for the test doesn't mean I'm going to get through! Like, there are a million people out there who're going to sit for it. So what are my chances of getting through? One in a million? Sounds like a cert, doesn't it?'

'I know you, Malhotra. If you say you're going to become a manager, you're going to become a manager. Don't forget me, that's all. People out there, I've heard, are very smart, not jhallas like us.'

'Listen to yourself,' I jeered. 'You're acting like I'm about to go to the moon.'

'Almost,' replied Lalita before burying herself back in the book, ending our discussion.

―⚊―

'No way,' said my father.

'But why not?'

'Because we don't want to see you go so far away from us. And anyway, India is still not ready for women managers. You can teach in the university, or become a journalist. You're good at writing, Shruti.'

I am always amazed at how parents do exactly the opposite of what they should be doing when it comes to their children. I mean, those children are born to them. Surely they should know how to manage their own offspring? But though my father was successfully managing a corporation with a thousand employees, he was clueless about how to deal with me. Had he gone along with my desire to go to the IIM, perhaps my ardour would have soon cooled off. His stick-in-the-mud attitude, on the other hand, only strengthened my resolve to get admission. I studied on the sly, in the college library, in my bed late at night, at Lalita's place, much against her protests.

'Why are you so keen to go all of a sudden?' asked Lalita.

'Because it's there,' I paraphrased George Mallory, the climber. 'And because I genuinely desire a good education.'

'Even at the cost of annoying your parents?'

'Oh, they'll come round,' I said breezily. 'They'll be so overcome by all the congratulatory messages when I reach the top that they'll send me off with a smile.'

'You're not going,' said my father flatly, when I waved the admission letter from IIM Bangalore in his face.

'Why not?'

The subliminal fear of all parents came out then. 'Arre, who knows what goes on over there? Drinking, drugs, what not? You're not going to do all that.'

'Dad, I give you my solemn oath, I'll never let any of that affect me.'

Since that day, I have ascribed my lack of acne to the choice of words in that promise I made.

But my father knew me better than I thought. 'I think we should wait for a year,' he said when I confronted him again. 'And if you're still sure, you can go.'

'Daddy, d'you know how difficult it is to get into the IIM? There's no chance I'm going to be offered admission next year. If it's gone now, it's gone. Look, I'm talking about studying business management, not getting married!' I was almost shouting by now. 'How can a year change my mind? For god's sake, you should be proud of me for achieving this! Anyone else would give their eye teeth for this honour!'

It came as a surprise to me that whereas I viewed the IIM as a centre of excellence, my parents had a completely different opinion. They were seeing it in the light of what harm it could do to me, not what good. For me, the harm was incidental. All profit came at some cost. But those costs were so irrelevant, somehow. Two years were such a small period of one's life. They would get over in a snap.

'Shruti,' said my mother, 'why do you need to become a manager? That isn't a very womanly profession. Besides, when you marry, it'll be so difficult! Men, you know! They aren't very keen to marry managers. Mrs Sharma's daughter....'

I interrupted hastily. I had no wish to enter into a discussion about Mrs Sharma's daughter, a misguided female, by all accounts. 'Mom, I promise I'll marry whoever you like. As soon as I return from the IIM, you can get me married off. In fact, why don't you hunt for a groom right away? Save you time.'

My parents, predictably, weren't amused by my facetiousness. Nor were they particularly convinced. I wasn't going, and that was that. They couldn't afford to let their innocent daughter go to a place that was, quite obviously, peopled by drug addicts and the like. At some point, it was better to bow to their superior judgement, even if it wasn't all that superior. Parents, one is taught very early in life by said parents, know best. I might as well, I informed Lalita tragically between bouts of crying, study French.

The date for joining the institute came and went. There was nothing to be done. About a week later, I had a visitor. It was a sultry July morning. The rain, as always, was playing hide and seek in Delhi, creating a few showers, then disappearing altogether, then returning with a vengeance to flood all the streets, and bring life to a complete standstill for a couple of days before doing the vanishing act again. I had decided to clean the verandah, which looked like the site of a major tornado attack in the wake of a long deluge the previous day. The activity would, I decided, take my mind off my biggest disappointment. I was dressed in a pair of cotton trousers held at the waist with a drawstring and a top that had lost its colour and shape many washes ago. A rag and a broom were my elegant accessories, and this was how the young girl who walked in found me.

She opened the gate and looked at me. Clearly, she

thought I was the help, for she asked me in Hindi, 'Is Shruti Malhotra here?'

I replied in English, 'I'm Shruti.'

'Hi,' said the girl easily. 'I'm Vandana. You're going to IIM, Bangalore, right?'

The statement was factually incorrect, since at that moment I wasn't going anywhere, but I didn't want to discuss that further. 'Yes.'

'Yeah, I got your name from college. Gosh! You're the only one from our college to have got through!' she gushed.

'Really?' I wasn't particularly interested in my status in college. My status at home was a bigger priority at the moment.

'Yes. I'm planning to join the IIM next year, so I wanted your guidance.'

My guidance? Was this girl deluded? I could perhaps guide her on how to antagonise her parents, but beyond that I felt like incompetence personified. I almost said so, but then I saw Vandana's face. She looked like I had probably looked before I started on the crazy adventure called 'How to get admission to the IIM'. She had a look of wonder and hope and excitement on her face, and in all conscience I couldn't prick that balloon. It would have been utterly heartless. And then another thought occurred to me. Perhaps Vandana could help me just as I was going to help her.

'Come along.' I said tersely. 'I need a favour from you.'

'Dad, Mom, this is Vandana. Vandana, go ahead. Tell

my parents why you've come to meet me,' I said, just a little abruptly. Perhaps if my parents heard from a complete stranger what a huge achievement it was to get into the IIM, they would be better convinced. To her credit, Vandana didn't let me down. She waxed eloquent about the IIM, about its significance as an institution of higher learning, about the prospects of the people who went there to study. She had done her research well. It seemed to me that she knew more about the IIM than I did. I was flattered that she thought so highly of my accomplishment. Who wouldn't be?

I shall remain in Vandana's debt forever, though I never met her after that day. That night, my mother came into my room while I was reading the prospectus for studying French at the Alliance Française.

'Beta, what are you doing?'

'Reading,' I said, waving the booklet at her.

'When are you supposed to join in Bangalore?'

'That's okay, Mom. I've decided I'm not going. I'll go to Alliance Française tomorrow and join French.'

'What? Why?'

'I don't know. I think French is a good option.'

'Beta, don't lie. I know, your father knows, what you really want. All this time, we thought you didn't know your own mind. But I can say it now. I think we were wrong, and you were right.'

'Oh, Mom! Don't say that!'

'Why not? You're no longer a child, and I can see that. You should do what your heart tells you. Why should we stand in your way? What kind of parent prevents her daughter from following her heart? I was never that kind, Shruti. So go ahead. Go to Bangalore. You haven't even told me when you are supposed to join.'

'Actually the joining date was last week.'

'Shruti! Now what are you going to do?'

I felt a bubble of happiness rise in me. It blocked my throat and brought a film of heat to my eyes. I hugged my mother tight, and told her, 'Don't worry. It's going to be fine. They'll wait.' After all, in a fit of optimism I had asked permission from the IIM to join late.

—⁂—

'Did you have to hug him so hard? His wife looked a bit broken up.' Kailash is, as usual, elegantly articulate. 'Come to think of it, many wives were looking shattered tonight. You people kicked up quite a storm. All that hugging and kissing and sharing IIM jokes that nobody else understood. Yeah, I think it was quite a reunion.'

'Are you broken up as well?' I tease Kailash, running my fingers through his thick hair as he gazes at me through smoke-narrowed eyes, his cigarette dangling from his fingers. He merely laughs and goes back to reading Bernard Shaw.

I stick my feet out towards Kailash. He massages them while he reads his book, and a current of pleasure shoots through me. Oh! My feet. I almost, but not quite, regret the heels that I wore to the dinner to give myself a few inches and lots of confidence.

'Was I looking different?'

Kailash looks up from his book. 'What do you mean?'

'Different. I mean, well, was I looking – different?'

'Let's see. I think what you really want to know is if you were sophisticated, beautiful, suave, confident,' Kailash counts off on his fingers. 'The answer is yes to all these. You were fantastic, and I was jealous, and now can I go back to my book?'

'Don't you want to talk?'

'About what?'

'About the party, what else. Did you figure out who's who?'

'That's a bit too much to expect, isn't it? I'm sure I'll know everyone by the end of the weekend, but as of now, all I can say is, the inventiveness of the nicknames has won my total admiration. Jaggu, Paxi, Tony, umm, let's see, Kutte, Mangu.... Was there someone called Monkey as well, or was that just my imagination?'

'Oh come on, Kailash! As though you didn't have some arbit nickname in college. We all had nicknames out here!' Am I actually defending my ex-classmates?

'Yes, I noticed, er, Ruts.'

'I had almost forgotten that's what I was called,' I reflect.

'Somehow I can quite see why they called you that. The name suits you.'

'Oh? How?'

'It's little, just like you!'

I punch my husband playfully. Darling Kailash! Do

you sense what is really bothering me at this moment? I wish I could explain it to you, but I'm not too clear myself. Is Xenia right? Have I been reluctant to come to this reunion because of history? I look at Kailash reading his book, oblivious to the turmoil inside me, and I'm suddenly very annoyed with myself, and as usual, I take my annoyance out on him.

'Stop kidding with me at this hour of the night,' I tell him, just a touch sharply. 'I'm really exhausted.'

'Go to sleep if you're tired, darling. Stop doing intellectual masturbation over the evening. It's over. You were great. Everything's fine, unless I'm missing something.'

I can't tell him. I look back upon the evening. Captain and Curry were there, my good old friends, who had held my hand so often in those early days, when I was a bewildered neophyte. They were eager to narrate their histories, attempting to cram the events of twenty years into a twenty minute chat, just like everyone else at the dinner. I was glad of my outfit then, my 'confidence building' dress, as I call the elegant affair that makes me look not even remotely like the raggedy girl of twenty years ago, glad of the matching sandals that added three inches to my height of five feet and a bit and brought me almost eye to eye with most of the people there, glad that I had thought of visiting a hairdresser in Delhi just the day before, and above all, glad that I had Kailash by my side all through.

I look at Kailash as he reads the play, fully engrossed, absent-mindedly rubbing his nose from time to time.

There's a lot to look at, almost all of it good – the nose, the smiling lips, the high forehead, the arched brows, all of these set beneath a brain that is as sharp as they come. He was one of the youngest people to have made it to an associate professorship at the University of Pennsylvania, and I'm not completely biased when I say that the honour was truly deserved. Kailash lives, breathes, eats theatre. He does not hold a very high opinion of management professionals. Most of them, he claims, have no imagination. For the most part, of course, he has nothing to do with that breed of humanity. A couple of times he has sought corporate sponsorship for some production in which he has been involved. These requests involved meeting the senior executives of the corporation. He has invariably come away feeling disgusted. The people he met did not share his ideas of what sponsorship of a play should entail. They couldn't understand his aversion to a banner on stage proudly proclaiming a well-known brand of single malt whisky for the duration of the production. He could not understand their refusal to give him large amounts of money without asking for anything in return.

On more than one occasion, my husband has told me about the girl from a local management school whom he dated briefly, before, as he puts it, 'latching' onto me. She was ambitious, suffered from a complex because she wasn't from one of the IIMs and made Kailash suffer too, since he couldn't claim that glory either. The issue came up frequently between them, and the girl never stopped being amazed that anyone would choose not to study management. Once I asked him why the girl had dated *him*. That's when Kailash explained, 'I guess because you management guys find the rest of the world a curiosity and can't resist the thought that you can certainly improve it. That's what I was to that female – a product, perhaps a system that needed improving through better management, something that she would supply. It might even have worked out if I hadn't believed that the world needed better actors, not better managers. If god had intended for managers to inhabit this planet, he would have vanished from it a long time ago. After all, he has proved to be a pretty hopeless manager himself. It is actors he wanted, people who are always pretending to be something they are not. Think about it, missy.'

Then I asked him, why me? He said it was because he recognized that I was acting something fierce, and he couldn't resist the temptation of coming backstage to find the real me.

Who *is* the real me? I was not like Rats, aka Ravi Saluja, whose middle name was smartness. Rats had defined what a management student should be, and set out to turn himself into one. For him, the only sport worth pursuing was golf, the only girl worth pursuing was the undergraduate college queen, the only subject worth pursuing was corporate finance, the only skill worth pursuing was conversation. Rats had practically written the reference manual for budding managers. Too bad I never read it. Perhaps life would have turned out differently if I had. But I have arranged life such that I can have things my own way, almost all the time. This weekend seems to be an exception. I wonder where Rats is now. Probably in the stratosphere. What would he think of the way I've turned out, I wonder. In all likelihood, nothing. People who did not reach at least cloud cover never did merit attention from Rats.

I don't know what Priya is doing these days, but perhaps someone like her would be a fitting companion for Rats. A brilliant executive in her own right, an achiever who can match his skills in the high stakes game of corporate wheeling and dealing, she will be a beauty and they will have no children since neither of them has the time to devote to raising a family. There, I have defined Ravi Saluja brilliantly. In twenty years I haven't met him once, but I don't think I'm all that off the mark where knowing him is concerned. People don't change, I've discovered, circumstances do. I shall be able to place Rats anywhere. For Rats, the steps only ever led up, and he had his foot firmly on the ladder even when I met him the first time as a classmate. There was something a little childish about Rats, even as a graduate student of business. It was as though he needed approval all the time, from everyone who mattered, teachers and even fellow students. 'I got admission to A,' he told me once, referring to IIM, Ahmedabad, the big daddy of all the IIMs. 'But I chose to come here. I wanted to understand rural marketing and agriculture management, so Bangalore it was.'

I did not offer any rebuttal to this blatant fib. What was the point? Rats and rural? Since when? But if lying made Rats happy, so be it. Who was I to show him the correct path? And how did I know it was correct? Perhaps raising your hand in select classes only, the ones most in demand amongst students, to make a good impression on your professor, was the correct thing to do. In a class of hundred, what other way was there to get noticed?

These thoughts drive away whatever sleep I think of getting. I try not to curse Rats for invading my mind at this hour. It is not his fault that I can conjure up his face so vividly. I try to think of Priya instead. She and Jaggu are my two reasons for coming to this reunion. And also for wanting to avoid it. Hell, the paradox is not worth deciphering this late at night. It must be past one o'clock. High time I slept. Just then my cell phone rings. Did I anticipate this when I adjusted its ringer to vibrate? I grab it and look at Kailash, who is fast asleep with his mouth open. Kailash doesn't stir and I whisper into the phone, 'What?'

'Ruts, come to Room 102. You're needed.'

'Jaggu, I'm sleeping,' I lie. 'Can't this wait till morning? It's one o' clock!'

My protest is ignored. 'Ruts, we're waiting for you. Now get dressed and get here fast. You need to be a part of this.' Jaggu is not going to be deterred by my reluctance.

Jaggu, Curry and Captain are lounging on the bed when I reach. Some things never change. Once more, they have managed to nose out an empty room for their various schemes. My entry does not affect their posture. The earlier formality, when we all behaved like long lost

CLOUD 9 MINUS ONE

strangers, might as well not exist. We are back to our earlier camaraderie, or at least the men are. I'm still ambiguous about what I'm doing here. Mild snorts of laughter emerge from Raghuraj Rao alias Captain's nose. It is the dwindling aftermath of a joke narrated by Kiran alias Curry, I guess. Curry himself looks gloomy, his expression belying his extremely risqué sense of humour. I've always enjoyed it only partially. There is something distasteful, in my mind, about grown men spouting anatomically graphic jokes, even smart ones. It was one more thing I had to get accustomed to as a female in a class of ninety-eight men and five women.

A space is created for me on the bed, and a glass is shoved into my hand. We're all set. Twenty years have dropped in a flash. I think of the *Cold Case* promos on TV in the US. From a Technicolor picture, we have reverted to the black and white version. Through some sleight of hand everyone just looks older. Everything else is the same. Age is suddenly irrelevant. Captain grins at me.

'Ruts, you're as vaguo as ever,' he says genially. 'What the hell have you been up to all these years?'

'What do you mean vaguo?' I reply hotly. 'I've actually kept track of many of you, though you don't know it. You vanished completely, you know that, don't you? But I know you were on television a couple of months ago, some talk show on global software companies.'

'Wow! Ruts! You actually saw me? Nobody else saw me on that show.'

'That doesn't have anything to do with you not telling anyone about it, I suppose?' asks Jaggu silkily.

'I saw your name during the promos,' I explain, 'and I thought it might be you.'

'Well, you could have shared the news with the rest of us,' says Jaggu.

Before I can reply, Curry interrupts. 'OK, forget the memory trip, guys. There's work to be done.'

Captain rolls a joint and lights up. I'm taken completely off-guard by this act.

'What are you doing?'

'Relax, Ruts. I need something to calm me down, okay dude?'

From being a woman, I am now a 'dude' once more. We're all dudes, mates, yaars, dosts, all the various monikers for 'friend' that we used for each other, and that I've never used since. Perhaps I should call Xenia 'yaar'. Why not? It might bring us to another level of intimacy altogether.

'Did you know Priya would be coming?' asks Curry, jerking me out of my reverie.

'I thought she might,' I reply cautiously, wondering what this is leading up to.

'And that doesn't bother you?' asks Captain, now puffing away.

'Why should it?'

'Forget it, people. We're talking to the wrong person. This one was always Priya's crony, a real special one,' says Jaggu with a yawn.

'Seriously, can you explain what's bothering you? So, Priya is coming to this do. So are a ton of other people, I assume. *We* have come. I really don't see the problem.'

Jaggu looks at me with narrowed eyes. 'Ruts, don't tell me you don't understand. Priya was trouble from day one. You don't think she could create problems here with her presence?'

'I think people can change,' I say carefully.

'So what are you saying, that Priya can change? And pigs can fly, fellows.'

'Umm, the fact is, none of us knows what's going to happen.' Curry takes the joint from Captain and puffs it.

Captain giggles. 'Can you imagine? What if Priya decides to have a conference with all the wives?'

It is a funny image and we all laugh, a little too hard. The tension is palpable. Priya's other name has always been Embarrassment; for others, of course. I doubt there is anything under the sun that could embarrass my former girlfriend. She was never wired that way. Anti middle-class probably sums it up nicely. But the three men in this room had always been immune to her charm, as she had been to theirs. I wonder what this mini-conference is really about. It can't be merely to discuss the sexual escapades of a misguided girl who is, in all likelihood, a respectable pillar of society now. Aren't we overreacting? After all, sleeping with one's classmate isn't really a crime these days. Though perhaps sleeping with about fifteen of them might be considered excessive.

'Why are we here?' I ask.

'To figure out what the fuck to do about that friend of yours,' says Jaggu.

'No, no, I mean, why are we all here, in Bangalore, after all these years? What was the need for this reunion?'

They all stare at me. 'Aw, come on Ruts! That's no way to talk. We needed to get together. It's been so long! Everyone has a reunion; schools, colleges, everyone.'

'Then why are you guys so pissed about Priya? Let her come. Face her. It was all twenty years ago, so forget about it. What are you so scared of? Student indiscretions, that's what they were, right? There has to be some difference between being twenty-five and being forty-five. Our *kids* are doing what we were doing then, for god's sake!'

'God! I hope not,' says Curry, while Captain breaks into applause, the effects of the marijuana now apparent.

'Hear, hear! The woman can talk, man! What a pure, bloody marvellous bit of oration! I'm actually scared, not of Priya, but of this lady here, this woman, this Ruts.'

'Shut up, Captain,' says Curry curtly. 'Okay, Ruts, if that's how you feel. Priya was always your blue-eyed friend, as I remember.'

'Curry, this isn't about the past. Haven't you got that? This is about now, about us. So what if Priya's coming here? We all have to face up to some things. We can't ignore the past selectively, that's all I'm saying. Let's be happy now. Let's not let the past trouble us. We're meeting to revive our friendships, aren't we? So why the fear? Let's just be friends now.' And not rivals, I add silently.

Apparently, I sound convincing. Jaggu smiles and says, 'Don't corner her, Curry. She's all right, aren't you, Ruts? It's good to see you too. Did I tell you, you look wonderful?'

Yes, you did, and I don't think I want to hear this. Let's not *talk* to each other. Let's just get this whole thing over with. Let's go back to where we were before we came here. Let me go back to Kailash.

Captain laughs and breaks into a song. 'Oh Priyaaaa.'

Suddenly, we're laughing hysterically. It's time for me to return to my room. As I get up to leave, Captain yells out, 'Hey, quitter! Come back! We've a lot of catching up to do.'

I ignore him. The smell of marijuana smoke and alcohol at such an odd hour are making my stomach churn. Besides, I want to delay entering the past as much as I can. I had wanted to avoid thinking about Priya, but now it seems I don't have a choice. She has shoved herself into my mind, and won't go away so easily. Priya was always a determined woman.

3

The wind is its usual noisy self, sounding like an inspired bagpipe. It finds music in the architecture of the stone campus of the IIM, making the most of the angles of the buildings. There's a certain hour when the music reaches a crescendo, and that's when I wake up.

The only thing that seems to have remained constant in the transformed IIM campus is the wind. It continues to invade the buildings of the institute, and relieves the torrid heat. I'm a little unsure about my feelings for the wind. It is capricious, and seems a bit of a tease. It blows you around and seems intent on terrorising everything that comes in its way. All these trees, lovingly nurtured over twenty years, must be struggling to survive this gusty onslaught. To me, the Bangalore breeze is remarkable for its sheer romance. If it is a little too aggressive, stamping its claim upon everything that comes its way, it is also just a tad mysterious, as though it brings in its wake something unknown. It is the precursor, I feel, to a fresh experience, one I will never forget.

Since I was joining the IIM a whole week late, I had no time to make a train reservation, and was taking a flight to Bangalore, a hugely expensive affair. As a result, I was travelling alone. It would have been an unthinkable extravagance for my parents to go with me. So with many tears and hugs, I left my parents at Delhi Airport, my last view of them of their noses crushed against the dark glass as my mother waved confusedly at the space in front of her.

I was petrified. A thousand times I told myself that Shruti Malhotra was what she was because she was never scared, but the hole in my stomach wasn't getting filled anytime soon. It was as much as I could do, after I landed in Bangalore, to find a taxi and explain to the driver where I wanted to go. The look on his face should have told me that my destination was unusual but I was far too busy trying to rehearse what I was going to say to the director of the Institute to notice.

It seemed like a few hours though it was just twenty-five minutes later that the taxi turned into the imposing gates set in a stone boundary wall, and discharged me onto the red gravel of the portico. Nothing that I saw there inspired me with confidence. There were no students sitting under trees, noses buried in books. As a matter of fact there were no trees. There was no bustle of professors walking around, intensely discussing the latest macroeconomic theory. There were no fliers hanging untidily from the notice board, exhorting everyone to come at eight in the evening to hear their own friend, Ramu so-and-so, read from his latest collection of poems. Instead, there was almost a void, with everything neatly laid out, bland and uninteresting. The place resembled a hospital more than a college, and my expectation of being called into the director's office as soon as I arrived vanished.

A neat signboard directed me to the 'Office', and I headed there, leaving my bags in an untidy heap in the middle of the vast entrance hall. They looked lost there, like they didn't matter, but I turned my back on them and went to meet whoever I was supposed to meet. I didn't care any longer about the Institute or the director or anything else. Within ten minutes of entering the portals of the Indian Institute of Management, I wanted to return to Delhi and never come back to this wretched place. I was homesick before I knew what I was homesick for.

The indifference of the clerk didn't make matters any easier. He didn't show any respect for the fact that I was one of God's Own People, blessed as I was with an admission to the IIM. He simply gave me a fleeting look, pushed a heap of paper towards me, asked me to fill it up, and didn't even wait for a reply before returning to his electronic typewriter. I swallowed my chagrin, and set to work filling up a hundred forms whose entire purpose seemed to be to ascertain my date of birth and gender. When I was done, a man in shirt and trousers and flip-flops on his feet materialised, a conversation was exchanged in Kannada, and I was told, 'Come.'

It hadn't taken much to transport me to cloud nine a

few weeks ago – just one sheet of paper with two sentences on it. The notice of admission had brought me to the brink of euphoria, as though now there was nothing else that life could offer me, ever. But now that feeling dissipated as I came face to face with the reality of being alone in an alien environment. Perhaps I was just imagining the hostility of the people I had met so far. They had no reason to dislike me. Nor, I told myself firmly, were they supposed to welcome me with open arms. I just wished the euphoria had lasted a little longer.

The slippered man walked briskly away, and I followed him, stammering, 'But my luggage... bags... I have to....'

I received no reply, but as we turned into the entrance hall, I found that my bags had disappeared. Instantly, I felt a surge of relief that my passport and money were in my handbag. Then I felt silly. Why would anyone want to steal two suitcases full of old clothes? I grappled with the mystery of my vanished bags as I followed my guide, noticing nothing around me as I hurried along, trying to keep up with his fast and easy pace. We entered another seemingly deserted building, though I could hear sounds coming from somewhere inside. Again, I was given no time to take in my surroundings as the man hopped up a flight of stairs, and finally came to a halt on the landing. He stood there, opened his mouth and shouted something, a name, at no one in particular, but within a minute, a dried-up old woman with a huge nose-pin and flowers in her hair emerged. The two exchanged words in Kannada, and the man turned on his heel and walked off. I began to follow him but the woman tapped my shoulder, and beckoned me to go with her. She led me to a room and went away, leaving me to stare at my first hostel accommodation in wonder. My bags stood neatly in one corner, next to the writing table. The bed was bare apart from a mattress and a pillow, both of which looked rough but clean, and in one corner stood a steel cupboard. These, apart from a straight-backed chair, were the only furniture in the room. The walls were painted a bilious yellow, and a nod to aesthetics had been made in the form of a pink-coloured alcove with a cement shelf, obviously meant to be used as a dressing table. The window was wide open, and I looked out to see an expanse of red earth, whirling up in places with the force of the wind. The wind blew a gust in my face, and I fell in love with it. I decided that perhaps I could give Bangalore a try, in spite of my spartan room and hostile environment. In my newfound optimism, I headed to the ground floor, where I had heard voices earlier. I bravely told myself that if I were ragged, I would put up with it. My fears proved groundless, as I discovered when I entered the source of the noise, the hostel dining room.

Nobody was bothered about me. Groups of men were gathered at various tables, in various outfits, from formal trousers to striped pyjamas, relaxing on this Sunday morning. Breakfast must have just got over, because the debris still lay there on a cement counter separating the kitchen from the dining area, rice idlis congealing in a steel bucket, blobs of coconut chutney carelessly spilt around the tub, a few coffee tumblers resting next to a steel drum with a tap. Empty jugs lay on the various dining tables, stray glasses giving them company, not telling if they had been used or not. Nobody offered me breakfast, but worse, nobody offered me recognition. I might as well have not existed. It was not an auspicious start. All my confidence drained away and lay about me in a pool, congealing as fast as the coconut chutney. A loud shout of laughter from one of the groups made me wonder if I was the subject of the merriment.

Was I offended or relieved to discover that I wasn't? It dawned on me that I was perhaps not expected to do anything except just be there, live my life, and stay out of everyone's way. Well, that wasn't me, never had been. I needed people, people who would support me, and would need my support. I wasn't overly gregarious, but nor was I a recluse. I thought of myself as just a regular kind of girl, the kind who made good friends as she went along, some of whom stayed by her side forever. If these friends wouldn't come to me well then.... 'Hi. Shruti Malhotra,' I said, going up to a random group.

I couldn't have caused more shock if I had walked in naked and said, 'Let's have sex.' It would have been funny if it weren't so tragic.

Sure, my conversation starter created interest, but not the kind I was looking for. I had hoped for some reciprocity, at least a vaguely enthusiastic greeting. All I received instead was a couple of mumbled hi's after an initial silence. There was not even a handshake. I could go back to being ignored. Nothing more was required from me. So I fled to the sanctuary of my room, the one that at first glance had appeared like a prison. Then I sat and waited, for what, I did not know.

It was evening before my presence was acknowledged. A shock-haired girl wearing bright red lipstick and not much else entered my room without knocking, sat heavily on my bed and said, 'Mind if I smoke?'

Priya Pathak was the first person with whom I exchanged a complete sentence on campus. And what a person! Can one change by meeting an individual? I don't mean a guru or thought leader. Just an ordinary individual. I did. The instant I laid eyes on Priya, I stopped being Shruti Malhotra from Delhi. I didn't know what I became then. I didn't even know I had changed. How could I? That wisdom came much later, twenty years later.

'You just came in, didn't you? I wasn't here this morning. Had something to do in town. I bet this bunch of assholes didn't even smile at you.'

To say I was taken aback by this diatribe would be understating it. I was stunned.

Before I could say anything, 'Assholes,' she muttered again darkly.

She didn't ask me my name or give hers. It didn't matter. The names could come later. She pushed back her heavy hair from her brow, and the long cylinder of bangles on her left forearm jingled madly. I didn't want to doubt her, but I couldn't do much else. She was doubtful, our Priya.

'I need a partner for tomorrow's POM 1 assignment. How about it?' she asked.

Assignments already? What did POM stand for? I dared not ask. I wanted, I didn't know why, to make a good impression on my new acquaintance. I was happy to assent. She told me to meet her in her room after dinner. It was the one with the Viennese mask on the door. She went out, leaving behind a cloud of cigarette smoke, Poison perfume and confusion. Watching her retreat from the slit in my doorway, I cursed myself for not asking her for more details.

At dinnertime, I looked around for my new friend. Perhaps she could be my dinner companion. She couldn't. She was busy seducing a willing male as I saw from a distance. Although there was no one else sitting at their long table, I knew there was no place for me there. In her own way Priya was being introduced to me. There was no other person whose companionship I could claim. I didn't know a soul in the dining room.

As I ate alone, feeling abandoned and friendless, I resolved to return to Delhi on the next flight. Whatever else the Indian Institute of Management, Bangalore may nurture, it wasn't friendliness, I decided. Two years of solitude, of not being spoken to, of being ignored by the only person with whom I had had a conversation. There was no choice. I must give up.

The POM assignment had been an excuse, as I discovered. Before going to Priya's room, I had armed myself with pens and a brand new notebook, having nothing else to arm myself with, not even my self-esteem. There wasn't any need, I discovered. Priya didn't even look at them. Within two minutes the Production and Operations Management professor, C. R. Chinnaswamy – Chinni to others and a prick to Priya – was dismissed as an asshole, this being Priya's favourite term for everyone that she considered beneath her, which was everyone.

'Ignore him,' she advised me. 'He's a sadist. Just read your text before going for class, always pages i to xi of the introduction, and you're safe. That's where the prick's name is mentioned twelve times, I counted, and he loves to talk about it. Why have you come here, to the IIM of B?' she asked, the subject of POM dismissed. I realized then that this was a test of sorts. The answer to this question was what would determine how I was viewed by Priya. I wasn't here to discuss POM, I was here to discuss me.

Priya saved me the bother of replying. 'You've come here because you're a sucker. Well, welcome to the club. You're going to see a bunch of brilliant suckers, some of the most brilliant in the whole country, perhaps the world, but still suckers. They believe they're going to rule the world. Boy, are they wrong! They're going to do nothing but lick ass all their lives. What a bunch of pricks!'

The combination of profanity and pop philosophy was heady. And I wanted more. 'This is the last refuge of the brilliant,' said my mentor bitterly, 'and this is where the dumbing down begins. POM indeed! What can this place offer? The students are opinionated sons-of-bitches, the professors are incompetent, the staff is indifferent, the facilities are not even of Indian standard, forget international ones.' At least the summing up was neat. I couldn't be open-minded after this. 'And the guys aren't even cute,' added Priya as an afterthought.

Priya was my senior by a whole week. I had no cause to disbelieve her, yet her way of thinking wasn't mine. I had come to the IIM in search of something. Her cynicism wasn't going to deprive me of that. But it wasn't long before I discovered that there was a measure of truth in Priya's opinion. I had expected to be taught by international celebrities from the world of management. Instead, the quality of the professors was erratic, and from day one, I found myself out of my depth in that world. From living in a world of economics and English literature, I was transported to the kingdoms of maths, financial accounting and of course, POM 1. And the journey of discovery began.

The maths professor, one B. R. Burman, or Berry, as we called him, was an international genius. For me, his genius lay in giving quizzes of the most bizarre complexity. In the first one, just a fortnight after I joined, I scored 2 out of 10. The passing score was 5. I had failed in my first quiz. Right. It was definitely time to return, admit defeat, and confess that I was mentally retarded, and had been so when I applied for admission to this facility for psychopaths. There were other downcast faces in the classroom when the answer papers were handed out. That didn't matter to me. Nobody could've done worse than me, I knew. The tears were close to the surface but needed to stay there for a while till I could retire to my room.

Priya walked in, as usual without knocking, when the waterworks were in full flow. She looked at me as a scientist looks at a pinned insect. I think the word is clinical. After a while she asked me, 'So, don't like your marks, huh? Don't worry, nobody does. The average is 4. Berry is Sadist No.1. Everyone knows that. He assumes everyone completed their PhD in Probs & Stats before joining this black hole. I wonder if he is the most hated guy on campus. Or it could be Pansy, I'm not sure. How about I take you for some real coffee instead of this sewage?'

I later discovered that Priya herself had scored 8, the highest in class. She was a genius, even if, to most people who didn't know her intimately, an evil one.

We walked across to Venky's, a tin shack that had come up in the middle of nowhere and served what we most wanted – wonderful coffee and hot, freshly cooked food of the snacky kind. I had a feeling this shack wasn't really legal, but who cared when there was no choice? It was open till one in the morning and served the best coffee I'd had in a long time. A filament bulb shone inside, suspended from an exposed wire, night and day. The shed had no windows and there was no natural light. A wooden table with a tin top performed the role of shop counter. On this were placed three glass jars containing orange lozenges in one, coconut cookies in the other and milk rusks in the third. None of the jars looked as though it had been touched by human hands since the tin structure first came up. In a tin tray covered by a dome-shaped wire mesh were freshly made vegetable fritters, the South Indian bhajjis, and those and the coffee that bubbled all day long on the kerosene stove were to die for. Our overall expectation in the department of food was low. There were only two choices offered to us – the luxury restaurants that were not within our reach and establishments like Venky's, where one could get a filling meal for just a few rupees. Those shacks weren't the last word on hygiene, but there wasn't much one could do about that. We were deprived, and our deprivation forced us to take whatever was offered.

Arrangement for the students' comfort at Venky's consisted of a few folding iron chairs, the kind whose back is only half-filled, leaving an indentation in your back if you sat in it too long, and some low stools to be used as tables. There was no flooring to speak of since the shack was built directly over the uneven ground. As a result, the chairs and the tables wobbled all the time. Priya said ironically that the place rocked.

We ordered two coffees, or rather, Priya ordered them in chaste Kannada, and we sat down at one of the tables. Of course, Priya would speak Kannada, a language as alien to me as Greek. Technically, she shouldn't have known it either since her native tongue was Marathi. But that was Priya. Two of the other tables were occupied. I saw with surprise that at one of them sat the man with whom my companion had been flirting so intensely the other day in the dining hall, but now she ignored him completely, while he stared at her hungrily, as though he hadn't eaten in a long time. It was embarrassing to watch. I almost wished she would go and sit with him, and relieve some of that naked desire, but she didn't. Instead, the two of us sat there and chatted for a long time, nursing our coffee and my sorely tested pride. Some more students came in. It was the same group to whom I had introduced myself on the first day. I cringed at the memory. I hoped they didn't remember that encounter. You could have knocked me down with a feather when one of the men got up from his chair and walked up to us. He shook my hand enthusiastically and, would you believe it, *ignored Priya*! 'Hi. I'm Dilip alias Jaggu.' There was a burst of laughter from the rest of the group.

'So, what're you guys doing for the welcome party?'

Priya continued to look bored and aloof while I was mystified. What welcome party?

'Come on, don't tell me you haven't heard of *the* welcome do?'

By now, Jaggu's friends were listening with avid interest. I came to know later that it was always Jaggu who made the first overtures for anything. He was the natural choice for Placement Rep in the second year, the man who was the liaison with the corporate organizations that came to campus to pick their new recruits.

There was going to be a party next Saturday, a kind of 'getting to know each other' affair, where the seniors would be formally introduced to the first years. It was tradition, said Jaggu. Bullshit, said another man who I later discovered was called Captain. Don't believe him. We've made up the tradition part. But yeah, it certainly is party time. We need *something* to forget Berry. My enthusiasm for the idea must have seemed incredibly juvenile to the cynical Priya. But I didn't care. Finally, I was being invited to the fraternity. I could, at long last, be a member of something other than class.

The rehearsals for the welcome party proceeded alongside the dreary lectures of Production Management. Suddenly the days, from being a series of lectures and assignments, became a hectic combination of rehearsals, party plans, project discussions for POM 1, where I was kindly included in Curry's group, and coffee sessions at Venky's.

I now, finally, belonged. I was twenty and lonely. The need to be a part of a group, a fraternity, was as strong in me as the next person, the exception to this rule being Priya. She could get by with anything and nothing. But I wasn't Priya, nothing like her. I was normal. Friendship with Priya, I felt, made me stick out like a sore thumb. It was high time I made some regular friends.

Priya made me uncomfortable, with her brooding and erratic behaviour. I was young enough that I could conveniently forget that it was she who had made my first few weeks in the institute bearable. I just moved on to newer friends. I would see her sometimes, in classes, most of which she skipped, or in the dining hall, sitting in a corner with a man, a different one almost every time. We were now almost three weeks into our first term. In another few weeks, it would be time for the mid-term exams, but right now the motif was the party, and the programme that went with it.

I was glad of that. Academics was not my favourite topic at present, though by now, my scores in the quizzes, from the initial dismal ones, had managed to crawl up to the halfway mark and had steadied there. I was tired of being told that things would improve slowly. I told myself that had I known things would be so tough at the IIM, I wouldn't have joined it in the first place. But I couldn't fool myself. I would have come no matter what.

'Stop worrying so much,' said Curry, trying to console me. 'This place is nothing compared to engineering college. That place is murder, man.'

I reminded him sharply that I was not from an engineering college and I found *this* place murder.

'You know what, you're too tense. You should learn to chill out a little. You won't last out the two years if you're so nervous all the time. And everyone says the first year is the hardest. Why don't you come to E6 tonight? There's some good stuff going on there in the evenings.'

I knew what the good stuff was, of course. I had never smoked marijuana before, but that didn't mean I wasn't willing to try. I was at the IIM, dammit, and I wanted to do everything that people did here, even drugs. A few weeks ago, I would have been shocked at my own thoughts, but something had changed since. The IIM had given me a different set of bifocals to see life with. The innocent girl who had entered the mighty gates of this institution just over a month before needed to be forgotten. I didn't wish to continue being Miss Know Nothing Graduate in Economics Honours from Delhi whose biggest adventure had been to go to an R rated movie at the age of sixteen, and who still slept with her mother after watching a late night horror movie. Yes, I missed my parents, desperately sometimes, and judging by their intense letters, my feelings were reciprocated with interest, but it was high time I grew up. I couldn't keep adulthood at bay forever. I was ready to forge a new identity. And that meant trying out every new experience, and then deciding what to do with it. I wanted to grow up because I saw I was still a child.

The day of the party finally dawned. The evening's entertainment consisted of the usual line up of musical talent, a skit, directed by Captain, loaded with double entendres and x-rated jokes, and some individual performances by my female classmates, Mangala and Radha. There was a delightful innocence about the whole programme, with everyone doing their bit to make it a success. I had never found any homogeneity in the way the class functioned. In fact, cliques were quick to form, and more than once, I had been on the verge of getting sucked into some childish backbiting myself. Intense competition, I discovered, created its own irrationality, and in many ways, though people behaved like mature managers, they revealed their insecurity in the pettiest of situations. That night, however, all was forgotten as the class bonded together to prove to the seniors that in this, as in everything else, we were a star company. I had a bit role in the skit, and another classmate, Kajri, was in the choir, belting out ghazals and Hindi film songs with surprising vigour. That accounted for four of the five women in class. Priya wasn't participating in anything.

The bar remained steadily crowded. After the skit,

Captain forced a glass of cheap beer on me, to celebrate, he said, his first dramatic success. Yet another first, the taste of alcohol on my tongue. By now the party was swinging. The professors, who were invited to every party, and for some strange reason, always attended, had left, and the students were getting into the mood to let their hair down.

Priya's hair was unravelling and her face looked shiny. Her pupils were pinpoints of light. It was obvious that she had imbibed much more than alcohol. A boy trailed behind Priya like a lost puppy. Somebody put on some music and Priya led the boy to the floor and started swaying. This was too much for the male students, all of whom had gathered around the little clearing in tight concentric circles to watch this spectacle, of a female taking the lead in something. Priya danced with abandon, her sari falling off to expose one breast in its miniature choli. She didn't bother to haul it up. Her dance companion stood in one spot, almost frozen as Priya's movements became more and more wild. She was giggling softly, not bothered that there was nobody else on the dance floor. A silence descended upon the gathered crowd, but it was just the calm before the storm. Suddenly, another body hurled itself in front of Priya. It was Ravi Saluja, our very own 'Dilliwallah', the man from Delhi. After a while, some more people started dancing, and the party became gay. Then I noticed that neither Priya nor Ravi were to be seen in the crowd. I drew my own conclusion and told myself it was none of my business. As for me, it was time to return to my room. I was tired but happy. I had made the acquaintance of quite

a few students, met some of the professors and drunk beer
for the first time in my life. It wasn't a bad score.

In the morning, when I went down for breakfast, a
group of students was hanging around the notice board.
There was a sheet of paper with some caricatures tacked
on it. I started to look at them but Curry hurried me into
the dining room. 'Come on, Shruts, stop gloating over last
night's success. Let's grab a bite.' It was the first time I had
heard my name abbreviated like this. Later on, it would
turn into a monosyllabic 'Ruts'.

'You carry on. I'll just take a look at these drawings.'
The crowd around the notice board had made me curious.
'Did you see them? What are they?'

'Never mind them, Shruts. Let's go have breakfast.'

'Why the hurry?' It was Sunday morning. Nobody
ever hurried for breakfast on Sundays. Half the class didn't
even *have* breakfast.

Curry was silent for a moment, and I had a feeling he
was trying to think of a good answer. 'I have a hangover
today, I wonder why, and both Eco and POM assignments
have to be handed in tomorrow. When the hell am I going
to do them? Last night's party rocked, didn't it? I haven't
had so much beer for three whole months now, not since I
celebrated my admission here.'

Curry was babbling and both of us knew it. There was
something on that notice board that he didn't want me
to see. One of the seniors was just about to take down
the mysterious sheet of paper. I pushed him aside a little
so I could see it. The sheet carried four sketches, one in

each corner. The first showed a girl sniffing something, the second sniffing and drinking, the third entwined with a man under whom was written in bold 'Sucker!', and the fourth showed the same girl vomiting, the man watching her while she did this. This time the word 'Sucker' was written below the girl. I was shocked to see the sketches. Which student had it in for Priya so badly, I wondered, for there was no doubt in my mind that the girl in the sketch was Priya. I was learning, and learning fast. There was a place for non-conformists, and the IIM wasn't it. And Priya was the standard-bearer for non-conformists. Her devil-may-care-I-certainly-don't attitude didn't go down too well with most of the students although that didn't seem to stop them from wanting to sleep with her. And bitchiness, it would appear, wasn't the prerogative of the female of the species. I was quite sure that the artist in question was male. I refused to believe that any of my female classmates could harbour so much spite.

I was hopping mad about the attack on my friend. I certainly didn't agree with, let alone approve of, many of the things she did. Sometimes she came to class totally stoned, and sat through the entire class in a trance. She never hid her contempt for the other students, and those whom she could have respected, she ignored instead. And since, on the IQ front, she was superior to almost everyone in class, her contempt wasn't misplaced, though it set people's backs up. She was abrasive in her behaviour and did not think the rules of polite society applied to her. If she could call a spade a bloody shovel, she did so. She was never shy, though her reserve was almost extreme. I doubt if she spoke openly even to her lovers. Often she made me uncomfortable with her rough language and unconventional ways. More than once I had felt out of my depth in her company. But how could I have forgotten that she was the first person who had taken the initiative to befriend me when I arrived? She had helped me make it through my first disastrous test, and there were other rough patches that she had smoothened out for me. I felt I owed something to her, though I wasn't clear what.

Priya only laughed when I spoke to her about my unease. 'Fuck it, yaar!' she said. 'Who cares what this bunch of wimps thinks? It's probably some guy who is despo to get into my pants.'

By now, I had stopped getting shocked by Priya's frankness. Her lack of concern should have been reassuring. Instead, I felt a sense of failure. I had failed to defend my friend.

I now think that this was the day I finally grew up. This was when I realized that I would have to shed all my notions of decency and morality if I wanted to survive the IIM. I think it was also the day I confirmed to myself what I had only faintly known before – that I hated the personal attacks that people made on Priya, even if I didn't stand up for her.

Judging by the uneasiness with which I listened to Jaggu and the others run Priya down earlier tonight, things haven't changed all that much.

4

The early morning is still sunless, with just a hint of brightness on the horizon. The Bangalore breeze is working its charm, and one could be deceived into thinking that one is in the countryside, although the treetops barely conceal the skyscrapers that surround the campus. A long time ago, there were coconut palms, houses with painted doors and colourful patterns of rangoli at the entrance, and further out of the city, fields of rice and other crops whose names I didn't know. Is there any point to thinking about what was? Whatever friendship I had with Bangalore must be transferred to this city. I have to look for things that I like now.

I don't remember when last I thought about the past so earnestly, nor wished for it to come back so much. Our lives were written on a blackboard, and they were wiped out as we moved on. Other things got written on the board, and the shadow of what was there before became fainter and fainter, until it was almost not discernible. To recall faded events is a fruitless struggle. We are not those people, these days aren't those days, this city isn't that city. Both Shruti Malhotra and Bangalore have changed, and I wonder which of the two is more unrecognisable. It's probably the latter. It's a reassuring realisation. I am a point in the continuum that is the life of Shruti Malhotra. Bangalore, on the other hand, shows no such continuity. I am released from the obligation of loving it as the city of my youth, although it's too soon to say if this carries into my association with the IIM as well. We shall just have to wait and see. After all, the campus has also morphed almost beyond recognition.

―✺―

But even now, in spite of the sweeping changes in its look, the lush green IIM campus offers respite from the ugliness and disorder outside. Now, as I look out my window, I can still believe that there are birds out there looking for snakes and rabbits to eat, that there are still rivers somewhere buried beneath the foundations of those ugly buildings, that will somehow spring to life when I walk upon that soil, that there are still shrubs sprouting out of hidden corners, waiting to assault one's senses with their perfume and colour.

I tell myself that there's no reason why I shouldn't be out there, amongst those tropical shrubs, getting my own feel of what it is like to be a part of the IIM now. Immediately, I pull on my jeans and wrap my hair in an untidy bun on top of my head. There's not a moment to be lost. I'm in a race with the sun to see who reaches that bank of trees faster. I win. The morning breeze is chilly, and goose bumps spring up on my arms. It is almost cool enough for a light sweater. I slow down to a sedate walk, picking my way through the tree-lined path that is still unpaved. Here and there are flowers that have fallen from the trees and are turning into mulch. I try not to tread on them but it's hard. There are so many. There are pebbles and the occasional stone, and I walk with my head bent, careful not to trip.

After a while I know I am lost within the campus. Twenty years is a long time in which to remember, and it is too early for me to come to terms with what I have forgotten. The changed look of the entire IIM complex doesn't help. Everything looks unfamiliar, though I know I should recognize it. The buildings in the distance seem new, as does the little shed with the asbestos roof that looms ahead. It has a window and as I approach closer, I can see heads moving about inside. There's a board above the doorway that says 'Shanthi Hotel'. So Venky's has been replaced by Shanthi Hotel. I step into the gloomy interior. There are four metal tables, each one with four chairs, spread out on the rough floor. The heads I had glimpsed belong to two young women who are noisily chopping vegetables at a table. It can't be much after six but the women look impeccable in their bright polyester saris, hair resplendent with fresh orange flowers, a hint of turmeric glistening on their chocolate faces. They stop chattering when they see me, though they don't look surprised to see a jeans-clad woman drifting into their 'hotel' at such an early hour. They smile at me, and I'm forced to smile back.

I don't know what to say. I have no Kannada with

which to apologize for intruding upon them. We stare at one another wordlessly. They have stopped chopping the vegetables, perhaps waiting for me to say something. When I remain silent, one of them returns to her task while the other continues to wait. I want to sit down inside that shack which, I can see, has been swept clean, each surface gleaming. But I don't know what I'll do after I sit down. I cannot enter into any conversation, ask questions or answer them. Restlessly, I wave goodbye, still smiling, but before I can leave, someone else enters the shack.

I don't know who it is. He wasn't there at the party last night.

'Ruts! What are you doing here?'

'Hi. And you are?'

Fortunately, the man doesn't take offence. He answers with a smile, 'Oh dear! I didn't think I was that forgettable!'

'I'm sorry.'

'That's okay. I was just teasing. Shridhar, Shridhar Acharya.'

'Of course! The five pointer!' That was what we called people who always received A's.

He laughs at my naïve exclamation. 'Was that what I was? I never knew.'

'I'm sorry,' I say again. 'I'm being really offensive this morning. Put it down to Bangalore.'

'Bangalore?'

'Yes, it was kind of a shock to see this new city, to be honest.'

'You haven't come here lately. I can see that. Otherwise you wouldn't be so shocked. I came here five years ago, and since then it's become even worse.'

'Where are the gardens?' I ask, referring to the huge green spaces that give Bangalore its name. 'Are they still there?'

'I think so. Haven't visited those, I'm afraid. I just fly in on work.'

'Work?'

'It's a long story. But back to my original question. What are you doing here?'

I don't think I have an answer. 'I was just walking around,' I answer vaguely.

'Would you like some tea?'

I would prefer coffee, but it looks demanding to ask for two different beverages for two people in that simple shack. I stick to tea.

Shridhar pulls up a couple of chairs and then tells the women something in fluent Kannada. Both of them give identical smiles that show their teeth gleaming between their cocoa-coloured lips and one of them walks up to a counter at one end of the shack. I watch curiously as she sets about lighting an oil stove. After some struggle, it lights up with a hiss and she puts a dented and discoloured pan on it. From a corner behind the counter she takes out two steel glasses and pours water into them from an earthen pitcher that is perched on a three-legged stool, and places the glasses in front of us. There is a profusion of the human touch in all this, and I feel myself almost visibly cringing. Taps and filters seem like alien machinery over here.

I watch in fascination as Shridhar gulps down the water. I am too conscious of the high bacterial content to do the same. There's something quite appropriate about Shridhar drinking the stuff though. In his ill-fitting shirt and cheap-looking trousers, he looks not quite urban, and certainly not the prototype of the typical IIM graduate. Where are the foreign brand shoes, the exclusive trousers, the casual tee that costs enough to buy a lesser person's wardrobe for an entire month, the gelled and set hair? Where is the signature pen peeping out of the breast-pocket, and the cellphone that has just been launched in the market? Instead, the full head of hair is oiled and combed neatly, the side-parting gleaming on the skull. On the feet are cheap leather chappals that look like they have been bought from a roadside vendor. There are no other accessories of any kind, and nothing in the overall appearance to indicate what the wearer does for a living, though he is certainly out to conserve his resources. That's about all I can judge from the way Shridhar looks, with his neat and unspectacular visage that can make him blend into the scenery anywhere he goes. The contrast with Jaggu couldn't be greater.

To my surprise, Shridhar has observed my inhibition regarding the water.

'You think this water isn't safe?' asks Shridhar.

'Yes, it isn't, frankly. You could fall sick.'

He throws his head back and laughs. Now I remember

Shridhar, quite vividly in fact. That laugh. I dreaded it in those years. It was usually the precursor to an argument that would always end in acrimony. It symbolized contempt for the speaker, and a certain arrogance. It was the laugh that had earned Shridhar the title 'Least Popular Boy of the Class'. Nobody was spared that jeering amusement, not the professors, and certainly not the students. Fortunately, I had escaped its slicing action, and retained my self-respect with Shridhar in those two years. Many others, I knew, hadn't been so fortunate. I tell myself that the sweat that has popped up suddenly on my brow is solely because of the heat, but who am I fooling? The temperature cannot be more than a pleasant twenty-five degrees. Shall I make my excuses and leave this shack? But the order for tea has already been placed, and I cannot dismiss that. Nor can I dismiss my renewed acquaintanceship so cravenly. For all I know, Shridhar might have changed. I steel myself to go through the tea ritual. I tell myself I'm no longer a vulnerable twenty-year-old. If I can deal with Banes, the miserly writer, the man in front of me is no big deal. For no reason, Xenia's face inserts itself into my mind, and I smile at the expression she would wear if she had to deal with a man like Shridhar. Wooden-faced describes it best.

The woman behind the counter fiddles with a small transistor radio. A song in Tamil echoes round the shack, and I come back to the here and now. The woman hums an occasional word, as she gets busy making our tea. In addition to Kannada, I don't know Tamil either, and the song gives me an excuse to stay silent. I don't know what to say to this man. He isn't exactly a great friend. To my surprise, Shridhar also hums a couple of bars of the song, which is apparently a famous one. It sounds familiar, and I realize why. There's a Hindi song with the same music. I smile at the thought, and Shridhar smiles back. The woman puts the tea in front of us, and walks back to her friend, resuming her task of vegetable chopping.

The tea is boiling hot and oddly delicious. It is extremely sweet, and normally I cringe at putting so much sugar in my body at such an unearthly hour. But now I sip the sweet brew with relish. I look around the small shack. There's a calendar with a picture of the trio of Ram, Laxman and Sita on one of the walls and the page is turned to the present month. On the wall next to the calendar is a shrine, mounted on the wall. An electric candle flickers in front of an oleograph of Lord Krishna that is garlanded with plastic flowers. One of the women, presumably, has lit two incense sticks and their ash falls onto the floor below. My examination of the shrine prompts one of the women to get up and go to it. She lifts a plate that has been placed in front of the idol and brings it to us. She offers us both pieces of coconut from the plate.

'Careful,' says Shridhar, after the woman returns to her spot, and just as I am about to put a coconut piece into my mouth, 'that's probably washed in the same water that you refused to drink earlier. The germs could easily be in that coconut as well.'

'I know.'

I eat the coconut. It is sweet and fresh and delicious, just as it should be.

Shridhar smiles as he chews on his piece. 'Is that it?'

'What do you want me to say?' I ask. 'Your logic is infallible. And I'm irrational enough to eat prasadam without questioning it.'

'So, you're religious.'

'Actually, I'm an atheist. But I still eat god's food,' I confess.

The laughter rings out again. 'It does taste good, doesn't it?'

'Delicious. I'm eating fresh coconut after so long.'

'How come?'

'Well, you don't find it back where I live.'

'And where's that?'

'Philadelphia. I've been there for fifteen years now. So it's been a really long time.'

'We should remain in touch then,' replies Shridhar. 'I live in Lawrence, Kansas.'

It is my turn to be curious. 'Doing what? Are you with some bank?'

'Why do you say that?'

'I don't know. I just assumed that's what you'd be doing. Wasn't that where all the bright students ended up?'

'Thanks,' he says.

'For what?' I'm confused.

'For the compliment. That I was bright.'

I laugh. 'I don't think that's a compliment. More like a fact.'

'Well, I didn't join a bank.' He pauses for a moment, looking down at his tea. Then he takes a slow sip. I get the impression that he is preparing himself to say something. It gives him a look of uncertainty, and I'm confused. The Shridhar I remember never looked uncertain about anything.

'How's Priya?' he says finally, taking me by surprise with the change of subject.

'Don't know,' I reply cautiously. 'We haven't exactly stayed in touch.'

'How come? I thought you two were really thick.'

'I don't know. Just one of those things, I guess. We never got round to exchanging details of our whereabouts, and then I moved about pretty often, in the early years. It isn't all that hard to lose contact.' Shridhar doesn't seem convinced and I'm not surprised. It is hard to believe that two friends as close as Priya and I could move so far apart. I almost find it hard to believe myself.

'I suppose not. I haven't met anyone from our batch in a long time now,' says Shridhar, interrupting my reverie. 'That's why I came to this do. I thought I'd look up everyone. I wonder if that's a good idea.'

'Yeah,' I reply weakly.

'I guess even you're not sure why you came here, right? I mean, it makes no sense, does it? We are all different people now. What's the point of going back to where we were? We can never do that. Isn't it ridiculous, wanting to be that young again? At least, I don't want to.'

'Yeah,' I say again.

'You look just the same.' There's a note of accusation in Shridhar's voice, and I make an effort to refrain from justifying my looks. Before I can think about it further, he continues speaking.

'I was surprised at how little people have changed, when I saw them last night. I could recognize all of them, well, almost all. There were a couple who have changed physically but they still talk in the same manner.'

'You haven't changed much either,' I say, hoping to flatter him.

'Well, thanks. I certainly feel a lot older.'

'I don't think there's anyone amongst us who doesn't.'

'Oh, I don't know. People claim to feel younger too, you know.'

'They are either lying or deluding themselves. They are the people who want to keep age at bay,' I say, rather passionately.

'Relax, Ruts, you and I both know how old we are.'

I sigh. 'Sometimes when I'm with my writers, I feel a hundred. They can be so naïve. It's like they haven't grown up in this world at all. And yet they treat us like aliens!' I explain to him what I do.

'Sounds like a hard job.'

'Yes, well, never mind. You were telling me what you do.'

Shridhar shrugs his shoulders. 'I teach at the University of Kansas.'

'A professor! I don't think there are too many of those in our batch.'

'I'm not a professor, not exactly. I just got denied my tenure, to be honest. Technically, I'm an assistant professor. Or rather, was. As things stand right now, I'm not anything.'

I don't know what to say to this. Being denied tenure is like being sacked. It's a professional stigma.

Shridhar is now looking out of the window, the same one through which I had seen the women's heads earlier on. The window is grainy and nothing much of the outside can be seen through it, except that it's daylight. The Tamil songs are still playing, and Shridhar's fingers tap a restless beat on the table. His eyes are crinkled as though he is trying to penetrate the bleariness of the window.

'I'm sorry to hear this,' I say, cursing myself for not being able to say more.

'Yeah, so am I. Twenty years of teaching and research, two continents, four different institutions and nothing to show for it.'

'And what about your family? Wife? Kids?'

'I'm not married.'

'Oh.'

'Yeah, no worries on that front. I'll only starve myself if I stop earning. Oh, and maybe my parents. I have to send them money every month.'

'You sound grim,' I say carefully. 'It can't be that bad. Don't you still have your job?'

'Not for very long.' Shridhar turns his face to the opposite wall and stares at it for some time. Then he faces me and gives a small smile, as though he knows I feel for him in spite of his aversion to any sympathy, and he appreciates that.

'Do you want some more tea?' he says.

'No thanks. It was good, wasn't it?'

'I thought you northies didn't like southie tea?'

'Well, normally I don't, but somehow, this tasted delicious.'

'I'll tell Vijaya that.'

'You know these people?'

'No. But I'm guessing that the owner of Shanthi Hotel has to be Vijaya.'

It is such a pointless thing to say, yet there's something funny in the way Shridhar says it. I laugh, as does Shridhar. This streak of humour comes as a surprise to me. Was it always there? He takes out his wallet and goes up to the women. They have a loud conversation and then Shridhar returns without paying.

'Ready? Let's go.'

'What was all that about?' I ask as we emerge in the sunlight, still only a mellow gloss rather than the fiery beam that it will turn into a little later.

'She said it was complimentary since we were the first customers of the day.'

'Oh, that was sweet! I should return the favour.'

'Don't worry about it, Ruts. The woman is sitting on IIM land, free of cost, I'm guessing. That's enough of a favour.'

'You know, I'd never have thought of that.'

'Yeah, I know. It's a certain kind of brain that moves in that direction, and you don't have it.'

'You make me sound stupid,' I protest.

'Not stupid, no. Honest maybe. A rare commodity in this place, honesty. I always believed the IIM needed more people like you and less like that Ravi.'

'You mean Rats?'

'Yeah. I mean, he was a trickster down to his last cell, but it worked for him. I heard somewhere that he is on the board of East-West Bank. I guess the IIM rewards people like him, people who are simply trying to beat the system all the time. That's all I saw him do, beat the system.'

The bitterness in his voice makes me uncomfortable.

'Remember how Ravi was always trying to be friendly with all the professors? I used to find that so disgusting, especially since he couldn't stand any of them, or so he claimed. And his deceit actually helped him!'

'He was always intelligent,' I say dubiously.

Shridhar laughs again. 'Ruts, everyone who manages to get admission to this place is intelligent, probably brilliant. So that's not the point. Rats was also brilliant in getting what he wanted, the means no issue. And those of us who were different suffered.'

'So you think ability isn't the key to success?'

'Not at all. The key to success is presentation, Ruts, and that's all. Everything else follows. Intelligence, intention, integrity, these are all of secondary value. If he were honest, Rats would agree.'

Shridhar reminds me now of the boy I used to know, the one who would engage in fiery debates in the classroom that had a certain bitterness in their tenor.

We are walking down a path that is well paved and clearly leading to some destination. I'm completely lost, though Shridhar seems to know the way. Changing the subject, I say, 'You seem to know this place well.'

'I've been visiting here for lectures.'

'That sounds great. It must make you feel happy, to teach where you studied. I know I'd like that.'

'Well, I was teaching earlier, when I was doing my fellowship here.'

'I didn't know that, the fellowship part, I mean. What made you join the programme?'

'I couldn't get a job and this seemed the next best option.'

Shridhar says this in a matter-of-fact manner that makes his words all the more shocking.

'What do you mean, you couldn't get a job?'

'Just that. I couldn't get placement.'

'I thought everyone got placement at this place. I got it.'

'Well, I did find a job, but it was pretty much a dead end thing. I don't even remember the name of the organization now. So I refused.'

'But why?'

'Why what?'

'Why couldn't you get a job? Your grades....'

'Were not enough. I found myself unable to suck up to the interviewers, and so they probably decided they didn't want an honest person in their midst.'

'Isn't that too harsh?'

'How else would you explain it? My knowledge was

never an issue. But I always advocated integrity, and I guess those people were uncomfortable with my approach.'

'But that's terrible!'

'I thought so too.' Shridhar smiles dimly. 'I knew I was far more capable than most of the other students and yet there I was, with nothing to show for the two years I spent at this place. I was clear I wasn't going to take up the placement I was offered. All they were offering was junior manager on the factory floor. It was a huge insult. Before joining the IIM, I had a decent job, much better than the placement I got here. It was a bit of an irony really. I quit my job to come here. A degree from the IIM always leads to better prospects, doesn't it? And look where I landed up.'

'And so?'

'And so I decided to get into research and teaching. I guess I wanted to do something more meaningful than suck up to corporate toady types. You look shocked,' he says as we arrive at our guesthouse through a circuitous route.

'I am. I never imagined....'

'No, neither did I. I thought just working hard would be enough to take me far. Even now I find it hard to believe that something else is required. By the way, you're the only one I've said all this to. I'd appreciate it not being spread around.'

Like I was going to go and tell the whole world what a loser this man was! I'm about to say something nasty but stop myself. I guess losing one's job does give one licence to be unpleasant. 'Don't worry on that front,' I tell him.

'I'm sorry,' he says, surprising me again. 'Of course you won't gossip about me.'

'I wish I could help.'

'Yeah, so do I. Anyway, fuck it. Let's have a blast while we're here, right? I can watch everyone get drunk all over again. So what about you?' he turns to look at me.

'What do you mean?'

'What are your plans for the weekend? Showing off the IIM to your family?'

The way he says it makes it sound like such a pedestrian exercise. Of course there's a need to show off. Isn't that partly why I'm here?

'Thanks for the tea,' I reply instead.

'Yeah. Seriously, though, how far down memory lane have you walked?'

'I'm sorry?'

'Like, are you looking at everyone and seeing their twenty year ago avatars? Remembering how someone dipped their toast in the coffee, or wore their pants high on the ankles? Like, are you here or in the past? And what does that handsome husband of yours think of your trip?'

So Shridhar was there at the party last night. I must have missed him. And why didn't he talk to me then? Was he afraid of all this stuff coming out in the presence of other people?

'Of course I'm here,' I lie. 'There's no point going back, is there?'

'I'm not sure others would agree with you.'

'Others don't matter.'

My companion smiles, a stray tooth gleaming through his closed lips. 'I agree. They don't.'

It's almost disgusting how easily I've started lying to people. What would Shridhar say if he knew what had crossed my mind when I saw Jaggu last night? The sight that rose in front of my eyes when I met him at the airport? The thought that leapt to the mind when he called me late at night, and the feeling I had when I saw not just Jaggu, but also Curry and Captain in that room? No, I don't think that is at all a fit description for Shridhar's ears.

Fortunately, we are back at the guesthouse before I can think of anything else to say to Shridhar. There's something strange about him, and I somehow can't figure him out. He is unmarried and unemployed, and embittered in the process. I wonder why he has chosen me for his confidences. I certainly can't offer any help, and I'm not sure I want to either. He seems determined to see the dark side of the moon all the time. And yet he's here. Surely that's a form of celebration?

—m—

Why is Shridhar unmarried still? It is odd for an Indian Brahmin from Tamil Nadu, a Tambram, as I guess Shridhar is, to remain single for so long. And there was something just a little odd about the way in which he described his marital state.

'Does a divorced man say he is not married?' I ask Kailash as I enter our room.

Kailash has just woken up and is still lying in bed, looking out of the window as he always does first thing in the morning. Communion with nature, he calls it, though all he sees from the window in our apartment block in Philadelphia are more apartment blocks.

'What are you talking about? And where were you?'

'I went for a walk,' I reply, snuggling up to him. 'Listen, explain this if you can. You ask a man about his wife and kids and he says he isn't married. What does that mean?'

'It means he is not married.'

'Why not?'

'Shruti, I think I need some tea.' Kailash sounds defeated.

'I'll order room service in a minute. Why doesn't a man marry?'

'Okay, I think this is all I can take. You need to explain yourself, woman. What the hell are you talking about?'

I tell him about my morning walk and Shridhar.

'All right, Sherlock, so now you have a mystery to solve about a man who didn't exist for you till half an hour ago. That's a bit excessive, isn't it?' Kailash says, putting his arm around me. He sounds amused.

'Excessive? Why?'

'Ask yourself what this Shridhar means to you. And why you're so bothered about him. Take it easy, Shruti. You're here for a fun weekend, touch base with some old cronies, relive some memories and then return to Philly, to Xenia and to that bunch of sociopaths you call writers.'

Xenia's name reminds me of Jaggu and the message I've just received. 'Gd mrng. C u at bfast. Heard P arriving 2day'. It's not the most indecipherable sms I've ever received but close.

'Kailash, do me a favour?'

'Anything after my tea,' he replies, his face caricaturing a mulish look.

'I heard there's an expedition going into town today, for the families, just after breakfast. Why don't you take the children with you?' I say after organising tea for the two of us, trying not to grimace at the peculiar flavour of burnt tea that's the hallmark of the brew in these parts.

'Getting us out of the way?' asks my husband, hitting really close to the mark.

'Yes. And trying to ensure you don't get sucked into reunion politics.'

'All right. You've sold the idea to me. I'll stay out of your way, while you go about charming the male population.'

'Yeah, like a forty-something woman is capable of that.'

I'm only half-joking. Since we landed at the airport, I've felt as though I've flown into never-never land, and the years have dropped off me until I'm twenty again. And then I'm back to being a mother and a wife, and Peter Pan once more turns into Mother Hubbard. I feel almost schizophrenic.

'So what do I wear today?' asks Kailash, looking at the clothes that are spilling out of his suitcase onto the floor.

I'm not sure what's going on. I've become used to being married to a man who thinks clothes were invented to irritate the wearer. 'What sort of question is that?'

'Look, I need to know this stuff, okay? I'm in the midst of all these corporate dudes. I need to understand power dressing.'

'Power dressing? Why?'

'That's how corporate executives dress, isn't it? Let's see, golf shirts or button downs, creaseless chinos, loafers, aftershave lotion.'

I look in amazement at Kailash. The last time I saw him wear any of these things was during his job interview at UPenn. A long time ago, Kailash stopped buying clothes. It saved him time, he said, and thinking. He was only in replacement mode, he told me once firmly. When something tore and couldn't be mended, he went and got a replacement that was as close as possible to the original, and that was that.

'I didn't even know you had those clothes,' I say, my head reeling.

'I don't. But they might not let me into this club if I don't have the right attire.'

'Don't be an idiot. The only attire you need is me, okay bonzo?'

'Okay. Incidentally, did I tell you I love my attire?'

I lean forward to kiss him and he pulls me closer. I could get carried away, as Kailash shows every sign of doing, but Rohan walks in to pop our balloon of romance. He leaps up on the bed and sprawls right on top of Kailash, neatly displacing me.

'Good morning. Where's Isha?' I ask, getting up from the bed, which is now the site of a mock fistfight.

'Asleep,' replies my twelve-year-old son with indifference. 'What are we doing today?'

'Your mother is going to be doing stuff with her classmates, and the three of us are free after breakfast to do what we like. So you and Isha can plan something. What would you like to do?'

'Mom, why do you have to hang out here?'

'Because that's what I've come for,' I explain.

'Are all of these people your friends?'

'No, not all. But we studied together many years ago.'

'So?'

'So, it's good fun to meet them, that's all.'

'And what're you going to do when you meet them?'

'I don't know. Talk maybe. Tell each other what we've been doing all these years. Something like that.'

'What a bore!' says Rohan dismissively. 'Can we go to a video game place?'

Kailash groans theatrically. 'Let's see. Maybe. Or maybe we'll explore the city.'

'Is it a nice city?'

'It used to be, once. We can find out today what remains of it.'

'Cool. Hurry up then. I'm hungry.'

Rohan scampers off to his room. 'I wish I could come with you guys,' I say. 'You're going to have so much fun.'

'And you aren't?' Kailash raises his eyebrows. 'Come on, you've been waiting to meet these people for so long. You can't fool me. I know you, my dear.'

—*—

Kailash and I are one of those unlikely pairings that one reads about in low-grade romance novels. I thought I was settled when I finished my business programme. I was going to have a good job that would pay me a good salary and eventually my parents would find me a good husband. I was nothing if not a conformist, and the IIM hadn't done anything to change that. But my marriage plans were all in the comfortable future. The single life suited me perfectly for the present. I wanted to do what I had trained myself for two years to do, work in an organization, give proof of my ability, and show the world that the IIM stamp wasn't just a stamp.

'You must think of marriage,' my mother said, two days after I returned from the institute, just half an hour after I was done putting my final book on my bookshelf. 'You are almost twenty-three now. High time you thought about your future.'

'Ma, I've been thinking about my future for almost three years now,' I replied.

'Oh, that!' said my mother dismissively, removing a book from my shelf, *Indian Economy* by Ruddar Dutt, and flipping through it carelessly, so that its pages dangled towards the ground, on the verge of separating from the cover. 'That's not what I meant. I meant your future. You should get settled now.'

Future, getting settled, having one's own home – so many euphemisms could be employed for the act of finding a man and marrying him. Before I could protest, I was presented with more wisdom on the subject.

'Look around you, Shruti. All your friends are in the process of settling down. You don't want to leave it too late. There's a time for everything, including marriage.'

'Mom, I've just returned! Don't you want me here with you?'

'Don't be foolish,' said my wise old mother. 'Of course it's a treat to have you back.'

'So let's keep it this way for some time. In any case, there's nobody I want to marry right now.'

'Don't worry about that. Just say the word. We have already found a few good boys. Something should work out.'

'Something should work out' – the words sounded as though they referred to finding a window seat in a full train, not my whole future. There was something almost casual in the way my life was being discussed. And alarmingly final.

There's a sort of melancholy that sets in after one returns from hostel. Life's colours are less vivid. There's a lack of expectation about the future. One almost feels like a soldier in mufti. While one has been away, the home has adjusted to one's absence, and the almost visible readjustment required to accommodate one back is also a depressing scene. In my absence, the family television had been shifted to my room. My cupboard, which had been bought long after my parents' cupboard, had now been exchanged with theirs. My clothes had been neatly stacked in one part of the cupboard, removed from their hangers, to make space for my mother's saris. My space had been taken away, in acknowledgment, perhaps, of the fact that it wouldn't be long before I would move out of that house for good. I had turned into an outsider. My heart was entwined around all my friends in Bangalore, and from this distance even the hostel mess waiters seemed closer to me than my acquaintances in Delhi. I thought of Priya all the time, and tried not to think of all the other stuff at all. My thoughts pricked me, since, in spite of the promise I had made on the last day, I had not written to Priya since I'd come home. And somewhere in my heart I knew I wouldn't.

When the phone rang, I was contemplating my wardrobe to decide what I should wear on my first day of work. It was Lalita. In my sadness and disorientation, I had omitted to call her as well.

'What's up? Why the silence?' she asked.

'Should I wear a sari or a salwar-kameez tomorrow?' I asked my newly appointed wardrobe consultant.

'And what's tomorrow?'

'The most important day of the rest of my life. I officially start work as a marketing executive tomorrow.'

'Shruti, that's exciting! You must be thrilled!'

'More scared than thrilled, Lals. I've never worked in an office before.'

'Hey, come on. Is this the woman who moved mountains to go to the IIM speaking? You'll handle it like a pro, don't worry. Wear a sari. The pink one. It looks good on you.'

'Thanks, yaar. So how are you?'

'Great. And missing you. Listen, I called to invite you.'

'To what?'

'My engagement party. This Sunday. Write down the address.'

I was stunned. It had always been the case that where Lalita led, I followed. She stood for 'womanhood' in my adolescent language. Her announcement of her engagement almost made her seem a traitor. After all, she had often declared that marriage and death were two sides of the same coin; the day you married was the day your ambitions died. I felt alone in my struggle to make my own decisions. My mother's nagging drove me to contemplate taking an apartment of my own, an unheard-of act in those days. Only airhostesses and models were supposed to live separately from their families when single. All respectable girls, especially in that bastion of conservative thought, Delhi, lived first with their parents and then with their husband. And after all, there was no real reason why I shouldn't marry. It wasn't as though, my mother pointed out, I had a boyfriend, only she called it 'someone special'. I was the right age, emotionally unattached and had a good job. I was the ideal candidate for the marriage bazaar. The most eligible bachelors were keen to woo me, and I wanted none of it.

'I'll get you a manager,' said my mother, trying to appease me.

I told her humorously that I could manage myself, but I knew what she meant, of course. She was referring to an

IIM graduate. She could produce one, she implied, if I so desired, as though they were a species that, though rare, could nonetheless be captured in the marriage jungle. I might have laughed if I wasn't involved.

'Is there anyone else?' asked my mother for the umpteenth time one night.

'No,' I replied with complete honesty. It was true. There was no one else, much as I wished there had been. I was destined to be one half of an arranged marriage, I thought dismally, and the thought rankled. In the end, it was theatre that rescued me.

I remember I had gone to see Tendulkar's *Ghasiram Kotwal* alone. I didn't mind going to the theatre alone. I actually preferred it. Being on my own allowed me to concentrate on the play rather than on my companion's preferences. I could watch the stage rather than the other person's face, evaluate the performance on its own merit rather than depend on his or her judgment. This time, I was even gladder that I had come alone. The performance, all two and a half hours of it, was riveting. I had seen two previous productions of *Ghasiram*, but this was the best of the lot.

It was a small production group and after the performance the main actors and the director were going to mingle with the audience, talk to them about what they liked about the play. Many people from the audience were trooping out at this point. I, on the other hand, as soon as I heard the announcement, decided to stay back. I wanted to meet the director.

To my disappointment he wasn't there. The actors were still in costume and couldn't be missed, but there was no one else who looked like the director to be found in that small auditorium. I felt I would know him when I saw him. He would be wearing Indian clothes, and have grey hair and a salt and pepper beard. Subconsciously, I think I was invoking an M S Sathyu kind of figure, elderly, stern, modish in a very Indian way. I could certainly make out who the audience was by their formal attire and eager expressions. Ah well, it was just my luck. Then I felt a sliver of annoyance nagging at me. They had announced that the director would be there. Where the hell was he?

'Excuse me,' I said, tapping the woman who played Gauri. 'I'd like to meet the director, please.'

'Kailash,' the woman called out casually. 'Someone here to see you.'

The first thing I noticed was the beard. The next was the emaciated body.

'Yes?' said Kailash.

Even as I looked at the man, I wondered if I was a groupie. I had an urge to hang on to his words, to emulate his gestures, to wear what he was wearing, grow a similar beard, and speak in the same gruff voice. I wished I could grow taller, that my feet could become bigger and wider so that I could wear the same casual chappals that he wore. I wondered, only six months into my first job, whether I could give it up in favour of theatre; if I could get a job with this man, this Kailash's group; and the thought that no theatre group in India actually paid any of its members,

I pushed to the back of my mind. I decided that I needed to see many more performances of the play in order to appreciate it fully, and I went to see every one of the eight shows, including two on Sunday.

My presence could not go unnoticed, particularly since the basement auditorium seated only about a hundred and fifty people. It was the woman who played Gauri, Ghasiram's beautiful wife, who accosted me on the last night. She had sent a man with a small note requesting my presence backstage. I had no plans of how I would continue my acquaintance with Kailash after the performances ended, so I was grateful for this invitation.

'Are you from theatre?' asked Gauri.

'No, but I would like to be,' I replied.

'What's your specialization?' she asked.

'I don't know,' I replied.

She laughed at my answer, and invited me to go with her to the last night party. We made our way in an autorickshaw to Volga Restaurant in Connaught Place, where the party was being held in the backroom. I stayed silent through the ride, unsure of what to expect. The festivities were already underway by the time we reached. Gauri introduced me to a number of people, and their easy self-confidence, instead of putting me at ease, made me nervous and self-conscious, and I immediately regretted accepting the invitation. Clearly, I was in alien territory, and I thought wistfully of home, where my mother was waiting for me, and where, when I went back, she would subject me to a full inquisition. I wondered how to get back home. It was already past ten, and there was no way I could go on my own. But how to look for an escort? The party was just beginning to warm up, and I didn't dare to break up anyone's fun by asking them to take me half way across the city. I lived in one of the most dangerous cities in the world, where sunset meant the law of the jungle taking over, and I knew I had no choice but to stay where I was and wait for some kind soul to give me a lift sometime during the evening. Once again I was annoyed with Kailash for not being there. The only reason I had come to the party was because of him, and now he was nowhere to be seen. And then I saw him, and I didn't know what to say to him, not even when he asked me if he could give me a lift home.

'Why are you late?' I asked when I found my tongue, only to realize what a foolish question it was.

'Excuse me?' he said.

'I'm sorry. I thought the director is a kind of host at these dos,' I said, trying to sound experienced, and also trying to cover up my confusion.

Kailash smiled as though he knew what was going through my mind. 'I heard you want a job with us,' he said, and I knew Gauri – I still didn't know her real name – had been busy. 'What do you like doing?'

'Watching,' I said with a smile, glad to get my wit and presence of mind back.

He was nothing like my classmates at the IIM, and I've never enjoyed a party so much.

I had no reason to fall in love with Kailash and that is

perhaps why I fell so hard. He was a theatre nobody at the time, living with and off his parents, and I was a middle-class, fairly unadventurous young girl, just the common or garden variety of Indian girl that you find in all large cities. I began to love theatre even more after Kailash and I met. Kailash also gave me a reason to ward off my parents' aspirations for me, as I guiltily acknowledged to myself. Though that wasn't the reason why I decided I had finally met my life partner. I loved him, and I still do, I tell myself as I see him and the children go off to breakfast, leaving me to get ready in peace. Kailash might have been an antidote in the beginning, but it wasn't long before he became the drug. He still is, for me.

5

'Madam,' says the heavily accented voice at the other end of the intercom. 'There's someone waiting in the lobby to meet you. Are you going to be long?'

I have just showered and am discarding one outfit after another in a bid to look my unrecognizable best when I go to meet all my former classmates, some of whom are now on the verge of becoming corporate celebrities. I didn't expect to meet anyone at this hour, and the interruption is slightly irritating. The beautifully carved elephant that has magically found its way into my luggage nestles in my left palm, my sweat making it shiny, as I think about my wardrobe. Over the years, it has become a habit to fidget with that elephant, as though it were some sort of charm, though I have never believed in that sort of thing. Now I put it down next to the telephone on the bedside table as I attend to the phone call.

'Who's waiting?'

'Madam, it is one Priya Madam.'

I stare at the phone in disbelief.

'Hello? Madam? What shall I say?'

I put the phone down without replying. It rings again

almost immediately but I don't pick up. There's other more important stuff that I need to do. Like pulling on the first set of clothes that comes to hand, running impatient fingers through my hair and then streaking out of the door.

I'm panting by the time I rush into the lobby. The man at the reception has the phone to his ear as he gazes into a computer. Perhaps he is still trying to call me. From the cafeteria beyond, I can hear the clink of cutlery and the mild dash of china as plate strikes against plate. Mingled with these sounds are the soft murmurs of various conversations. But the lobby is silent. In one corner, there is a large, attractive wooden statue of Ganesha. It is bedecked with fresh flowers and someone has lit incense sticks near it. The perfume of the incense pervades the entire lobby. I glance around, and it is hard to subdue the rush of disappointment that overcomes me when I discover that the receptionist is indeed my only companion. The vision of a wild-haired girl rises before my eyes. Her perfectly proportioned body, black eyes glinting under a pair of arched brows, the lashes sweeping her cheekbones, her sharp nose and stretched lips whose smile seldom reached her eyes, unless it was to laugh at something foolish I did, were all designed to drive a man off his path, into the thorny side lanes of desire. With women, it was a different story. With them, Priya was rationality and kindness itself, and I often wondered how a person could change moods and attitudes so quickly.

I had no wish to emulate Priya. One cannot be a song,

only sing it. I am amazed that I not only knew her, but for a while she was my closest friend, before other matters intervened. The human heart can show its pettiness at the most random moment and I know who is responsible for my losing Priya for twenty years and it isn't Priya.

I have now got my breath back but there is a heaviness in my chest at the anticlimax of finding myself alone. The thought of meeting Priya before anyone else did was somehow delightful. Now, of course, she has gone inside, and I shall have to meet her in a public encounter, possibly in the dining room, a somewhat anonymous meeting where the veils will be well in place. As I stand there, in the middle of the large, aseptic lobby, a little blank in my head, a girl comes and stands before me. She cannot be more than fourteen. She is wearing a smocked top with spaghetti straps in an attractive shade of pink, and denim capris. She looks like she is going to grow taller than her present height of five-four or thereabouts. She is dark-skinned, and has a flawless complexion. Her thick black hair is cut short and she has a fringe falling over her almond-shaped eyes. She is beautiful. I do not remember seeing her at last night's dinner. Obviously she is someone's daughter and has just arrived.

She looks at me speculatively. She is carrying a duffel bag on her shoulder. Now she puts it down and continues to look at me until I have no choice but to say, 'Hello. Can I help you?'

'Are you Ruts?'

I'm not sure how to respond to this. Perhaps a simple

yes will do. But I don't think I want to do that. I want to explain that I *was* Ruts, that nobody calls me that now, that my identity is now something else. Before I can articulate any of these thoughts, someone covers my eyes with their hands, and the last thing I remember seeing is the broad smile on the beautiful girl's face.

'Guess who,' says a voice in my ear.

The hammering of my heart almost drowns the voice. 'Priya Pathak,' I say in a measured tone.

The hands are removed, the voice gets embodied into a figure that I almost wouldn't have recognized. It's the eyes. The eyes give her away. They haven't changed, in their sparkle, their shape, the excitement they portray as though they are seeing something the rest of the world is missing. As for the rest of Priya, it is no longer the person I last met almost exactly twenty years ago. The transformation has nothing to do with age. It is not the maturing of the skin that I'm referring to, or the sober cotton sari with its handloom border, a far cry from the fashionable Western clothing of yesteryear, that is draped around the slender figure. No, this is something more fundamental. I finally nail it. It is the expression on her face. It is tranquil, as though all the world's issues have been examined, brought into the light, and then resolved. That is not the expression that I recall ever seeing on Priya's face. It makes her look like a new person.

'Ruts! Ruts!' she says repeatedly, her famed coherence gone.

'Priya, you look great,' I say, careful to keep all

exuberance out of my voice. Though she sounds enthusiastic, I'm not entirely sure how my friend feels about seeing me after so long.

'Wait, let me look at you. Hmm, gorgeous, as always.'

'Thanks.'

Priya's eyes laugh, though her voice is sober. 'Haven't you forgotten something?'

'Forgotten? No, I don't think so.'

Now she really does laugh. 'Ruts! You're not wearing your shoes!'

The words slip out, 'I don't care.'

Priya laughs again. 'That's the Ruts I remember!'

I had forgotten all about the girl who knows my identity. Now Priya holds out her hand to her and she comes forward. 'Ruts, meet Anya, my daughter.'

'Hello, Anya.'

'Hello, Ruts.'

Priya is moved to protest, 'Now Anya, is that the way you address people?'

But I am charmed. 'No, Priya. Let her call me Ruts. I guess that's how she thinks of me. It's okay, Anya. I'm delighted to meet you. Really. I have a feeling we'll be talking about lots of things over the next couple of days. But first, let's find some breakfast. Would you like to go in there? I hope you're hungry. The food's good for a change.'

'Ruts, you've forgotten your shoes!' exclaims Priya. 'I know, I'll take Anya inside and show her around, and then wait for you to come down after you're properly dressed.'

In the event, Priya comes up to my room after dropping

Anya off in the cafeteria and introducing her to some of the folks there. She cannot resist chatting with me while I get ready. There is so much catching up to do, twenty years to be crammed into twenty minutes. We chatter continuously. One talks and the other listens by turns. It is almost like reading out the laundry list of events in our respective lives. 'Where's your husband?' I ask, when we come to the subject of families.

'Don't have one.'

For a moment I'm halted in my tracks. 'What?'

'Oh, don't look like that, Ruts. My god! You still haven't lost the ability to be shocked easily. It isn't what you think. I didn't marry, but I decided to adopt Anya. I wanted a child.'

'You wanted a child?' I repeat stupidly.

'Is that so unusual?' asks Priya. She has picked up the miniature elephant, and is looking at it curiously, a puzzled frown between her brows.

'Well, one normally associates children with marriage, so I guess it is a little unusual,' I say carefully.

Priya looks up from her appraisal of the carved animal to stare at me. 'All right, maybe. But I didn't think like that, still don't as a matter of fact. After putting in a few years of work, I found that there wasn't a single man I could bear to have as a husband. But kids are a different ballgame. And I wanted one, someone to love, someone in whom I could instil the values I care for.'

'And?'

'And I met a long lost cousin for whom Anya was the

fourth girl child. Anyone could see that this baby had no future, she would be lucky to escape with her life; she would probably die of some vitamin deficiency if malnutrition didn't get her first. It was as though I had been presented with my dream, and I wasn't going to let up on that. Here was a woman with all the love that a baby could possibly ever want, and there was an unwanted baby. What do you think? Could I seriously give up the opportunity?'

'Good for you, Priya. But doesn't a child need two parents?'

'Of course she does. But before that she needs a life. Anya was probably going to lose it. I decided I would do the vital thing first, which was to get Anya away from that hellhole, and then get married later.'

I can't help it. I have to laugh at this. I laugh so much that tears stream down my cheeks. Priya smiles but clearly doesn't understand the joke.

'What? Ruts, stop it! Ruts!'

'All right, wait, let me get my breath back. It's just the way you said it. I'll get the baby then I'll get the husband. Only you could talk like that, Priya.'

She smiles and then frowns a little. 'You're right. Once I had Anya, all I could think of was what would be right for her. You know my feelings about marriage. But I decided to go for that compromise for Anya's sake. She needed a father, and I was willing to get one for her. But men don't think that way, Ruts, let me tell you. Once they saw me with Anya, they quickly backed off, every one of them. Men don't want entanglement, Ruts, just some fun.

So I got tired of looking and decided to raise Anya on my own.'

'Well, it looks like you've done a good job of it. Anya looks really smart. But let me be honest. I couldn't have done what you did. Adopt a kid when I was single, I mean.'

Priya looks at me meditatively. 'Tell me, how did you meet your husband?'

'Kailash? Well, let me see. I think we first met at the theatre. He was directing his first play.'

'And when did you know he was the one?'

I laugh. 'I think almost instantly. I saw him, and I knew it.'

'So it was love at first sight?'

'I guess so.'

'It was exactly the same for me when I saw that five-month-old baby. She had been bawling, and her face was still red when I saw her. All that crying had made her sleepy, and she gave this giant yawn that covered her whole face. And that's it. That's when I knew she was the one for me.'

I laugh. 'I suppose I know what you mean, though it's certainly not the same thing. I wish you weren't still so bitter about men, though. I thought you'd have changed your opinion by now.'

'Honestly, I did try. But I don't think I'm as radically against marriage as I used to be. If the right man comes along, I could always change my mind.'

'How would you know it's the right man?' I counter. 'You have to start by giving the relationship a chance.

Or rather, a second chance.' Both of us know what I'm referring to.

—⁊⁊⁊—

Berry's lectures on maths were nightmarish. He called our public humiliation 'class participation'. The questions that Berry asked were always within the scope of what we were supposed to know. And therein lay their beauty. We were supposed to know stuff but we didn't. The situation mirrored life almost exactly. As I watched people breaking out in a sweat while staring blindly at the professor, who strolled about the classroom indifferently, a look of supreme disdain on his face, I wondered when I would be the target. The very thought turned me cold. The inevitable couldn't be put off forever, and I was almost expecting it when Berry said in his soft voice, 'Miss Malhotra, could you come to the board to solve this problem? It was in the exercise on page 61. I'm sure all of you have solved it but I just want to make sure that your method is correct.'

What he really meant, of course, was that he was sure all of us hadn't solved it, and he was right. I for one hadn't done about sixty per cent of the exercise. The problems were hard beyond belief, and this one seemed to be written in a language that definitely wasn't English.

I wondered why I had been singled out for the special honour of going up to the board. Usually people just squirmed in their chairs while mumbling something incomprehensible. The torture lasted for barely a few seconds. But in my case, I was in for the whole nine yards. It was as bad as I had known it would be.

But I was determined to return to class the next day with the solution. Gradually, it had begun to dawn upon me that if we were expected to solve impossibly difficult problems, it was because that was the stuff we were made of. We had been selected to join the IIM because we were supposed to be the best of the best. And by god, I was determined to prove that I could do it. Eventually I would discover that life contained much tougher problems compared to the bookish stuff that we were confronted with at the institute, but the mental hardihood required to deal with whatever circumstances threw our way was developed in those two years, not just within the classroom but also outside it.

In the evening, Priya walked into my room, and told me she had the solution to the maths problem.

'Then why didn't you say so in class when Berry asked?' I asked.

'Do you want the solution?' she asked, skirting my question.

'Sure. But you'll have to explain it to me.'

'Not a problem. Step into my room after tea.'

And that's how I found myself in Priya's room, an unusual occurrence, since she was almost never there when there was some hot quarry in sight.

The days had started growing shorter now, and it was twilight. I was glad of Priya's help, but it was also nice to have her company. She had been going steady with a senior for some time now, and was never to be seen in her room. Her presence that day indicated that the affair was over.

Rooms indicate a lot about the occupier's personality. I remember going to Rats's room once. He was, as usual, trying to wheedle something out of me, something that would further his prospects and grades, and he had decided to bribe me with expensive books, that he kept on his impeccable writing table, in his impeccable room. He had succeeded in impressing me but only temporarily. The room was as big a sham as its owner – all style, no substance.

While Rats's room looked as though it was a company president's abode, and my own looked like a humble hostel room, Priya's domain looked like the mad fantasy of a slob. In addition to the rock star posters, there was an assortment of clutter in every corner of the room. Discarded socks, laundry, both washed and unwashed, books and papers and pencil shavings, cigarette ends and matches, empty matchboxes, empty bottles, a few dishes from the mess, and many other things lay scattered about the room. The bed was unmade, and had perhaps been so for weeks. I knew that nobody came to clean the room, and it was evident in the overall appearance. There was a kind of wildness in that room, and it seemed to gel well with Priya's own approach to life. As for me, I felt uncomfortable and out of my depth, sitting on the unmade bed amidst rumpled sheets. Priya was smoking, and the ash dripped onto the mosaic floor. Absentmindedly, she brushed it aside with her foot, but it stayed there, now smeared. On the ledge was a picture of Priya's parents and a much younger, cheerful Priya. The face that smiled out of the frame looked innocent and so different from the jaded, cynical visage in front of me. Priya couldn't have been more than twenty-two, having joined the institute almost as soon as she had completed her Bachelors' degree from VJTI, one of the best known engineering colleges in Bombay. But she looked older, and contrastingly, much younger as well.

The dirty room was getting to me pretty strongly. For a while I sat quietly and allowed my friend to take me through calculus problems. Then I couldn't resist it any longer. 'Why don't I clean up your room for you?' I offered.

'Chill, man. The room's just fine.'

'No, really. I'll tidy it up, make the bed and so on. You don't have to do anything if you don't want to. Just sit and chat with me. My repayment for helping me with maths.'

The deal was done except that Priya didn't sit. As usual, when she put her mind to it, she could do things quite well, and I discovered that her housekeeping skills were much better than mine. I picked up some books to dust them, and some papers fell out in a startling shower. There was no option but to go down on my hands and knees to pick up everything, and since the papers had scattered in all directions, I had to crawl everywhere to hunt them down, a disgusting task. That was when I saw the picture. It had slid behind the bedpost, and was positioned there vertically, all too easy to miss. A coloured postcard-sized picture of a girl and boy in wedding finery smiling into the camera. There was dust on the photograph, a thick layer of it, but in spite of that I could recognize Priya as the girl, a much younger Priya, of course, but Priya nonetheless. I kept looking at the picture, my mind blank.

'Ruts, get out of that corner! I know it's filthy.'

Priya's voice seemed to be coming from a great distance, as though it was traversing ether. I stood up with the picture in hand and said in an oddly constricted voice, 'You never said you're married. Who's the lucky guy?'

There was never any emotion to be seen in Priya. To me, she symbolized a cold ball of fire. There was everything in her, but one only felt it. But now there was a new stillness about her, and I felt the presence of an enormous force, which just might blow me away. Instinctively, I stepped back, though Priya hadn't moved, hadn't said a word. The room stood still, and I don't recall sitting down on the unmade bed, but there I was, and there was Priya sitting right next to me, holding my left hand by the fingertips. I was greatly moved, as one is by the presence of a sorrow that transcends everything, every being, mind, sense, rationality, and leaves behind just a hole that one then has to spend the rest of one's life filling up. It is the kind of sorrow that one has on seeing the incomplete painting of a great artist. There can never be resolution.

It was a rare sight to see Priya in complete inaction. Normally, she would be either smoking or cussing or walking in and out of rooms. Now, she just sat on the bed, holding my hand loosely, so that I could have withdrawn it at any moment of my choice, and that moment never came. Then, finally, she took the photo from my other hand and looked at it. And then she lifted her head and she looked at me, staring deep into my eyes as though trying to solve some unfathomable puzzle.

'I'm not married,' she said finally. 'That photo is a lie, and I keep it merely to remind myself that people can go to any extent to cheat someone. It gives me a shield for the future. Ruts, to be cheated is as bad as to cheat, and ten times more stupid. I would much rather cheat others myself.'

'You don't mean that,' I said weakly.

'Well, maybe I don't. But you don't want to know about me, you want to know the story behind this photo. So let's not talk about irrelevant things. I'll tell you the whole story. You never know, it might do you good.'

In all the while that I had known Priya, it was always I who had gone to her with my troubles. Priya came across as this supremely confident woman who knew what she was doing. Yet now I got the feeling that I was in the presence of someone who was probably more vulnerable than I was. I was almost scared of hearing the story behind that picture. I sensed there was something there that was large in its implications, possibly too large for me to grasp.

Priya stared at a poster of a laughing rock star, her visage completely at odds with his. Then she turned her face to me and smiled. There was no humour in that smile. Oddly, it was a smile of pity as though she knew I didn't understand. But why did she pity me? And why should I pity her, the brilliant, beautiful, sexy Priya who could put a roomful of people in the shade?

'You know I'm from Bombay?'

I nodded, unwilling to speak.

'My father works in a nationalized bank there. My mother teaches maths in a government aided school.' She smiled gently. 'Maybe that's where my maths ability comes from. As long as I can remember, we've lived in Malad. It's a nice Bombay suburb, and I loved our housing complex. All the neighbours knew each other. I had known Rohit, our neighbour, forever. He was four years older than me, but we did a lot of things together, and by the time I was fifteen, I had begun to think of him as something more than a neighbour-slash-friend. It was inevitable, I suppose. But at the time, it was the most beautiful thing that had ever happened to me. I was sure Rohit was the one for me, and it seemed the most marvellous thing when he confessed that he too felt the same way. I was still a year away from completing high school, but we promised each other that we would marry once I finished with school. Rohit was in college with no clear plans for the future, but that didn't matter. Even the fact that we were from different castes didn't matter. Rohit was sure his parents would never allow this marriage. He was quite scared of his parents. I convinced him that we should present them with a fait accompli. Surely they would have to accept their daughter-in-law when they had no choice.'

Priya lit another cigarette. It was her third so far. I was counting for want of anything better to do. For some odd reason, it seemed that my friend was laughing silently. It was a bewildering sensation. For the life of me, I couldn't understand what there was to laugh about in this narrative. I couldn't imagine a lovelorn Priya, wide eyed and rose spectacled. But that's what change is all about, I suppose.

'On the day of my last high school exam,' continued Priya, taking a deep pull at her cigarette, 'Rohit came to pick me up from the exam centre. I was carrying a change of clothes in my bag. It was a wedding sari that I had bought after saving up my pocket money for a year. That's how long I had planned this. We went to a small temple, and I changed into my wedding outfit behind a tree. It all seemed so romantic, getting married in this way. I remember, I laughed all the time, and the priest had to ask me to be sober. It was not fitting, he admonished me, for a bride to laugh on her wedding day. But I didn't care. I was just so happy. I wanted to kiss Rohit then and there, but somehow I knew the priest wouldn't approve. When the priest asked my age, I said I was eighteen. I think he knew I was lying but he continued to conduct the ceremony. It was a short ceremony, but it seemed endless at the time. From the temple we went to a photo studio and had our picture taken. I was all for going straight back home to tell my parents, but Rohit wouldn't agree. He said we must spend our wedding night together and then go home. He couldn't bear to be away from me, he said. The thought of consummating our marriage was unbearably exciting. Before that day, I hadn't even kissed Rohit. We went to a hotel in Bandra. Rohit had found out about the place earlier. I was proud to sign my name as Mrs Sinha. I called my parents and told them I would be spending the night with a friend, and would return the next day.'

Priya turned to look at me through a haze of cigarette smoke. 'Are you shocked?' she asked.

I swallowed the saliva that had collected in my mouth and asked, 'Shocked? At what?'

'My behaviour? The wedding, the wedding night, the lies, the whole nine yards of deceit?'

'Why? I'm not your mother,' I said, pretending an indifference I was far from feeling. Somehow, I knew where this story was heading, and I didn't want to bring in my own feelings, and muddy the waters further. I could swear then that I saw gratitude in Priya's eyes, and I wondered at this girl. There was nothing that I had said or done that invited gratitude from her. Why, I had barely uttered a word throughout. We were sitting on the bed, side by side, and the warmth I felt in my left palm was from Priya's hand nestling there, touching but not clenching my fingers. Our hands rested like that for a while, still and warm.

Then Priya stood up, and I had to stand with her. She looked around her, at the dismally untidy room and said, 'Let's get out of here. I can't stand this room sometimes.'

'Where do you want to go? We can move to my room, if you like.'

'No, I don't want these walls to listen. But you're busy, I know. We can do this another time.'

I refused to take the way out that was offered. I *was*

busy, and the thought of the three assignments that were waiting for me crossed my mind briefly, but Chinni and HR, I told myself firmly, could wait.

We started walking towards our inevitable destination whenever we needed to talk, Venky's. It was always soothing to sit there with a cup of the ambrosia called coffee and contemplate life's tricks. After two sips, they all seemed manageable, somehow. As we placed our order and took our seats, Priya said, 'It's funny how sure one is of oneself and one's life at seventeen. I was absolutely convinced that that ridiculous marriage was the best thing I had done in my life. But then, I was just seventeen. Rohit was older. Surely he should have understood the enormity of what we had done. But he went along with everything I said. The next morning we went home. I didn't feel at all nervous at the thought of confronting his family. I didn't think about my parents at all. All through life they had done exactly what I had asked them to, and why should this time be any different.

'In spite of what I had done, I knew I was a decent and honest person. This was the first time I had actually lied by design. And because I knew that, I was so sure of myself, and certain that nothing could go wrong for me, nothing big. I was prepared for the recriminations that would come my way, but I had Rohit to protect and shield me, and my own love.'

In all the time I had known Priya, the last word I could have associated with her was love. There was a dog that had sort of been adopted by the hostel. He was an ugly mongrel, and followed anyone who bothered to throw a scrap of food at him. But for some reason, whenever he saw Priya, he abandoned everything and followed her, his eyes dripping with sentiment, and I almost expected him to growl at every lover she took, he was so in love with her. Yet all Priya did was treat him with a casual indifference that set my teeth on edge. I like animals, and within a few days of coming to the IIM, I had started making friendly overtures towards the dog, but he did no more than acknowledge my presence with a little wag of his tail whenever he saw me. None of the devotion that he reserved for Priya came my way. Sometimes I almost felt like shaking my friend and asking her what her intention was. And here she was, talking about love as though she had believed in it once. It was also the first time she had spoken of her parents. I had got the impression that that domain was closed off, not just for me, but also for her, that she was cut off from her parents. It was not anything she said or did but what she didn't say. Apart from that picture in her room, there was nothing to show that she even had parents. I had assumed they lived far away, maybe in a foreign country, and now it surprised me that I hadn't inquired about them before this. I thought of asking now, but I didn't want to distract Priya.

A piece of cardboard hung on a thick string from one of the window stoppers in the tin and asbestos coffee shack. It said in red lettering, 'no Smokeing'. Everyone who sat there ignored the sign, and Priya was no exception. For some time, she just smoked and stared out of the window, though I knew there was nothing to see, since the panes were covered in grime.

Then she looked at me and smiled. 'Of course, there was a blazing row. Rohit was from a really conservative family, and the less than half a dozen times that I had been to his house, I had always felt uncomfortable. This was a bank colony that we lived in and his father was a sort of junior clerk there. All kinds of accusations flew thick and fast, but I was so proud of my new husband when he stood his ground about what we had done. Finally, my parents were called in. I didn't want them there. Some instinct, I suppose, made me want to protect them from the ugliness I was facing. But their presence actually helped. They were stunned by what I had done, and their obvious hurt made Rohit's parents calm down. In the whole process, I stopped feeling as grown up as I had just a few hours earlier. Rohit's father treated me as though I was an errant schoolchild and he was the headmaster. I almost felt I would be made to stand in a corner. It was humiliating, and there wasn't a thing I could do about it. Finally, I was sent home with my parents, and I had the feeling my punishment would be announced soon. My marriage had already started appearing like a dream to me. I wanted my parents to say something to me, but they didn't. That evening, Rohit and I were told the decision. A proper marriage ceremony would be held three weeks later, and until then we would have to live separately, so that we gave no cause for gossip.

'I was overjoyed, and so was Rohit. I didn't want to risk his parents' displeasure so I forced myself not to even see him for the next three weeks, and in a way it was a wonderful feeling. There was a sort of warmth in being so close to him, knowing he would be mine in just a short while, and yet staying away from him. But it was hard, too. Then I heard that Rohit had gone out of town for a few days, and that made it easier for me. I patched up with my parents, and they encouraged me to go the full nine yards for the wedding. They even managed to put together some sort of dowry, including a motorcycle for Rohit. After all, every parent wants to see their daughter married. I was, in a way, happy with these arrangements. They all signified a formality about the marriage, making it more official, I suppose. When, a couple of days before the ceremony, I saw hectic activity at Rohit's place, I thought it was all part of the same thing on their side. I was curious about what was going on, but there was no one I could ask. I never thought about why my in-laws never made contact with either me or my parents in those weeks. It didn't seem to matter then. We, too, had a house full of guests to look after, aunts and uncles and cousins who had all descended upon us for the occasion. That evening, Rohit finally came over. There were so many claims to his attention from my parents, and from the myriad relatives gathered at home, but I held back. I felt shy in my husband's presence, who almost seemed a stranger now. Rohit ignored all the attention. He asked to see me alone, and I, fool that I was, felt almost flattered. Here, for a change, was someone who wanted me to the exclusion of everything else. We went into my bedroom, messy with all the packaging of my trousseau scattered everywhere. I sat on the bed, while he stood next to the window and said that he had got married to another girl from his village. It wasn't his fault, he told me. He had been dead against the marriage but his uncle had almost kidnapped him to push the wedding through. He had now returned with the bride.'

I had half-expected this turn of events, or something equally dramatic, for there was nothing in Priya's demeanour to indicate that she wasn't single. Nonetheless, a thrill of shock ran down my spine as Priya's unemotional voice spoke these words.

'The prick!' I cried out instinctively, though I had vowed to remain silent.

Much to my amazement, Priya laughed at this. 'Ruts! You'll need to wash your mouth out with soap and water! But I know what you mean. Though that wasn't what I thought at that time. I didn't think anything, really. Rohit apologized, saying sorry many times over, and then finally left, much to my relief. I wanted to be alone, so that I could swallow the three strips of analgesics that were lying in my room, and go to sleep forever. But before the tablets could take effect, my parents discovered me.

'In any case, my death would have been pointless. I'm glad I didn't stay married to Rohit. He turned out to be a complete loser. I sometimes catch sight of him when I go home. I think he works as a shop assistant in a clothing store, and continues to live with those awful parents of his. I don't think I would have made a good shop assistant's wife. No, this is much more fun.'

Fun? Nothing about Priya struck me as being any fun, least of all what I had just learnt about her.

'And your parents?'

'Yeah, my parents. What about them? They are there, still trying to find a groom for a girl whom no boy will marry. Word had got round, in spite of all the secrecy.'

'But it wasn't your fault!' I exclaimed.

'Wasn't it? Why did I elope with Rohit? Didn't I tempt him into being irresponsible?'

'Is that what he said about you?'

'Yeah, but none of that mattered. I was living in a hostel in VJTI in Bombay a year later, and I found my new world so different from Rohit and his family that I didn't care any more. But my parents continued to live there, continued to put up with the humiliation of having that family next door with all their stupid, petty insults. Why? That's what I still haven't understood, Ruts. Why?'

'And that's why you don't talk to them?' I asked incredulously.

'How do you know I don't talk to them?' she asked. I just looked at her and she looked away, frowning slightly.

It was dark now. We had been sitting in Venky's for more than two hours. Other students had come and gone. Jaggu had been there also, but I had ignored him.

The past few hours had changed my outlook towards life. I said as much to Priya over the coffee. 'Has it taught you not to trust men?' she asked. 'Because that's the only lesson you should learn. That, and that the only virtue is being a conformist. You can do any shit, even murder, but you're safe as long as you don't show the world that there is something different about you. Never rebel, Ruts. But hey, who am I talking to? This is Ruts, the original conformist. You wouldn't ever go against the current, now would you? You'll always be virtuous and kind to animals and old people. You'll prosper, Ruts, wait and see.'

I was forced to protest against this judgment. 'Don't we all rebel at some point?'

'No,' corrected Priya, 'no, we think of rebelling often, but we don't because of fear; fear that we might end up making enemies.'

'And is that a good thing? Making enemies?'

'No. But is it a good thing to live in fear? We have only this life. Can't we stand up for what we believe in? Is compromise the only way of living?'

Then I decided to say something that had been preying on my mind for some time. I felt I had earned the right to say it. 'And do you think what you are doing, this lifestyle of yours, is principled? What principles are you standing up for now?'

She smiled at my angry question. 'Actually, I'm performing an experiment.'

'Oh yeah? What? How men differ in their styles of love making?' I said sarcastically.

'No, that's the conclusion. The experiment is to find out whether there's any depth in the male of the species at all, or whether he is just led by his organ.'

'So, what's the conclusion?'

'Oh, I'm still doing the experiment, but I think I can safely say that a man lives by his dick alone.'

What I knew about men sexually then could have been written on the back of a postage stamp. But it didn't take a Cleopatra to know that Priya was erroneous in her thinking. I wanted to point out that her experiment was wrong since it presumed the conclusion. She knew men were led by their dick, and she was setting out to prove it. What sense did that make?

I often wondered about the whole business of sex. I might not have had intercourse, but masturbation had its own delights and I was certainly no stranger to those. But there was an implied intimacy in the sexual act that was belied by the kind of behaviour I witnessed in Priya. She had made love to a man with whom she was genuinely in love or so she believed. Was the quality of that passion different from the one she experienced during her 'experiments'? Of course, it was none of my business, but the question interested me intellectually. What would sex be like? When I had sex with a man, would it change the way he looked at me? And who would be my first lover? Would I know him well enough to sleep with him? I knew enough to know that a real orgasm pulled off all the veils that one covered oneself with. That was the moment when one was truly naked. Did I want to be that naked with someone I did not really want to be intimate with? The answer was enough to put me off sexual experimentation for that moment. I needed to keep myself hidden, I decided. My unveiling could not be casual. Priya seemed able to segregate her orgasmed self from her sober self with ease. I wasn't sure if I could do that.

—※—

'You and superbitch are really thick these days,' said Jaggu one evening about two weeks after Priya had revealed her secret to me.

'Jaggu, for god's sake, stop calling her that.'

'Oh, what should I call her then, Mother Teresa?'

'Just call her Priya, okay?'

'Why are you so fond of her? She's nothing but trouble. Half the hostel is on the verge of committing suicide because she ditched them. How can you call someone like that your friend?'

'Jaggu, it's none of our business what she does here with the others. She isn't hassling you, so stay out of it. She doesn't even *talk* to you, for god's sake!'

'Correction,' said Jaggu coldly. '*I* don't talk to her. I wonder why you do.'

We were on the terrace, our usual haunt. Jaggu and I had become friendlier with the passage of time, and shared our thoughts on almost everything. We sat on the terrace most nights, talking about our problems and offering help to each other, on things like behavioural science for him and production management for me, or just how to bargain effectively with the autorickshaw-wallah. It had become a habit to sit in that small, cool corner of the terrace, if only for fifteen minutes. The longest we sat there was six hours. I clocked it. It was a night not to be forgotten, nor to be repeated.

Jaggu stared moodily at the floor of the terrace as he leaned against the parapet. I was in my favourite posture, reclining against the wall, my knees drawn up to my chin. It was soothing to sit like that. I always took care not to sit too close to Jaggu. I disliked the cigarette smoke, and he, like most of the men there, smoked continuously.

'Have you ever been jilted?' asked Jaggu, suddenly.

This was a tricky question. I could always say the truth, of course, that I had never had a boyfriend to jilt me, but somehow I felt that that would not go down well with him.

'No.'

'So, have you ever ditched anyone, Ruts?'

'No.' I was starting to feel uncomfortable now.

'Lucky you! You don't know what it's like to have someone tell you to get lost. It's worse than being slapped in public by your mother.'

'You seem to know a lot about it,' I said.

'I should,' said Jaggu, bitterly. 'My girlfriend told me six months after we were going steady that she loved someone else. Love! What did she know about it? She just found another great body with a fatter wallet.'

'Or maybe she really was in love with someone else.'

'Yeah! And it's just a coincidence that that person was far richer, while I was just a struggling student at IIT.'

'It could be a coincidence,' I said.

Jaggu flared up. 'Ruts, you don't understand, okay?

I was in love with this female, and I thought she felt the
same way. She slept with me, not once but many times.
Doesn't that mean something? And then she just threw
me off, just like that, and took off with someone else. She
just wanted a good time, believe me. When she thought I
could give it to her, she went along with me, and when she
found bigger fish, she left. What does that show you?'

I remained silent.

'Women!' he exclaimed, bitterly. 'They really know
how to turn a man on and then give him a kick.'

I forbore to point out that he was sitting with one such
from the accursed species.

'Ruts, meet a regular guy and get married. That's what
I've planned for my sisters as well. You shouldn't be in this
place. It's sick. Don't you find the men here twisted? And
the women also. Like your friend Priya. You'll become
as bad as the rest of them, if you stay with them long
enough. Why should you come to the IIM? What's in it
for you? Eventually you're going to get married, and have
kids. You're not going to pursue any hotshot career, that's
for sure.'

I was getting more and more angry as Jaggu spoke.
'Jaggu, I want to get one thing straight. I'm not going to
get married, not in the near future. I don't know what
century you live in but I'm definitely in the twentieth.
Women don't just get married nowadays, in case you
hadn't noticed; they live their lives.'

'Like Priya, you mean?'

'Why not? I doubt you would be so censorious if a

man were doing what she is. Anyway, forget it, Jaggu. You don't like Priya, I get it. Now shut up.'

Before this, Jaggu and I had had our usual share of arguments. There were many things on which we didn't agree. But this time I felt we had crossed some limit. Jaggu had never revealed such intimate details about himself before, and I had never spoken to him so sharply. Now he looked at me, and something in his look alarmed me. I could feel some change in the atmosphere. We no longer seemed like two friends just having an argument. After a minute, Jaggu turned his back on me and walked off, leaving me alone on that deserted terrace. That was also a first. Usually we went back together. There was nothing unsafe about sitting alone in any part of the hostel, but for some reason Jaggu never left me on my own, especially at night. I wondered what had come over him. I almost went after him to ask, but something held me back. This was a different Jaggu, and I wasn't too sure if I wanted to find out what was going on.

6

'So, do you still write stuff?' asks someone behind me. For a moment I'm lost and then I recognize the voice.

'Ravi!'

'Ah, come on! I believe it's all nicknames out here. Jaggu, Golu, Paxi!' he sneers.

'All right then, Rats. You look good.'

He doesn't return the compliment. 'God! This place is still the same old dump! I swear I counted at least twenty flies in the lobby this morning.'

There are several replies I can give to this, but don't. 'So you're with a bank, aren't you?'

'Yup. I just moved to East-West Banking Corporation.' He whisks out a card that says 'Ravi Saluja, Chief Executive Officer – Asia Pacific'.

'I saw you on CNBC.'

'That! That was a while ago. Not a very good piece of journalism, I thought. There's one coming up next Saturday on CNN. You should watch that. The one on NDTV two weeks from now can be skipped. I prefer American broadcasters.'

Rats was never one to hide his light under a bushel. If there's one thing Rats has ever cared about, it is Ravi Saluja.

'Hey, Jaggu is around, I see,' he says as we walk out of the dining room.

'So?'

'Kind of awkward, I would say.'

'Awkward? Why?'

'So that's how you want to play it. Well, all right. Mum's the word. Hey, did you get my email? I think I sent it a couple of months ago.'

'No,' I lie.

'Funny! I'm sure I had the right address. Are you sure you didn't get it?'

'Are you here alone?' I ask in a bid to change the subject.

'No. Anyway, I was curious to find out if you were planning on coming here.'

'Of course I was. And why shouldn't I?'

'It might be embarrassing, that's all.'

'Rats, what are you getting at?'

'Has your hubby come with you?'

'Has your wife?' I counter.

'So where's the great novel?' he asks, changing tack.

'Didn't you read it? The rest of the world has,' I say with a deadpan expression.

'Really? What's it called?'

'*The Da Vinci Code*. I've used a pseudonym.'

Even Rats has to laugh then. I leave him there with a

smile on his face. Conversations with Ravi Saluja always left me feeling like I needed to put on a few more clothes. Or rather armour. Dealing with Rats, one had to be combat ready, as though one were in a battle zone. My smartness quotient was definitely inadequate when it came to him. Rats has always had that effect on me, and I am still amazed that I thought he wanted me for a lover. Anyone less lover-like I have yet to see. Just because he cosied up to me to copy the only coherent notes I had in all of the two years that I studied at the IIM, in Organization Behaviour, I started to believe that I was an attractive woman in this Greek god's eyes. Nature plays strange games with us. Rats may have been many things but ugly wasn't one of them. In his case, his face *was* his fortune. Unfortunately for him, his mouth came in the way of his face more than once. It was Jaggu who warned me against Rats. And like everything else, in this also I questioned Jaggu's judgment.

─────

Maths might have been a mystery to me the entire time that I was at the IIM, and production management a non-starter, but the study of organization behaviour was something I cottoned onto in the very first class. Here was something that I knew I would be using for the rest of my life, and suddenly life started making sense to me. The subject was interesting, the professors were good, the textbooks were readable. For the first time, I did not try to crawl under my chair whenever a question was asked. That ominous grading feature, 'class participation', no longer seemed like a threat. Finally, I too, could score on that criterion. And I did. With bells on. And Rats Saluja knew that.

I frequently found myself in the company of the most eligible bachelor in class. And that can be a fairly big ego kick for a twenty-something girl with the sexual knowledge of a ten year old.

'So, Rats and you are becoming real pally these days,' said Priya, walking into my room one evening after dinner.

I had just returned from Rats's room. He had procured a bottle of wine from somewhere, and had invited me specially to share it with him.

'It isn't Rats and I, not yet anyway,' I laughed.

'No? Tongues are wagging, you know.'

'Yeah, like that's so strange. When did tongues not wag out here?' Campus gossip at the IIM was an occupation in itself, and there were people who, I could have sworn, intended to make a career out of it.

'Well, Rats is a snake, just so you know.'

'Are you jealous?' I asked slyly.

Priya threw her head back and laughed. 'Right! Well, have a good time with him, okay? Get him to buy you lots of goodies, at least.'

'Hey, I'm not that kind of girl,' I protested.

'You need to be, if you want to stick with him,' was all Priya would say.

I could ignore Priya, but it was Jaggu who really got my back up.

'I didn't know you'd changed your name,' he said one

night as we sat in our usual corner of the terrace. His tone should have warned me, but it didn't. Our trysts had become irregular now, for some reason I couldn't fathom.

'I haven't,' I replied.

'I heard different. I heard it was Ratsy, the feminine of Rats. At least that's what the buzz is.'

'Jaggu, don't listen to gossip, for heaven's sake. I thought better of you. Rats is just a good friend.' Even now when I look back, I cannot help cringing at the cliché. And Jaggu wasn't slow to catch on.

'Good friend? Is that what they call it these days?'

'Call what?'

'Living in each other's pockets?'

I rose to my feet in anger. Jaggu's tone was offensive and I wasn't prepared to listen to any more of this. But I still felt I had to explain my point of view. 'I'm just trying to help Rats with some OB fundas,' I said.

'Over wine?'

I wasn't surprised Jaggu knew about the wine. Nothing in the hostel, and practically nothing on campus, could be kept secret.

'He just happened to have the wine and he offered it to me. You'd have done the same. Oh, why do I bother explaining things to you? You're not my keeper.'

'Yeah, lucky you. You don't need a keeper, do you? You're a free bird, just like that bitch, Priya. You can choose the richest customer, right? Oh, you women! You make me sick.'

'How dare you?' I couldn't utter another word. My throat was clogged, whether with anger or humiliation, I didn't know. What had I done to warrant such a nasty attack? As I stomped off the terrace, I thought I heard Jaggu call after me, but I didn't pause. I was in no mood to show him what a devastating effect his words had had on me.

After that debacle, I wished I didn't have to meet Jaggu ever again, but that was impossible. In a community of barely a couple of hundred students, not a day passed when we didn't see every other person there. Who received phone calls from whom, who got the most mail, who slept in the day and studied in the evening and who did exactly the reverse, everything was public knowledge.

I tried not to miss Jaggu. The vacuum he left was filled by Rats only partially. One day, Rats met me after class, as I was returning to the hostel. He seemed out of breath, but I didn't ask him why. It was a hot day, and there were almost no trees to cast their shade upon the red earth on which the stone buildings had been constructed. There was nothing more serious on my mind than how to cross the long path without getting sunburnt.

'I've found a gem,' Rats panted when he was next to me. 'In the library. The new book that HR asked us to read. Let's go and get it.'

'Now?' I looked at the distance I had already walked away from the library block. 'Why can't we get it in the evening?'

'Look, it's the only copy. Someone else is bound to get

it, and then our chance is gone. Let's go now. It'll only take a minute.'

'But, Rats.... Okay, why don't you go and get it. I'll save a place for you in the lunch queue.'

'Do you think I would have asked you if I could borrow it myself? My quota of books is over. You'll have to get it. Come on, Ruts. God! I hate that name! Anyway... it'll only take five minutes!'

I gave in. There was no sense in making a fuss. The sun was making me irritable, and by the time we entered the cool library, I was in a foul temper. Rats, on the other hand, seemed almost mellow, and my irritation with him and with the rest of the world grew. The behavioural management section was in the basement, and was usually deserted. Not today. There were two people sitting at one of the tables, and one of them was Jaggu. I hadn't seen him for a few days, and was conscious of both curiosity and relief. He looked up and then down again so quickly that I wasn't sure he had even seen us. I wondered at the coincidence of finding him there at such an odd hour of the day. But then, perhaps it wasn't so odd. Why shouldn't he go to the library after class?

'What do you think Jaggu was doing there?' asked Rats after we had taken the book and left.

'I don't know. What do you suppose one does in a library?'

I regretted my sarcasm when I saw Rats look down. But it was always hard to apologize to Rats, for some reason. I didn't notice, but though I had borrowed the book from the library, it was Rats who laid claim to it. I only thought about it after I'd returned to my room. I contemplated going to his room and asking for it, but after the quarrel with Jaggu, I was reluctant to visit Rats in his room more than strictly necessary. I tried to study. There was an economics assignment due the next day, and I knew it would take at least four hours to complete it, but my concentration had been shot. All I could see was Jaggu's expressionless face when he saw me in the library. I felt annoyed, with him, with myself, with the institute. It was he who had insulted me. I failed to understand why I should feel guilty. I told myself there was nothing in the least romantic about my friendship with Rats, and if Jaggu chose to have a problem with it, that was his business. I was certainly not going to go out of my way to appease him. An hour later, I realized I had read the first sentence of the chapter a hundred times, and I closed my books. It was better to go for a walk, clear my head and then return to work. Perhaps I could complete it if I skipped dinner. I was not a nocturnal person, but tonight I felt I would have to pull an all-nighter if I was to complete the assignment.

When I returned to my room, there was a note lying under my door. It said, 'I need to meet you. Usual time and place.' I knew who it was from, of course, and I was tempted to ignore it. Its peremptory tone put me off. The man could have at least apologized to me before ordering me to go to the terrace. It would serve him right if I didn't respond to the summons.

The smell of cigarette smoke on the dark terrace told me that Jaggu was there, though I couldn't see him. I walked to the terrace wall and leaned over to look down at the dark, peaceful campus, mysterious in the moonlight.

'I hope you aren't thinking of jumping,' said Jaggu, walking up to me.

'Why should I? Someone should be allowed to push me over,' I retorted and he laughed.

'It won't be worth it. Killing you and going to jail, I mean. So what's up?'

'Up? Nothing.'

Jaggu seemed ill at ease, a first for him, I thought. 'I mean, the last few days. How's work?'

'Good,' I replied without elaborating.

'Eco all right?'

'Yes.'

'Great. I got screwed in the last quiz.'

I didn't reply.

'Your superwoman friend did good, though. Naturally.'

Again, I didn't say anything. In earlier days, I would have lodged a vocal protest against his manner of referring to Priya, but today I didn't want to get into any distractions. We both stared out towards the dark land, the lights of a neighbouring village twinkling in the distance, and sounds from the local cinema hall wafting across the still air faintly. Finally, I said, 'I don't know about you, but I need to get back to finish my assignment.'

As I stepped out towards the terrace door, I felt a clamp on my upper arm. I looked up but in the darkness it was hard to see his face. All of a sudden, I was desperate to get out of there. That hand on my arm was doing something to me. I didn't understand what it was doing there, but whatever it was, I was uncomfortable with it. 'Don't go. Please. I got something from you from Cauvery. You love that store, don't you?'

It was true. I had almost a passion for the handicrafts boutique of the Karnataka government. I tried to buy something from it every time I went there. There wasn't much I could afford, but I looked upon every purchase as an investment.

Now Jaggu held out his palm, and in it lay an exquisitely carved elephant, redolent with the scent of sandalwood. A small string was tied to its trunk. Threaded through the string was a tiny piece of paper.

'Jaggu! That's awesome! I'm not sure I should be taking it from you. It must have cost the earth.'

'Do you like it?'

I was speechless. I literally didn't know how to thank Jaggu for the gift, and I felt graceless when I remained silent. Perhaps he guessed what was going through my head. At least, I hoped he did.

'I had better be getting back,' I said foolishly.

'I know. Eco calls.'

'I'll see you around.'

I returned to my room, and looked at the elephant properly in the light. Then I unfolded the slip of paper dangling from its trunk. There was one word written on it. 'Sorry'. I put the elephant and the note at the back of my cupboard. I had no desire to think about why Jaggu should feel compelled to get me such an expensive gift.

'So, you and Jaggu are back together again?' asked Rats a couple of days later while we were drinking tea.

I disliked his tone. 'That book,' I said, ignoring him, 'I thought I could go through it before HR's next lecture. Are you done with it?'

'I haven't had time to do more than glance through it. But come to my room tonight after dinner. I should be able to return it then.'

I had no desire to go to Rats's room. He could just as easily bring it down to dinner and give it to me. I said so.

'Yeah, but if the others get to see it, they'll want it too. I haven't let out that we have it with us, though people have been asking for it.'

I wasn't sure I liked being made part of this conspiracy to hoard comparatively rare books. But I had no wish to enter into an argument at this stage.

'All right. I'll see you after dinner.'

That night Jaggu chose to give me company over dinner. 'Coming?' he asked after we were done. I knew what he meant. Many times we headed for the terrace straight after dinner, and then proceeded to go back to study.

'No,' I said. 'I have to go to Rats's room.'

I saw his face close and resume the blank expression that I had spotted in the library that day. It made me angry. I didn't see why I should have to justify myself to him again. He had offered an apology for his earlier rudeness but the root cause remained, and the apology seemed hollow now.

He continued to suspect me of being on more than 'just friends' terms with Rats.

Rats chose to be at his irritating worst when I went to his room to pick up the book. I was in a hurry to get out of there. Jaggu might still be on the terrace, and I could join him, thus proving that my tryst with Rats was strictly business. Instead, I found myself making polite conversation with Rats till I felt I could scream. He went on discussing what he had discovered in the book, all of which seemed superficial and repetitive, and I wondered at the denseness with which he chose to ignore my lack of interest in what he was saying. Finally, I was offered respite and I sped out of his room, waving aside his offer of coffee. I went straight to the terrace but there was no sign of Jaggu, and then, feeling annoyed, I decided to go to his room.

His door was open, and he was sitting at his desk with an open book in front of him. I shut the door behind me, and said, 'You shouldn't have got me the elephant. Elephants are benign animals and there's nothing benign about the way you are treating me.'

'Oh yeah? And what about the way you've ignored me? Instead of appreciating what I did, you just cut me out. Just like that. I wasn't wrong in thinking that women are a selfish breed.'

'If that's what you believe, why did you apologize? Why the drama? If being insulting is your way of winning friends, then I can say nothing except that it's really funny.'

'So laugh, why don't you. You are being matey with the king prick of this place, and you dare laugh at me?'

Before I knew it, we were shouting at each other, hurling all sorts of insults, until a whistle and the sound of applause outside the door told us we had an audience. Then Jaggu yelled, 'Shut the fuck up, assholes!' There were a few more catcalls at this, but by now I was doubling up with laughter. Jaggu stared at me for a minute, and then the humour of the situation struck him, and both of us were rolling around hysterically.

It is hard to say when that laughter changed into awareness, awareness into intimacy, and intimacy into torrid sex. One moment we were laughing fit to tear a muscle, the next our lips were locked into each other's and we were doing everything we could to enter each other's bodies. We were both taken aback by the suddenness of the encounter, and its fury. I was a virgin but that didn't seem to matter. In that moment, this was what we both wanted with equal intensity. Nothing seemed enough. The red-hot desire that arced through me had its mate in Jaggu's feverish fumblings. Finally, we slowed down and then just lay on the narrow bed, our arms around each other. It seemed like only minutes had passed, but there was a faint glow in the sky that told me it was almost dawn. I had spent the night in Jaggu's arms and in his bed.

'Where were you last night?' asked Rats as we emerged from breakfast in the morning. I could barely keep my eyes open, and were it not for a quiz that had been announced for that day's marketing management class, I would probably have gone back to bed after breakfast and slept.

'I was in my room, of course,' I said, avoiding Rats's eye.

'No you were not. I came looking for you. You weren't there.'

'Perhaps I didn't hear you. I fell asleep early. Anyway, what did you want?'

'Some of us were going for chai to Venky's. I wanted to ask if you cared to join us.'

'Thanks. Next time.'

Rats's gang of friends changed depending on the season. During marketing heavy semesters, it consisted of the marketing whizzes in class, when the emphasis was on finance courses, Rats could be seen hobnobbing with all the potential bankers, and so on. I had accompanied Rats on a couple of occasions to these chai sessions, and it was almost embarrassing to watch him pretend an affinity he didn't have with his 'friends' of the moment.

'So, how's the book?'

'Which one?'

'Ruts! Is something wrong? I'm talking about the one you were so anxious to get your hands on. How did you find it?'

'Oh that! Wonderful!'

'The chapter on game theory, isn't it original?'

'Yup!'

Rats smirked and said, 'Caught you! You haven't even opened the book, have you? So what were you doing last night then?'

'I told you! I was sleeping! So, I haven't had time to go through the text. Big deal! Now can we get into class?'

'After you've told me what you were doing last night.'

'Rats, do me a favour. Fuck off.'

—∞—

I still smile when I think of Rats's face when I used the F-word on him. A mixture of disbelief, outrage and plain stupidity, as though he didn't understand what he had just heard, remained on his face for the rest of the class. It was also the moment I knew that Rats and I as a team were over. Perhaps he too is remembering that day. Rats's behaviour is always dependent on what he can extract from an encounter. The spite he showed earlier on has a purpose. It now remains for me to find out what that is.

7

It couldn't have been more than a couple of days after my night with Jaggu that Priya accosted me one evening in my room. As usual, she walked in without knocking. Like her, I never locked my room, whether I was in or not. Though it gave people the licence to walk in at any time, I was never one to bother about either intrusions or thieves.

'So, how was it?' she asked as soon as she had lit a cigarette and ensconced her body on my bed in her favourite position, sitting cross-legged at one end, hugging the pillow.

'I'm sorry?'

'The sex? How was it?'

I just stared at her in amazement.

'Oh, come on. It's obvious from your face that something's happened,' she explained.

'Obvious?'

'To me, at least. Your nose is shining.'

I rubbed my nose vigorously. 'As are your eyes,' she said. I closed my eyes. 'And your hips are swinging a little more.'

'Can we not talk about this?' I said eventually.

'Why not?'

'Because.'

'Not good enough. You have to do better than that.'

'All right. What do you want to know?'

'Are you happy?' she asked, stunning me.

'I think I am, actually.'

'Then I am glad for you. I'm glad you aren't into that guilt shit.'

'Why would I feel guilty? I haven't murdered anyone, Priya!'

'Come on, Ruts! This is India, remember?'

'And this is the IIM, remember?' I countered.

'So what? People here are the same moralistic pricks that they are anywhere else in this country. They'll cheat in exams, but raise a stink at a kiss.'

She was right, of course. Education didn't seem to have a significant effect on people's value systems. As long as I wasn't hurting anyone, I failed to see what business it was of theirs who I slept with. But that wasn't how the crowd looked at things.

'So, do you want to talk about it?' she asked, getting up to open the window and let out the cigarette fumes. 'About your boyfriend?'

'That's not how I think of him,' I said slowly.

Priya laughed at that. 'You mean you haven't slept with your boyfriend?'

'I mean I slept with someone. I'm not even sure I want to do it again.'

'Why? Wasn't it good?'

'It was amazing,' I confessed. 'It was the best few hours I've had here till now. But now what?'

'You mean you want to leave him?'

'I don't know. It's hard to explain. It's like eating at a gourmet restaurant. One meal is fantastic, but you don't want to eat there for the rest of your life. I'm not sure I'm in my own kitchen right now. Do you get what I'm saying?'

Priya was chuckling now. 'Well, this could certainly be the first time anyone has compared sex to food in this way,' she laughed. 'But if you don't want this to go any further, you'd better tell your man right away. Otherwise there could be trouble ahead.'

I noted that Priya didn't ask me the name of my lover. Perhaps she guessed who it was. Anyone else in her place would have tried to dig out all the details, but Priya was Priya. She stuck to the point and didn't go beyond it. I was grateful for that. And I trusted her more than ever. I don't know if I would have sought her out if I needed advice on true love. I doubted her expertise on that score, for all that she had had a million lovers. Of all her boyfriends, I never knew who it was that had a true claim to her affections. It was as though she was in the business of performing an act. The partner didn't really matter. She never expressed any sentiment for anyone, dismissing all her male acquaintances with equal indifference.

The exception to this was Sasi. Professor I. Sasikant was the instructor of macroeconomics. He was young and modest about his achievements, which were considerable. He couldn't have been much more than thirty but he had already completed his Ph.D. from the London School of Economics. During some research I had had to do for a paper, I had come across references to him in the journal of a well-known American university. That was quite an achievement, and I knew he could have chosen to teach at any of the top universities anywhere in the world. Instead, he had chosen to return to India and be a part of the best here.

Of course, we were all his admirers. He was modest and engaging and so very down to earth. He was the same age as some of the students, and we would often meet up with him outside the classroom and chat with him about anything under the sun. He never stood on ceremony with us, and crossed the teacher-student divide with ease. After the stiff formality of Chinni and Berry, Sasi was a refreshing change. He was never shy about answering our questions about his personal life. Thus we knew that his parents still lived in a village near Pondicherry, that his father was a physics teacher in the village high school and his mother ran a women's self-help group, that his brother was a farmer who used the most modern farming techniques, that he himself had only studied when he got a scholarship, that he was passionate about India and what he thought his contribution to it could be, that he wasn't married since he had been busy earlier and then hadn't managed to find the right woman but still hoped to, that he was vegetarian and his biggest vice was smoking.

Nobody unacquainted with Professor I. Sasikant would have believed he was an associate professor at the

Indian Institute of Management. With his oiled hair, dark rimmed glasses, scuffed chappals and synthetic shirts, he looked like a clerk in the lower division of a government office in the mofussil. All that changed, of course, as soon as he opened his mouth. From it emerged the most elegant English, spoken with a faint British accent that he had probably acquired during his years at the LSE.

Sasi was endearing and bright. I didn't see any reason why Priya shouldn't like him. She was probably the only one who didn't.

'He's such a self-conscious prick,' she told me, as we were returning from his class one day.

'I thought his lecture went off so well. I mean, how could anyone explain the concepts better than he does?' I protested.

'I'm not talking about the lecture,' said Priya.

'Then what?'

'Doesn't he strike you as being smug?'

'Smug? Sasi? Priya, what's wrong with you? What do you find smug about him?'

'His whole attitude. As though he knows it all. You guys don't see it, I guess. You're too overawed by his qualifications. You can't see beyond that.'

'Yeah, right. You're the only one smart enough to see through his façade.'

'Maybe I am.'

'So tell me what exactly you don't like about him. Let me try to understand this.'

'Okay. How about this? He talks too much. He has an

opinion about everything. He is too personal. He thinks every word he says is wisdom. Want more?'

'I think you're insane if you think these are all things that work against Sasi. Anyway, let us agree to disagree. You hate him, I get it. Let's stay with that.'

'Hey, guess what!' Priya said, changing the subject. 'I've got my summer job. In Delhi.'

'Wonderful! But why not Bombay?'

'Well, this came along first, and it's a really meaty assignment, so I'm taking it.'

It seemed a perfectly reasonable explanation, except that I knew it wasn't the truth. Priya tried to stay away from her parents as much as possible, and in the seven years since she had left home, she hadn't gone back more than a couple of times. I felt pained by her continuing anger towards them, but there wasn't anything I could do, except to support my friend in whatever she did.

'So, do you want to stay at my place? I have an extra room, and my parents would be glad to have another person around.' As soon as I made my offer, I regretted it. Priya wasn't the most conventional of people, and I dreaded the effect she might have on my parents. But the delight on her face when I invited her forbade me from retracting the invitation. I would simply have to face the situation as diplomatically as I could, and hope that my parents didn't base their impression of the IIM on my most extraordinary friend there.

But I had underestimated Priya, as I soon discovered. While she lived at my place during the summer break, she did her share of the chores, helping out my mother in the kitchen, running errands for my father, keeping her room so tidy that I wondered if this was the same person who lived in the cluttered room at the IIM. With her first stipend, she bought generous gifts for all of us. My parents thought the world of her, and were sad to see her leave when the two month break ended. Though I wished Priya had mended fences with her parents and spent the summer with them, I was glad of her company in those two months, glad of the opportunity to know her better. She intrigued me, this girl, and made me despair, and then made me wish I had some of her generosity and open-heartedness.

—✳—

We are what we are because of our teachers. I can remember even my first grade teacher to this date. She cast me as the black fairy, I remember, in *Sleeping Beauty* and I cried because I thought she had done it because I was ugly. And then she did something that changed the way I looked at myself for the rest of my life. After the pageant, she made me stand on her table and declared to the rest of the class that I had performed a very difficult role wonderfully, and made them all clap for me.

It is said that as one grows older, the role of one's teachers becomes less pivotal and that of one's friends more so. However, at the IIM, I found myself admiring, to the point of almost worshipping, a lot of the professors. There was HR, the man who taught me all I knew about

human behaviour, and whose words still reverberate in
my ears when I have to deal with difficult situations or
people, and there was Berry, whose initial sadism turned
into sympathy in the second year, when he was no longer
concerned with turning us into the best mathematicians in
the world, only into the best human beings. Berry took it
upon himself to talk to us about the world outside, many
times in mathematical terms, to tell us what to expect when
we became 'real people' as he put it. Berry was a true blue
genius, and my admiration was for both his intelligence
and his humanity. Both Berry and HR are now dead, one
from cancer and the other from a massive heart attack.
There are many others who are still around, Chinni being
one of them. Chinni is now the director and has turned
almost fanatical in his bid to take the institute to ever-
higher planes of fame. But of all the professors, I think it is
Sasi who has been, for me, the icon of what a professor at
the Indian Institute of Management should be.

Within the first few weeks of studying at the IIM,
the scales had fallen from my eyes as far as the quality of
the teaching staff was concerned. It ranged from brilliant
to downright bad, and like the rest of the students, my
loyalties were firmly with the former. I can admit it now. I
did idolise Sasi. He had just the right mix of scholarship and
communication skills and his connection with his students
was almost magical. And he was always in the vanguard of
any changes to improve the institute. If there'd been a vote
for the most respected faculty member, mine would have
definitely gone to him. From what I've seen now, things

haven't changed all that much. It is no surprise, therefore, that the choice of professor for felicitating by the batch has almost unanimously fallen upon Prof. Sasikant.

For some reason, I am the one who has been selected to hand over the award and citation to the professor.

'Me?' I squeak. 'Why me? I wasn't exactly brilliant at Eco, if I remember right.'

'Hey, who cares a fuck about Eco?' says Captain, when we're sitting together after breakfast to talk about this. 'You could give a kickass speech, I remember, and I guess those things don't change much. And Sasi always liked you for some reason. He'll be happy if you give him the citation.'

There was a reason for Sasi liking me, though perhaps nobody apart from me, including Sasi himself, knew what it was. I was appalled by Priya's dislike for my favourite professor. On the whole, for all her dry wit and ruthless opinions, she was fair-minded when it came to evaluating individuals. It was only in Sasi's case that she wore blinkers that just wouldn't come off. Eventually, I gave up trying to persuade her that she had no cause to dislike Sasi and that her prejudices were baseless. To offset Priya's rudeness, and because I liked him so much, I often socialized more with him than with any other professor on campus, a fact that annoyed Priya no end.

'Just look at you. You didn't strike me as being a teacher's pet,' she sneered.

'Not just any teacher,' I replied with a smirk. 'Good old Sasi.'

'He isn't that old, darling.'

'Oh, so you've noticed his age? I'm surprised!'

'Stop being cute, Ruts. It doesn't suit you. You should watch out. The other students think Sasi is favouring you.'

'Since when did you start getting concerned about what people think, Priya? Sasi is a good friend, that's all. He is one of the nicest people on campus, as you would realize if you weren't so stubborn.'

'Yes, well, to each his, or rather her, own.'

Sasi wasn't too impressed with Priya either, though she was, as usual, academically exceptional. In class he needled her more than once, raising arguments with her that left me, for one, completely bemused. The two would enter into highly technical discussions in which I understood just one in every five terms. Sometimes Sasi would become uncharacteristically sarcastic, and I got the feeling that he was willing to go to any lengths to win an argument. But even though I was on friendly terms with him, I could not go so far as to ask him why he was trying to corner Priya, for that was exactly what he was doing.

The citation given to me to read says, 'This award is being given to Professor I. Sasikant for his sterling service to the cause of the Indian Institute of Management, Bangalore. His dedication to taking the institute forward has made us more proud than ever to be a part of the IIMB family. Professor Sasikant is an inspiration to all of us, and this award recognizes that.' Oh phooey! Trust a bunch of management graduates to come up with the driest piece of word craft that has been heard in a long time.

We are in the auditorium where the director is addressing the gathering. For the last few minutes, I have been feeling nervous, and with good reason. I am due to go onstage next, and the prospect is daunting. I tell myself I am among friends, and it's really Sasi who needs to be nervous. It is his spotlight.

It is time. I go up to the dais. The rest of the auditorium is in darkness, filled with the ghosts of yesterday and the actual audience. I can see myself and the rest of the people on the stage, the director, Chinni, a couple of other professors, Sasi himself, and two members of the alumni. It occurs to me that the lighting is unnecessarily dramatic. It is not as though this is a performance. But then, perhaps it is, especially when I start to speak.

'Brilliance has no value here. Everyone is brilliant or they wouldn't be at the Indian Institute of Management. I do not state that as flattery, merely as fact. Perhaps once upon a time, when we were merely children, we enjoyed the acknowledgement of our unusual talents. That is no longer the case. None of us has any need to prove ourselves on that scale any longer. Once we were here, safely installed within the walls of this hallowed institution, each of us made one of three choices – to mix ambition and ability with compassion and prove that one's own success can benefit others, to use others for one's own success wilfully, or to simply meander through life without thought or purpose.

'Professor Sasikant, Sasi to many of us, made his choice about the same time that the rest of us made ours. We honour him today for creating the right mix of integrity, ambition and sense of purpose for himself. His choices have benefited him, true, else he wouldn't have made them. But what is a lesson to all of us assembled here is that they have also benefited the institute, and hundreds of students like us. Perhaps then, the right kind of self-interest is a type of mantra for success. In honouring you, professor, we, the former students of the Indian Institute of Management, remind ourselves of this particular road. I hope we all find our way on it.'

For a moment there is deathly silence, and then there is applause, the kind that rises up to the rafters and comes down like a shower of rain. I am pleased with the effect my words have had, especially since I mean every one of them. Sasi has a folded paper in his hand, perhaps his acceptance speech, but it stays folded, and when he speaks, it is in response to my own little oration. He has no need for any training in saying the right thing in the right manner and I am enthralled.

I don't know why people are so enthusiastic about my speech. Almost always, words that ask others to be honest have hypocrisy lining them, and I'm not sure if I should have chosen a pulpit to say what I did. Perhaps I have touched a nerve in my former classmates, each one of who falls in one of the three categories that I identified. Now I wish Kailash were by my side. He would certainly know what I'm talking about, and I could have shared with him the humour of seeing people applaud something that points a finger of accusation at them. But I was eager to have Kailash out of the way this morning, so that I could get on with the day's work without any hindrance.

It is natural for me to turn to Kailash for advice in almost everything, and this surreptitiousness is somewhat unusual for me. There's nothing to hide, I have told myself resolutely at least a dozen times since last night, but my deeds speak for themselves. Why, I ask myself, have I not told him what I'm planning to do some time during the day today? What am I afraid of?

Before I can work myself up into a proper mess, I find myself at lunch. We are dining with the professors and a few students who, I assume, have been specially chosen for this affair, to fraternise with the illustrious members of a twenty-year-old batch. I'm with Priya and Anya, the latter busy listening to our conversation, which has naturally veered to past days. Another person joins us. It is, I note with resignation, Rats. Now his eyes are all for Priya, his one-time girlfriend. I become silent, feeling like an intruder. I wonder, incredulously, whether these two still like each other the way they used to. I observe with fascination the pantomime of Priya introducing Anya and Rats to each other. I feel like I am in the way and stand up to join another table, but Priya stops me and says, 'Ruts, where are you off to? I can't let you go now. Anya has heard so much about you from me. Both of us want to chat with you.' She ignores Rats, who looks at her with an expressionless face for a moment and then walks away.

Though Rats has gone, the situation remains fraught, for soon thereafter it is none other than Sasi who joins us. Sasi was water to Priya's oil when I last saw them together, and I wonder if civilities are possible with so much bitterness in their history. I thought I had forgotten that episode, but as I watch Sasi turning on that famous smile at Anya, it comes back to me. Sasi starts asking Anya something about her school, and soon the two are engrossed in conversation, leaving Priya and me to talk about everything and nothing.

I am relieved that Priya and Sasi are on cordial terms, relieved and surprised. I had half expected to be acting as referee for the sparring match that used to be conversation for them, but none of that is in evidence, and for a moment I feel like I have missed a couple of steps here.

As I walk out of the lunchroom, leaving Priya and Sasi engaged in an intense conversation about managing voluntary organizations, I am accosted by Rats. 'That was a great speech,' he says.

It was targeted at you, I say silently. The job Rats holds with its posting in Hong Kong, I've discovered, is his fifth in as many years. Before that he worked in an FMCG company in India and then in South Africa. Rats has truly seen the world.

'I'd forgotten your debating stuff. Not surprising since we haven't touched base in all this time. You should come to Hong Kong. It's a great city, really on the move. There's nothing in India to compare.'

I have seen Hong Kong. Kailash wrote a play that

travelled to that city four years ago. For a change, all of us went along to share Kailash's excitement. I don't comment on the comparison with India. It's the sort of thing that would lead to a debate and Rats doesn't awaken my usual combative self.

'Why didn't you call me? We could have done something together,' he says when I tell him about my visit.

He skims over the fact that I had no contact details, but that doesn't seem to be material to the purpose, which is 'to do something together'. This is just an aside to myself, and not pertinent. Even if I did know how to find Rats, I do not believe I would have done it. He has never excited me, not even in the capacity of an old 'buddy'.

'I almost couldn't come for this do. In any case, I'm going to have to miss tomorrow's session. Catching the early morning flight back to Delhi and on to New York. An urgent meeting.'

Why is he volunteering this information to me? I'm in a hurry to put the first part of my plan in action, but I forbear to say so to Rats. However, he senses my impatience. He looks at me moodily. 'You're really busy, Ruts. My wife and kids have landed up. I thought to introduce them to you.'

Me? Why? Rats and I are hardly college pals. I'm sure there are many other people here who are more intimate with this man. Nonetheless, I agree to meet them for tea. It might be fun for us to meet at the local Barista coffee shop, I suggest. A chain of these has sprung up across the new Bangalore, model coffee shops gleaming with anonymity, trying hard but failing, I'm glad to see, to drive the old 'kaapi' houses into obscurity.

'How about the coffee shop at the Westend? That's where they are staying. I thought it might be better if we put up there. This place isn't really all that great.'

In the new Bangalore of traffic jams, this means an hour's drive each way. I'm not sure if I can spare the time, but I'm left with no choice. Rats is insistent, and I agree. Also, I'm curious to see Rats' wife. My phone rings as I'm working out the details with Rats.

'Tee!' squeals a familiar voice.

'Xenia! What's going on? It must be four in the morning there!'

'Yeah, I couldn't sleep. Hey listen! They showed something about your college on CNBC today.'

'IIM?' I ask incredulously.

'Yes. I knew I'd got it right. Hey, your campus looks neat!'

'And you're calling me at four in the morning to tell me this?'

'Well, I was wondering if all was well. How are things with the ex? Does Lash know what's going on? Are you in big trouble?'

I'm sure my friend can be heard for miles around. There are a few faces that look in my direction curiously and then walk off. Fortunately, Rats has moved away to talk on his phone.

'Xenia, can we talk later? I'll call you.'

'Why, is the ex around?'

'No. But I'm busy right now.'

'Hey, listen, I remembered why I wanted to speak to you. Gunther Rowe is coming next month.'

I almost do a little two-step right there in the lobby. 'He is? Xenia, that's fantastic. Wow!'

'Yes, and all because you wrote him some letter, it seems, that he couldn't ignore. He called yesterday asking for you.'

I kick myself for being in Bangalore and missing the opportunity to speak to my idol. Gunther is a writer whom I have admired for over ten years now. In the past, I have failed on more than one occasion to get him to come to the Big Creek.

'That's the best news you could have given me!'

'Better than the ex saying he still likes you?'

I don't dignify that with a reply. Xenia's teasing can be excessive sometimes. 'Write a thank you note to Gunther, and ask him if he has any special preferences for his stay. Attach the brochure with a list of all our facilities.' My voice has turned crisp as I give Xenia instructions on how to handle the next few days.

'Tee,' says Xenia after I'm done. 'Is everything all right with you?'

'Yes,' I answer, though not for long, but I don't say that.

Xenia's call has put a new spring in my step, and once again I wish Kailash were there to share the good news with me. He knows how I have longed to have Gunther in my stable of writers, and how hard I have worked to achieve that goal. Big Creek isn't exactly a five star facility with writers clamouring to get in. Though it has been around for quite a few years, it has still not achieved the status I desire. The last couple of years have seen small successes in this direction. Gunther's acceptance is a big number though. He can lead me to confirmed success with his presence. There are other writers whom I have chased, but none with as much avidity as Gunther.

In the whole excitement, I've almost forgotten about Rats and Jaggu. A quick look at my watch shows me that I am running late for both appointments. In fact, there's no way I can keep both.

I call up Jaggu on his cellphone. 'I have to go out with Rats,' I explain. 'I'll see you later.'

There's a moment of silence at the other end. 'Hello?' I say loudly.

'I heard you, Ruts,' says Jaggu quietly. 'Let me know when you are free.'

'All right.' I should have told him why I'm going out with Rats but I'm chary of explaining my actions to Jaggu or anyone else. Why can't people take me at face value? I feel annoyed with Jaggu and resist charging up to him and giving him a piece of my mind. It takes some effort to remind myself that I am now on the wrong side of forty and indulging my impulses is no longer such a good idea.

—*≡*—

I am more than twenty minutes late. Rats is sitting alone in the dining room, reading a newspaper. I apologize for keeping him waiting. He doesn't respond, as though that isn't what's on his mind. I wonder what is. He ushers me into the waiting car and we are driven in the direction of the hotel, towards his family. I devote myself to the sights of Bangalore, most of which are unfamiliar to me, expressing no curiosity about Rats's family. Rats volunteers no information on his own, and I am none the wiser about his personal life.

'So, have you started writing your memoirs yet?' he asks as the car weaves rapidly in and out of traffic, making me a little sick.

'I don't think anyone would be interested in my life.'

'Oh, come on, going to the IIM, getting laid, marrying a theatre hotshot, somewhere in there lies a story, don't you think?'

I have no intention of falling into Rats's trap.

'Thanks for the idea. I'll think about it,' I reply with a grin.

'Yeah, you do that. And don't forget to mention my name.'

I certainly shan't, Rats, never fear.

Mrs Saluja (I don't know her first name) has been told to expect us, but though we are late, she is not there. A boy of fourteen, iPod attached to his ears and cellphone to his fingers, sits in the lobby, gazing euphorically at nothing. He is dressed the way most teenagers dress these days, as though clothes are an insult to their intelligence. A pair of shapeless jeans loosely hangs on his hips, their legs and his dissociated from each other. I would say the jeans are a few sizes too loose for him, but what do I know about it. His

T-shirt bears the legend 'I Need Sex. What About You?'. It is too big for his bony frame, and looks like it is meant for someone older. Scruffy though his appearance might be, it is a deliberate, expensive scruffiness. The boy's hair is cut in a sort of layered style that succeeds in falling over his face in different places. I can make out he is Rats's son. Nothing can camouflage those eyes or those sharply rising cheekbones. The girl, sitting on a different sofa, is less easy to place. She is younger, equally expensively dressed in a flowery sundress and open-toed shoes, in which her painted toes are displayed to advantage. I can see that there is some parental influence at work here. The whole appearance is normal and pleasing to the eye, though the pout on the lips and the glittering eyes display an anger that is being held under check with difficulty. I have seen too many girlish tantrums not to recognize one, even a repressed one. The furious expression does not sit well on the slightly flabby face, which would be more suited to a smile. The girl cannot be more than twelve years old, and I see signs of future plumpness in her. She is exceedingly fair, almost Caucasian in appearance, especially since her hair, which hangs till her shoulders, is slightly blonde. The brother-sister duo look what they are, the offspring of well-to-do parents. The girl, too, has her own iPod and cellphone, but both of these are lying by her side, toys whose ability to entertain is now suspect.

I stand to one side, uncertain if I should be intruding into whatever was going on before we arrived, but Rats has no such scruples. 'Gautam, meet Shruti Malhotra. Shruti was my classmate at IIM. I told you in the morning that I would be bringing her to meet you.' That's typical Rats. He had assumed I would consent to join him even before he had asked me.

Gautam stands up, and I'm relieved. It embarrasses me when parents have to prompt their children to show good manners. It makes me feel like the cause of the conflict.

'Hi. It's Shruti Narayan now, not Malhotra.'

Gautam makes a sound that I assume to be a greeting and retreats into his iPod. The girl does not get up. She has not been introduced to me. I wonder at the omission.

'Where's Shaina, Khushi?'

'I don't know. Why can't we eat pizza for dinner?'

'Shut up, Khushi. There are guests around, can't you see,' pipes up Gautam.

Khushi doesn't heed her brother. They are both equally rude, to each other and to the environment. 'Dad, why can't we get pizza and ice-cream for dinner? Restaurants out here suck.'

I have no part in this family conversation. I wonder why Rats has brought me. Perhaps Rats is thinking the same thing. We go to the coffee shop. It looks like a pleasant place, with solid wood furniture that gives it a colonial club-like appearance. Shaina's absence is not commented upon anymore. The children have retreated into their own worlds, their role in this gathering over. I am anxious to get back. This absurd tea party holds no interest for me. Rats forces a cup of tea on me, while the children order some exotic fruit juice cocktails that come in tall glasses with umbrellas. Rats himself is a coffee man, it seems, and gives the waiter complicated instructions about preparing it. Once again there is a vacuum. There is a small dilemma here. If I talk to Rats, the children will be excluded, something I do not desire. And there is nothing to say to Gautam and Khushi, both of whom are sulking over their drinks, nothing in the cocktails exciting their admiration.

'Gautam, take that damn thing out of your ears, for god's sake!'

Gautam can't hear him, though I can hear the music coming out of his ears, it is so loud. Rats gestures, looking ridiculous, and Gautam takes out one earphone inquiringly.

'Can you switch that thing off? I brought Shruti particularly to meet you.'

Is Rats lying? He has not done anything to encourage interaction between his children and me. All of us are under the impression that having introduced us, he has decided that nothing more is required. I really cannot blame the children for ignoring me. Their father also seems to be doing the same.

I decide to salvage the evening, for my as well as the children's sakes. 'Your father is being polite,' I smile. 'He never called me Shruti and I never knew him as Ravi. I am Ruts and he is Rats.'

It is an interesting opening gambit and it works. There is a flood of questions about our student days, and I am happy to indulge in a bout of nostalgia with strangers. The children are not too knowledgeable about their father's youthful exploits. Rats has not told them much, I gather. I wonder at such reticence.

'Did you like the college?' asks Khushi, and I stop in my tracks. I have nothing to say.

I am surprised when Rats enters the conversation. 'What's not to like? It is one of the world's best institutions. The students there are brilliant, the teachers are also good. Once you are in it, you know that you belong to the best. IIM graduates, young lady, are special.'

I do not like this assessment. 'Well, initially I didn't like it, but after some time, when I had made a few friends, I became really comfortable there.'

'Were you and dad friends then?'

I can always object to Gautam's snide tone. There is some hidden agenda he is pursuing that isn't hard to fathom. I feel like telling him that I wouldn't have gone near Rats for all the tea in China. 'I knew your father quite well, yes. We were together in many classes. We helped each other in a lot of things.' No harm in a few white lies.

'We were people who worked hard. We knew if we did that we could achieve success. Life is all about going after what you want. Ruts, Gautam is clueless about what he wants. You should talk to him about it.'

I look at Rats. This is the worst a child can suffer, being derided by his parents in front of strangers. I catch a look of despair in Gautam's eyes. 'Oh, I'm no role model, believe me. I think it is important to make the most of the moment. I wish I had done more of that when I was your age. Now I want to do all those things but I can't. Dancing, for instance. You should know what you like, I think. I liked writing, and now I've taken it up seriously. I love it. Your father likes making money,' I joke, 'and look how well he is doing.' Rats looks almost murderous at my levity but I ignore him. He shouldn't have invited me in the first place. Now I will not shut up to suit him.

'Gautam likes looking at himself in the mirror,' giggles Khushi.

'Shut up, fatso,' says Gautam angrily.

Khushi, fortunately, does just that and we are back to being adults. 'I've decided what I want to do,' says Gautam, looking at me. I know he isn't talking to me now.

'Yes, well, let's not get into that right now,' says Rats edgily.

'Why not? I want to be a fashion designer,' he tells me.

There is silence, an appalled one. Gautam seems to have crossed some hidden boundary of propriety, judging by the expressions on the family's faces.

'Gautam,' says Rats. There is anger in his voice. This subject has been visited before. I can make out. And there is going to be an altercation about it right now. I don't know if I should intervene. I wonder if Gautam is choosing his career out of spite. It is a possibility, but I'm not sure if I care to know the details. It is fortunate that matters are not allowed to go any further.

'Hi. What's up?'

The woman standing next to our table is perfect. Her

skin, her hair, her eyes, her shape, her clothes, her lipstick, her *being* is perfect. This can be none other than Rats's wife. Rats has always sought what he thinks to be perfection. By no stretch of imagination does Shaina look like the mother of two teenage children. For a wild moment I wonder if she is Rats's second wife. She looks so *young*.

'Hi, Mum. Where were you?' asks Khushi with a pout.

'Darling, I just had to go to the new mall on Brigade Road. It has a fantastic Bulgari showroom.'

I wonder if children of Khushi's age know what Bulgari stands for. Perhaps they do.

'Gautam says he is going to be a fashion designer,' says Khushi, not interested in Bulgari.

A quick look passes between Gautam and his mother. Something is going on here that I am not aware of. Rats is flushed with anger. 'We are not here to talk about Gautam,' he hisses through clenched teeth. 'Shaina, did you forget I had asked Shruti to have tea with us?'

'Well, I had forgotten. I am so sorry.' The smile that flashes is charm defined. 'Hi. I'm Shaina.'

I smile and there is peace. The act of ordering and getting more tea eliminates the need for talk. I am not unaware that Rats is furious. Everybody, even his wife, is busy ignoring him and with a mental shrug, I join them. The conversation picks up tentatively. We skirt around the elephant in the room, Gautam's stated career choice. Shaina is an expert on small talk, and I know she is drawing me out. Her presence has certainly energized the children. Gautam even smiles a couple of times.

'Shaina is heir apparent to the Katwal empire,' sneers Rats. 'Next month she is going to become the chairman, oops, sorry, chairperson, I should say. We're talking serious money here, Ruts. Remember how we used to talk about the perfect, rich life? Well, Shaina actually lives it.'

Rats waits for a reaction to this but there is none. Gautam has gone back to his overloud iPod and Khushi is slurping her drink through the crushed ice in a bid to be noisy. The gurgle cannot drown Rats's words.

'Ruts, you and I went to B-school to do what Shaina is doing today. She has five thousand six hundred and forty eight people reporting to her. Am I right?'

'Ravi, you are embarrassing your friend. I'm sure she hasn't come to hear about what I do. Ravi can be a bit overbearing at times.' Shaina smiles. I am amazed at her ability to ignore her husband's jibes. 'He's just upset that we have moved to Delhi now. Ignore him. I'm really not doing anything that great. Dad has professionals to do everything.' She waves a manicured hand. 'But going to his office is one way of keeping busy, I suppose. I'm nothing as accomplished as you guys. Am I, Gautam?'

Gautam is immersed in his music and ignores his mother. But Shaina can't help ruffling his hair in a madly maternal gesture that has me warming to her instantly. It is obvious that Gautam is not unhappy with his mother's display of affection.

'Khushi is also set on going to B-school. That's why I brought her along.'

'Yes, but we still haven't been to the ins-ti-tute, Daddy.'

The girl's lisp and pout are sure to kill some gentlemen some day.

'You should have stayed on campus,' I say. 'You would have seen how we lived twenty years ago.' I can't help smiling.

'Dad, let's go and stay at the inst-whatever it is. This aunty says so.'

'Oh, don't call me aunty, call me Ruts,' I say instinctively.

'We can't go tonight, Khushi. We have to leave in the morning. We'll go for a couple of hours, and then sleep here,' says Rats.

Shaina intervenes. 'Considering we've come all the way for the get-together, I think you're being ridiculous about not staying on campus. The children will enjoy it, Ravi. We'll check out of here now and go to the campus guesthouse.'

The decision is made. There is a flurry of activity. Rats is silent. He has been overruled, and I think he is unused to that. He ushers me out to the waiting car, while the others follow in a second car. I wonder about this arrangement. I don't know why Rats wants my company. We have almost nothing to say to each other.

'They're going to hate it, you know. They are used to better arrangements. This place is tacky.' His cellphone rings and he barks into it, some business lingo that allows me to collect my thoughts. His tone is one that is employed with a distinct subordinate, short and crisp and barely disguising his impatience. The conversation ends, but I do not wish to engage with Rats. I am happier looking at the changed Bangalore landscape. I am obviously out of place with Rats and his family, though for a moment, as I talked to the children, I sensed a spark of animation. Rats has married well, I think. I would have expected him to. He is from a humble background, his father a manager in a small company when Rats was a student, a two-bedroom house in Punjabi Bagh in West Delhi the pinnacle of achievement for this Punjabi migrant family. Rats has worked hard to exit that environment. There is nothing now in his persona to indicate those migrant, refugee roots. He is a man of the world, in the true sense.

I wonder about Shaina. Why did she marry Rats? Well, he does have a seductive profile. Twenty years ago, he was a young man about town, educated at some of the best institutions the world had to offer. Most women would be thrilled to have him. For many, quality education is more seductive than wealth. Wealth is finite, while education can keep capitalizing on itself. So it is believed. But what if education is only a means to wealth?

The receptionist gives me several messages when I return. Kailash and the children are back, and are searching for me. There's a message from Jaggu. 'Need to see you asap' says the small slip of paper. Priya has also left word that she needs to tell me something. The tea at the hotel was good, but I feel the need for another cup before I take on all these challenges. Rats has disappeared somewhere, much to my relief, and I'm left alone for some time.

Priya manages to nose me out while I'm having tea in the cafeteria. 'Where on earth have you been?'

I explain.

'That creep! Why did you agree to go with him? Was he showing you off in front of his wife? You should have given him the boot.'

The thought of Shaina makes me smile.

'What are you grinning for?'

'Wait till you see Shaina.'

'Who is Shaina?'

I go into the Saluja family history with Priya. She has a right to know and be warned that she will very soon be confronted by her former lover's family. Priya grins, and her eyes sparkle with mischief.

'Should I tell his wife who I am? Her expression will be worth it. And his too.'

Both of us laugh at the thought of Rats's dismay. I know Priya is only joking. I cannot even begin to guess the number of men she has been intimate with in the past. It was something we never talked about. Priya's life could not but be a source of curiosity for me, inexperienced as I was in matters of sex, but I could never muster up the nerve to ask her. Except that one time, when she told me the story of her aborted marriage. It is something I haven't told anyone, not even Kailash. Some things are better left buried.

'You were looking for me?'

'Can Anya be with you for the rest of the evening? She can play with your kids,' says Priya.

'Of course.'

As though guessing that she owes me some explanation, she adds, 'I have to go out. Anya is used to being on her own. She won't hassle you. I should be back after dinner.'

I do not ask what Priya is up to. Anya will certainly have to look after herself. I'm going to be occupied with other things for the rest of the evening. But Priya's daughter doesn't seem to be a problem child. She looks as self-assured as her mother. Priya and I are just getting up when Shaina walks in with Gautam and Khushi. It is typical of Rats that he has not bothered to be there to meet his family. Shaina looks pleased to see me.

'This place is a dream!' is her first remark.

A thrill of pride runs down my spine. It is many years since I obtained my Post Graduate Diploma in Business Management or PGDM from the IIM, but I still feel proud of the institute. I never own up to its weaknesses in front of strangers.

Khushi actually offers her hand to be shaken. 'Hi, Ruts, once again. Are you going to show us around?'

I believe this should have been Rats's job, but he is nowhere to be seen. I have to meet Kailash and Jaggu and have no time. Priya guesses my dilemma. She holds out a hand. 'Hi, I'm Priya. I was also with Rats, I mean Ravi. I can take you around the campus. It'll be my pleasure.'

'Are you sure?' I ask Priya, pulling her aside. 'I thought you had to go somewhere.'

'Did you see that kid's face? I can imagine how Anya would feel if I abandoned her like this. The kid doesn't need this, does she? She deserves to know where her papa studied. What if she wants to come here some day? The least we can do is tell her something about IIM.'

Wow! Priya *has* changed. I remember my own introduction to the place through Priya's eyes. Her sentiments seem to have... amended, somewhat.

It seems the same thought is running through everybody's mind today, that perhaps someday their children will also choose to study at this institution, though the other way round is more proper, that maybe their children will be found good enough to be admitted to this place.

I ignore Jaggu's note as I head back to my room to look for Kailash. He is sitting placidly by the window, glancing through one of his books while the children lounge around playing Pictionary. It is a scene of careless domesticity, and I feel soothed by it. After the charged atmosphere within Rats's family, my own looks so normal, and I feel almost an outsider in it. The last adjective I would use for myself at this stage is normal. For an insane moment, I wonder if my entry won't disturb this placid scene. But then Kailash looks up and gives his smile, the one he reserves only for me, a combination of query, smirk and laughter that indicates somehow that he loves me for all my sins, and I manage to shake off my guilt for his sake. Considering that it is at his behest that we have decided to attend this event, the least I can do is make my husband feel welcome here.

'I believe,' says Kailash with a twinkle, 'that we have an actress in our midst now.'

'I'll pretend you didn't say that,' I reply, not entirely in jest.

'Why not? Rumour has it that there's a performance scheduled for this evening, and you are one of the cast.'

We are having a replay of the performance that all of us put up at our welcome party twenty years ago. Someone thought up this brilliant idea. Though this time the audience will consist of the families of the performers. I'm not looking forward to having my husband witness my juvenile attempts at acting.

'As long as you don't boo me off,' I tell Kailash.

'Darling! I'm not really that mean, am I?'

Before I can reply, my cellphone rings. I'm all for ignoring it but something tells me that it will just go on ringing until I take the call.

'What?'

'Didn't you get my message?'

'I did.'

Kailash is listening to the conversation avidly.

'Then why haven't you met me?'

'Yeah,' I say. 'See you at the party. Kailash and I can't wait.'

'Who was that?' asks Kailash as I turn my phone off.

'No one you know. Just another batchie.'

8

'**Y**o! Ruts! Come on! Take it off! Be a sport! We want
some fun! We want Ruts! We want Ruts!'

The calls emanate from the audience. They are all men
in their forties or even older, and for one evening they have
decided to behave like overgrown adolescents.

The skit goes on uninterrupted by the cheers, the jokes
getting bawdier and more uninhibited with each dialogue.
We are re-enacting the skit that we did in our first term
here. As then, it is a big hit now, with everyone rolling in
the aisles.

Kailash is the first one to come backstage and slapping
me on the back, he says, 'Congrats, er, Ruts! I should cast
you in one of my plays! Why didn't you tell me before
what a great actor you are! That was simply marvellous!
Totally artistic!'

'Shut up, Kailash!' I laugh. 'I'm glad you enjoyed
yourself. I hope Isha and Rohan did not see this bilge.
I don't fancy explaining to them why everyone was
laughing.'

'Don't worry! The children are having their own party
somewhere. Some wise person realized what a disaster it

would be to have them present here. But seriously, I haven't laughed so much in a long time. You guys must have had some fun back then.'

Captain walks up to us and I introduce him to Kailash. 'Meet the director of our play.'

'I am truly honoured,' says Kailash with a twinkle. 'You show great talent. I must take a few lessons from you.'

'Kailash teaches theatre at UPenn,' I explain.

Captain has a huge grin plastered on his face. 'Hey man! I think I want to join theatre as a profession.'

'I completely agree,' says Kailash. 'I think your talents are wasted in the corporate world.'

Rats walks up to us in the middle of all this, as we head to the buffet. I think Rats is never comfortable unless he knows exactly what each person is doing or talking about. A moment ago he was in the middle of another group, trying to make himself the centre of attention there, and then he abandoned them to walk to us. He probably calls it networking.

I look around and see his family huddled together. I wave at Shaina.

'Your family looks lost,' I tell Rats, pulling him aside. 'You should introduce them around.'

'They'll be okay,' he shrugs. 'Incidentally, whose fucking idea was it for Priya to take Shaina around? Couldn't you have done it?'

'I was busy. Anyway, why the concern? I would have thought in some ways Priya might be a better guide than me. She has visited this place a few times in the past, it seems, to give some visiting faculty lectures. Whereas I'm returning after twenty years.'

'That's not the point, is it?'

I do not understand. 'What is the point then, Rats?'

'I'm talking about why my wife and that bitch should never be alone together. I know you were never very bright but surely you can see that.'

I lose no time in reassuring him. 'Rats! Priya isn't going to talk about ancient history to your wife. She isn't so thoughtless.'

'What would you know about it?'

It's a rhetorical question. Priya isn't the only one who has broken off relationships. I, too, know what it is to leave behind a sundered heart, and the memory of that night on the terrace runs through me now like a sharply honed knife, leaving in its wake an oozing wound that I believed had healed over the years. I'm not going to think about it, I'm not. I don't wish to, and Jaggu can call me till kingdom come, I'm not going to go. It's only a few more hours. Surely I can survive them. What are a few hours compared to twenty years? I have lived all these years, haven't I? And I shall continue to do so. And nothing in this weekend can change that. So, Mr Rats, I do know a few things, contrary to your belief, and one of the things I know better than you is how to judge a person. You have nothing to fear from Priya. I have seen the way Shaina looks at you. But perhaps women thinks differently from men. There's only one way of finding out.

'Kailash,' I say, catching him when he's alone. 'If your

ex-girlfriend showed up, the one who did management studies, how would you feel about her talking to me?'

Kailash gives me an inscrutable look and says, 'Awful. Why?'

'Why would you feel awful?'

'Shruti, if I knew why you were asking me this question, perhaps I might have a better answer.'

'I'll tell you. But just for the sake of argument, if she and I were to meet, would you get mad when you found out?'

'Yes. She had hate in her heart, darling, real hate. And hate poisons, if you don't know. That female could spew venom and kill.'

'Oh. But if she weren't that kind...' I suddenly realize how ridiculous I sound and stop.

'Shruti, you're making no sense. What's going on?'

'I don't know what's going on, really. Did you know Priya had a thing with Rats one time?'

'Help me out here. Who is Rats?'

'The well-dressed one? The one who was with us a while ago?'

'The one with the manicure?'

'Yeah, the very same. He got really mad when he found out that Priya had taken his wife around the campus.'

'Wow! That was a dicey thing to do, wouldn't you agree?'

'Normally, yes. But you don't know Priya. She is just not like that. I mean, she isn't the vengeful kind. She would never dream of saying anything indiscreet to Rats's wife.'

'So why is he so angry?'

'That's what I'm wondering myself. He has to know Priya is not the type to step in between his wife and him. I'm sure there's something else that's bothering him.'

'Wait. Isn't he the man you think is a category A jerk?'

'I'm sure I didn't say that!' I exclaim.

'No, but I can read between the lines. So then the problem may not be at Priya's end at all. It could be this Rats's problem in some way.'

What would that be, I wonder. I'm sure I will find out.

There have been times in these past few hours when I wished I had never known any of these people. As strangers, they are an impressive lot, all my classmates, movers and shakers who can move and shake with the best of them. Take Priya, for instance. Who would believe that underneath that calm demeanour lies a person who once attempted to take her own life? Does her daughter know how many shattered hearts her mother left behind wherever she went? Is she aware of the many scandals that accompanied Priya's career at the IIM? Today's Priya is a former finance wizard and a current leader in the voluntary sector, looking at microfinance distribution, I'm told; a mother, albeit a single one, and a thorough professional. What wouldn't I give to know her just like this, not to have her earlier avatar superimpose itself on this image, and so respect her for what she is today. Perhaps that is still possible. Perhaps I will return to Philadelphia believing that my friend has successfully laid the ghosts of the past to rest. Just as she will go back home carrying an image of my happy family with her.

We are all selective about what we reveal of ourselves, and our persona changes with our audience. Even our closest relatives are shown only one aspect of our lives, the most suitable one. Now when I contemplate the sophisticated men and women with whom I spent two years of my life, I cannot help wonder if their spouses, and children, and parents know what I know about them. Does Shaina see the womanizing opportunist behind the elegant façade of her husband? Does Jaggu's wife guess the deep hatred he is capable of carrying in his heart? I know that Kailash doesn't know the depths of anxiety I am prone to sometimes, though Priya was never far in coming to my rescue the moment she saw signs of something eating away at my soul. These deceptions, large and small, are perhaps an inevitable part of our experience, but that doesn't make them any more acceptable. I realize this at night when I take Kailash out for a stroll, once again ignoring Jaggu's appeal for a tête-à-tête. The cheerful end to the day hasn't rid me of a feeling of dread, as though I'm being led towards a dark place in my past. The only person who has always succeeded in ridding me of my strange 'fancies', as he calls them, is Kailash. Tonight, however, Kailash is silent, almost moody, a fact that initially escapes my notice as I unload all my pent up anxiety on him, chattering on about Priya and Sasi, giving long, unedited descriptions of our past life, and narrating the tea party experience with Rats and his family. Kailash interrupts me mid-sentence.

'That Jaggu. He seemed a little keen on you, I thought. Tell me, what's up?'

'What's up? What could be up?' I try to supress the shiver that goes down my spine, and am only partially successful.

'I noticed a little, umm, eagerness?'

'Did you? I didn't. Jaggu always talks like that.'

'Didn't seem like it,' says my husband, doggedly.

'Kailash, stop imagining things! Jaggu's just a friend, that's all,' I reply, trying to believe what I'm saying.

'Are you sure he thinks the same way?'

'I think your mind is a bit twisted, and I think you should do something about it.' I don't know why I'm getting so angry. If there's one person with whom I should be honey itself, it is my dear husband.

'Hey! Keep your hair on!' says Kailash, raising his hands as though to protect himself from assault. 'You are an attractive woman, sexy, mysterious, gentle, friendly, humorous! You have everything that will attract a red-blooded man. Something could be up. You should like it.'

'Nothing's up and I don't like it,' I say, and that's the end of that. Perhaps I should meet Jaggu and repeat these words to him as well.

The feeling of dread has been growing even as I have this conversation with Kailash. I love you, I feel like telling my husband, and then feel silly. He knows I love him. I have no intention of stating the obvious. But perhaps it isn't so obvious anymore.

How our insecurities turn us into selfish monsters! Here I am thinking only about myself, with no desire to console my husband beyond stating the obvious. I put myself into his shoes for a moment, and conclude the obvious, that he has been far more generous to me than I would have been to him under similar circumstances. While I relive the past with my erstwhile friends, and once again connect to their present lives, he has stood patiently by my side, content to let me be, going along with whatever demands I make on his time and patience. And now when he does demand accountability from me, how quick I have been to rap him on the knuckles for going beyond his brief!

Kailash is staring into the distance where an obliging moon is staring back at him, its face a large grin. In the distance a bird squawks, forgetting that it is supposed to be a time for silence and rest. The uneven ground beneath our feet sways a little more as I stand on tiptoe to give my husband a generous kiss. 'I love you,' I tell him.

He smiles at me and says, 'I know.'

'Is that all?'

'What do you mean?'

'I mean, what about you? What are you supposed to say?' I'm only partially teasing.

'I love you too, darling. Does that make you happy?'

More than you will know. There's a danger now that we will get carried away right in the middle of the path. It is still not too late for some stray passer-by to stroll past, and we turn back towards our guesthouse. The children are in bed now, and the two of us will be able to resume our moment of intimacy in the privacy of our room.

Since it is already quite late, most of the lights have been switched off in the lobby and it carries an air of mystery. It makes me start when I see a figure rising from one of the sofas in a corner. A sigh escapes me when I see who it is.

'Jaggu! What are you doing here?' It is Kailash who speaks.

'I wanted a word with your wife, actually,' says the man.

'What, now?' I protest.

'It won't take more than a couple of minutes, Ruts. It's about Priya.'

I can smell a lie a mile off and now my nose is twitching madly. But before I can say anything, Kailash says, 'I'll leave you to it then.'

'Kailash!' I call out to my already disappearing husband. 'You can stay here too.'

'That's okay, Shruti. I need to do some reading. Goodnight, Jaggu.'

And with that Kailash goes off in the elevator, leaving me to face my classmate.

'Shall we go for a walk?' asks Jaggu.

'Actually my feet are....'

But Jaggu is already heading towards the exit and I have no option but to follow him. He whips out a pack of cigarettes and offers me one. The first and last time I smoked was on this same campus twenty years ago. Jaggu doesn't heed my comment to this effect as he quickly lights up and inhales deeply.

'So, what about Priya?' I ask after we have walked a few steps. My mind is torn between my aching heels and my curiosity. I'm not sure which is winning. I wish I could say honestly that it is the heels.

'Fuck Priya, okay? That dame has done enough damage already.'

'What are you talking about?'

'Don't pretend you don't know.'

'Well, if we aren't here to discuss Priya, then what's up?'

'Why haven't you answered my calls?'

'I've been busy.' Why am I even explaining myself to this man? I wish I could just say it's none of his business but somehow I can't.

'Not busy enough to go off with Rats, apparently.'

Am I sure I'm not imagining the note of jealousy in Jaggu's voice? 'He wanted to introduce his family to me.'

'And that was more important than meeting me?'

'Not really, no.'

'Then what's going on?'

'Look, it's no big deal, okay? He asked, and he was obviously anxious, and I took a spur of the moment decision to go. Now if that's all you wanted to know then can we go back? Kailash is probably waiting for me.'

'As is Vijay, my wife. I told her I was going to meet a prof.'

This doesn't sound good at all. But before I can say anything, Jaggu says, 'Do you remember coming to the library one time? With Rats?'

'Yeah.'

'You do know he brought you because he knew I was there.'

'What do you mean?'

'He came to the library looking for some book. I

remember he was searching through the shelves for quite some time. I was just glad to be sitting in a quiet corner until the bugger came up to me and started chatting. It pissed me off to be disturbed like that, and I was so glad when he went off. I had been feeling restless for quite a few days, without knowing why and I was desperate for some peace. And the next thing I know, you came sauntering in with him. I was furious, and it took a lot out of me not to punch both of you on the nose right then and there.'

'I'm sorry,' I say, regretting the inadequacy of my words.

'Why should you be? You were always ignorant of the games that sicko insisted on playing with you. He knew how I would feel seeing the two of you together, and he made me see it. Snake is a better name for him than rat.'

'I'm sorry,' I repeat. 'No wonder he was so eager to take me to the library. I wondered at the time what the urgency was.'

'So, can we talk?' asks Jaggu, flicking the cigarette butt into some nearby bushes.

'Talk? I thought that's what we were doing.'

'I guess I mean talk about us.'

'Us?'

'Yeah. You and me. Us.'

I can see a jam when I'm in one. If I say no, then I'm acknowledging the 'us'. And I certainly can't say yes. Fortunately or otherwise, I'm not given an option.

'You didn't do right by me, Ruts. Just because your friend poisoned your ears against me....'

'Leave Priya out of this.'

'All right. Then why did you ditch me like that?'

'Jaggu, let the past be over, please. I didn't come here to resurrect it.'

'No? Well, I did. In fact, the only reason I came to this reunion was to see you.'

Now I am genuinely shocked. 'And what about your wife and daughter? Why have you brought them along?'

'Because I care about them. Because I want them to see and admire this place. Because a lot of what I am today is linked to this institute, and I'm proud of that. I'm not a heel, contrary to what you believe.'

'Of course I don't believe that. But then don't say you came here because of me.'

'I'll change my words then. If you hadn't come, then I might not have come either.'

'I can't believe you waited twenty years to meet me.'

'Having met you now, I can't believe it either. I don't know why I didn't try before. I think I was trying to put it all behind me, trying to convince myself that perhaps what we were wasn't really reality. The right time to meet you was, of course, right after we passed out. But I didn't do it then. I needed to breathe and you seemed to take away my oxygen. And then it was too late. By the time I felt I could go back to you, I heard you were already with someone else.' There's a pause and then, 'I called you. Did you know that?'

'No. When?'

'I don't remember. But I was told, I think it was your

mother, that you had moved out to your husband's. I don't know. I felt guilty when I heard that. As though it was somehow my fault that I hadn't even known you were married. The way I felt back then, I should have known in my gut when you got married. And I didn't. And that sort of seemed to prove that I wasn't as serious about you as I should have been. Till then I had felt tied to you. Even though you were far away, I felt my fortunes were linked to yours, that I couldn't do anything independently. But after hearing about your marriage, I felt a sense of release also. The first thing I did was get a smoke. The minute I put the phone down, I went to the corner shop and bought a pack of twenties.'

It was I who had persuaded Jaggu to give up smoking. If I'm honest I'll confess that it was out of a sense of vanity that I had made him quit. I wanted to prove to myself that I had so much power over him that he could kick a decade old habit at my behest. Silly, feminine vanity. What did I care if Jaggu smoked? But it did my ego good to know that I could make him do my bidding.

'I can't say that makes me feel good,' I say honestly. Jaggu's lips are almost purple and his fingers are nicotine stained. He has been smoking forever, I can see that. 'I'm not sure I like the thought of being the agent who drove you to your grave.'

'Oh, don't kill yourself. I could have quit any time these past twenty years. Vijay keeps telling me to. I guess I will, one of these days.'

'What's she like, your wife?'

'An angel who rescued me from hell. She knew there was something up with me, and she helped me with my demons.'

'Is she aware...?'

'Oh no, no, of course not. I never told anyone about all that. So you can be at peace.'

I tell Jaggu about the conversation with Rats this morning.

'That bastard! Some people never change! I wish I really had punched him that day! At least that face of his wouldn't have remained so beautiful!'

I laugh at the thought of the violence that Jaggu desires. Jaggu laughs as well. And before I know it he has grabbed me and is kissing me hard. Grab, hard, adjectives that fall short of describing the invasion of my senses. I can't say I am taken by surprise. A walk down a moonlit path with a former lover is the right setting for what is happening now.

I allow the kiss to dissipate, and then disengage Jaggu's arms from around my waist. I'm more than usually slow, and a sense of clumsiness overcomes me. I have nothing to say, and I wish that my response were less neutral. I should have either become angry or welcomed this assault. If nothing else, flattery at still being desirable should have governed my reaction. But the emptiness that I feel humiliates me, and I feel guilty that it probably humiliates my friend as well. This wasn't how it was supposed to be. We were never supposed to meet like this. Actually, we were never supposed to meet at all. Perhaps that was the premise on which I based my decisions all those years ago, that once we crossed the portals of the IIM, we would never cross them again.

We stand well apart now and my eyes go to the moon, now far up in the sky, so high up that I have to crane my neck to see it. It gives me something to do, and I tell myself this is the most important thing I have ever done, looking up at the moon.

Jaggu makes a great show of lighting up another cigarette, almost dropping the lighter, and setting himself on fire in the process. Finally, we are done avoiding each other's eyes.

'Same old Ruts. Nothing fazes you, does it?'

'I think we should go back now.'

'You should shower before going to bed. Your husband might smell the nicotine.'

There's no fear of that at least, though I don't say so to Jaggu. Kailash is a smoker himself. It's funny how Jaggu is more concerned about what my husband will think rather than what I will think. I, on the other hand, am more concerned with myself at the moment. Why am I not more moved?

'My question is still unanswered. And now I suppose it will remain that way.'

But I have my answer. I know now that my decision at that time was the right one. And I'm glad that I didn't allow my judgment to be clouded by the fact that I did what relatively few women in eighties India did, experiment with sex. Jaggu was not for me, either then or now. The revelation makes me smile, and I feel almost kindly towards him.

'You should relax a little,' I tell him. 'Try and enjoy the rest of the weekend. I'll be around. We'll keep meeting. Now I really must go.'

Jaggu throws his head back and laughs. 'Ruts, you are priceless, really. I should have been slapped for what I just did.'

'Yeah, well, don't try it on anyone else. You might just get it.'

I move the conversation away from us towards Jaggu's family. His wife is a gynaecologist, he tells me. His sisters both work for financial institutions as senior managers. I laugh.

'What?' he asks.

'I just remembered your views on women working. You were adamant that your sisters should just marry and get pregnant.'

'Did I really say that? I must have sounded like a real prick.'

'You were annoyed with women at the time.'

'I was annoyed with women for a long time. Speaking of which, how's your friend Priya doing? Any more scandals?'

'She seems to be very chummy with Sasi for some reason.'

'The grapevine is that they are really close. They've been seen together before this as well.'

'Oh, that could just be a coincidence. I mean, Priya has been visiting this place for lectures and so on.'

'If you say so. But there's something in the air, if you must know. Don't say you weren't warned.'

I'm sure Jaggu is simply pulling my leg. After all, he has never been well disposed towards Priya. In any case, I have no desire to prolong this conversation. We are back at the guesthouse, and I am relieved to return to my room, where my beloved Kailash is, I'm glad to see, waiting up for me. Jaggu, I tell myself, can go to hell.

—※—

I have told Kailash that I had an affair with a man in college, but not who it was. I think he now suspects the identity of that person, but neither of us talks about it. Besides, I was never very involved with Jaggu, and even then, I was aware that our relationship was an uneven one. Priya was the one who pointed this out to me.

'Jaggu looks like a new born pup around you these days. Like the world is threatening him and only you can offer protection.'

We were walking back from the last of the mid-term exams. Priya, as usual, had plans for the evening, but all I looked forward to was washing my hair and going to bed at the ridiculous hour of nine. Jaggu was the last thing on my mind as I thought about the mistakes I had made in the exam.

'You're just imagining things,' I said. 'Not all men behave like your various boyfriends.'

'Ruts, you had better watch out. You are in deeper

water than you think. I hope you are serious about Jaggu. Otherwise tell him now before it goes too far.'

'Why are you so concerned about Jaggu?' I asked. 'He keeps warning me against you.'

'Sometimes I think you should follow his advice. But we are not discussing me; we're talking about you. When are you going to tell Jaggu that he is just a nice toy for you?'

'Priya!'

'Oh, come on! You're playing with him, Ruts. Surely you can see that?'

'I'm not playing! Jaggu is a wonderful friend, a dear one.'

'Just listen to yourself,' jeered Priya. 'All right, so you're having sex with a dear friend. It's the same thing as playing with him. Listen, I should know, all right? I've been there several times. You'll break his pitiful heart, darling, if you aren't careful. And that's no way to treat him unless you intend to.'

We were sitting on a ledge in the middle of a parched piece of land a little distance away from the hostel building. The sun was going down, and on the horizon I could make out its slow movement into darkness. It was as though it was deliberating whether to leave us in peace for another night or not. I kept my eyes focused on its ochre face, a welcome relief from Priya's own grim visage. A trickle of sweat flowed down between my breasts, and I rubbed my shirt.

'Speaking of boyfriends, have you broken off with Shastri? He was looking really grim in class.'

But Priya wasn't to be put off so easily. 'Never mind Shastri. He is going to flunk his next exam. I'm putting him in the cooler for some time, so that he can come to his senses. And you should do the same with Jaggu, if you know what's good for you. Tell him it's for his own good. They always like to hear that. Give him a nice present. And then let him go.'

I had just finished reading *Wuthering Heights*, and I knew that what I felt for Jaggu could not even remotely be called passion. I enjoyed his company, he was fun, but I could spend time without him just as easily as with him. So Priya's advice made a lot of sense. Especially since my boyfriend had started alluding to our future as a common one. So, though Jaggu could be Heathcliff, I was certainly no Catherine.

But before I could tell Jaggu what I really felt, something else came up that drove all thoughts of my own affairs out of my head.

9

'Some tea?' asks the bearer.

'Yes, please.' I smile at his retreating back. In the early morning, the dining room is empty.

'Here you are, madam. Enjoy.' The bearer speaks in English. I never could learn Kannada, unlike Priya and Jaggu. I don't remember it ever being a handicap though. Bangalore was always a fairly cosmopolitan town. That is why I loved it so much.

As the bearer fetches my tea, I see Rats walk in. I sigh. I don't wish for a companion to break my peace, and I certainly don't wish for Rats.

'Bearer, tea please,' calls out Rats, another non-Kannada speaker, in English.

Then he notices me. 'What are you doing up so early?' he asks, sounding irritated.

'I could ask you the same thing,' I reply.

'Don't be smart, Ruts. God! Life is a shit. Fuck life, man, that's what I say.'

The bearer is smirking at the graphic language. Rats is, as usual, oblivious to such things.

'You look upset,' I comment though I'm not really

concentrating on Rats at the moment. I'm still thinking about last night and Jaggu. So is Rats, as it turns out.

'So, lover boy is still keen on you?'

'I don't know what you are talking about.'

'I'm talking about the moonlit stroll last night when the whole world was asleep.'

But not, apparently, Ravi Saluja. However, it's been a long time since Rats could provoke me into being indiscreet. Some lessons are never forgotten.

'Does your family like this place?' I ask, moving to a neutral topic.

'They'd be fools to. The infra is completely shot. I mean, talk about being in the Third World. I couldn't sleep in that miserable bed last night.'

I let go the topic of comfort. Obviously I'm not going to make much headway there. 'Tell me more about your work,' I offer next. No man is averse to talking about his job, I've learnt.

But Rats looks at me with something bordering contempt in his eyes. 'I'm the Asia MD of my bank. It's a Chinese bank. I'm the first Indian to head it.'

'Congratulations. Your family must feel proud of you. That's quite an achievement.'

'My family, or rather my wife, is, even as we talk, in the process of leaving me for good. That's how proud she is.'

Having dropped this bombshell, Rats proceeds to look at his watch. 'Fuck!' he says. 'I think I'm going to miss my flight.' He doesn't stir from his chair.

'Well,' I say. 'If you'll excuse me....'

'Oh, sit down Ruts,' he says in exasperation. 'I'm in the middle of a fucking crisis here. Can't you see that? And what's your hurry anyway? Nothing's happening in this dump, is it?'

That's not the way I remember last night's merrymaking that had Ravi Saluja turning into the belle, or rather, beau of the ball, charming all his suitors, i.e. all the people who he thought could be of some use to him in the distant future. I had seen the pre-dinner drinking binge from a distance. The only thing that had changed in twenty years was the quality of the liquor.

'I'm sorry I ever came to this motherfucking place. It stank then, and it stinks now.' Rats stares down at his tea. It has gone cold, I'm sure. He doesn't seem bothered. 'I believe only morons could think of this place as great. God's gift to mankind. What crap!'

'Then why did you come here, Rats?'

For a moment, Rats looks as though he hasn't even heard. Then a frown creases his forehead. 'I came because that was the only way to get a good job. It still is, damn it! But hey, why the hell are we talking about this shit hole? I'm not interested in that, hell no! Listen, did Shaina talk to you last night? You two seemed pretty chummy, from what I could make out.'

'Talk about what? She told me she liked this place a lot. She's hoping Khushi will come here as well.'

'No way am I sending my daughter to this fucked up place! Did she say anything else?'

I feel a little annoyed. I wish he would just get to the

point. 'No, we didn't really speak to each other much, actually.'

'It has to be that bitch, Priya.'

'You're not serious?'

'Of course I'm serious. You always were dumb, Ruts. You maxed organization behaviour but you can't tell when a person is serious.'

Rats is being nasty but I choose to ignore it. There are other things on my mind at the moment. Like what to say to Rats, how to console him. Although I'm not sure he needs consolation. He seems more angry than sad. 'Rats, I'm really sorry to hear this. What happened?'

'I wish I knew. One minute we were discussing today's departure plans, and the next she was telling me she's filing for divorce.'

'But why?'

'How the bloody hell do I know why? You'll have to ask her. I bet Priya's behind this, the fucking whore.' Rats bangs the table angrily as he says these words.

'Oh, Rats, you seriously can't believe Priya has anything to do with this. All that happened in the past.'

'You always were that bitch's tail, god knows why. Miss Goody Two Shoes and the nympho. What a pizza and coke combo.'

I don't know why I'm even talking to this man. He means nothing to me, and he has made it clear that he reciprocates my sentiment. He looks at me, a strange expression in his eyes. 'You are the first person I'm telling this to. You should feel proud,' he says, his face twisting into a mockery of a grin. 'Of all the people in the world, it has to be Ruts, the great fucking Ruts, who first gets to know that Ravi Saluja is soon going to be single again.'

The same thought has crossed my mind. 'I'm sorry,' I say again.

'Why? It's not your fault. And it damn well isn't mine. In fact if there's anyone who should be filing for divorce, it should be me. My wife thinks I don't know about all the men who've warmed her bed. Of course I know. I knew from the start. She made no attempt to hide it, either. She was almost flaunting it. I thought if I ignored the whole thing, she would settle down. And look where *that* got me! Fuck man!' He bangs the table again, and our tea cups rattle violently. 'The bitch! I could have had any woman I wanted. All these years women have been throwing themselves at me. But no, I chose to be faithful. And for what? Tell me that. I feel like such a sucker.'

It is hard to imagine Rats remaining faithful out of love, or his feeling like a loser. That wasn't the Rats I knew, the Rats who always ensured that everyone around him was aware of all his triumphs. He was always eager to latch on to a female when it suited him, at least when last I saw him. Over the years I have come to the conclusion that people do not change all that much. I believe that Rats clung to Shaina because it suited him and for no other reason.

Rats's head is bent over his tea. His left thumb is frantically caressing his index finger. The nails are perfectly manicured. Even at this hour of the morning, Rats looks perfectly groomed, nothing in his appearance indicating that a major hurricane has hit his life. Only the frown on his face gives a hint that he has something on his mind. After a while he looks up, and there is a smile on his lips and a hard look in his eyes.

'So, does hubby dear know that there's trouble in Eden?' he says, once again training his guns on me.

I cannot see where this conversation is leading up to. More fool I.

'Kailash knows I went for a walk with Jaggu, if that's what you're asking.'

'And does he also know that relations have resumed, shall we say, between you two?'

'What are you talking about?'

The grin on Rats's face grows wider. 'I'm talking about the passionate smooch that set the garden ablaze. I bet your spouses would love to know what that was all about.'

I want to tell Rats that none of this is his business, but for the moment I hold my peace.

'Look, we are all friends here, right?' he continues. 'What you do with Jaggu is your business. I appreciate that. But I would really like some help from you. Like this fucking divorce business is going to make life hard for me, you know?'

I feel a twinge of sympathy for Rats, even though he makes my blood boil. I wonder how he knows about that kiss.

'I'm sorry. I don't know how I can help.'

'You could talk to Shaina, tell her to hold off for some time. I'm up for promotion next month. These chinks, they are sticky about divorce and stuff, they like a man to have a happy family. So I can't have this shit going on right now.'

I can't believe what I'm hearing. All along, in the last two days, I have tried to remain on top of things. Even that ridiculous encounter with Jaggu didn't make me lose it. But now I feel truly defeated. Does nothing crack the cast iron shell that Rats has wrapped around himself? She is talking divorce and he is talking career. I can quite see why she would like to leave this low life.

'Your children will take it hard,' I offer by way of saying something.

'My children! I don't think they'll really care. They are with her all the time, in any case. Why should they bother about what happens? As long as I pay for their education and their expensive tastes, I won't be missed. It's not as though they are all that fond of me. She's made sure of that.'

His cellphone rings, and Rats barks into it, 'What? Hong Kong? The HO? Man, you guys really fuck up, don't you? Why couldn't you have called earlier? I don't care what time it is. You have to call me whether I'm in the shower, sleeping, or attending my goddamn mother's funeral. I think I've said this before. I have to be told, regardless. Remember that for the future, okay? Don't wait to make a mess before informing me. Call up the options guy, what's his name, and tell him to buy stat. I know it's Sunday. That's the whole point, isn't it?'

I have no idea what this gobbledygook is but for about fifteen minutes Rats is talking simultaneously on his two cellphones. He seems to be good at what he does, and is obviously an important man, but for some reason he can't seem to get by without letting the other person know what an incompetent asshole that person is. It seems to be a strange way of functioning. I know he has forgotten that I'm sitting there. I have an urge to get up and leave, but that doesn't seem the best way to treat Rats's problem.

'Okay, so where were we?' Rats looks at me as though he has no idea why I'm sitting there. I don't enlighten him. 'Oh yeah. You're gonna talk to my wife, tell her to loosen up, and I'll try and forget the love triangle, or should we call it a quadrangle?' He laughs as he walks out of the dining room. 'Oh, and if we need to talk, I'll be available after five. I've decided to work from the Bangalore office today. Something urgent's come up. I'm not going to New York, not right away.'

I try to say something but he has already left, and I can see him getting into his car. Then he is gone, and I'm left with a curse on my lips. Rats's crude attempt at blackmail doesn't scare me, but I still need to tell Jaggu about it. The really tricky part will be talking to Shaina. Of the two evils, of having Kailash know about last night and embarrassing myself with Shaina, I think I prefer the former.

This whole drama has made me thirsty, but in twenty years the catering arrangement at the IIM hasn't discovered a recipe for good tea, and I regretfully discard the idea of asking the bearer for another cup. Hotel Shanthi seems like a better alternative. Should I wake Kailash up and carry him along with me? I know what he would say to the whole Rats business. He would ask me to leave well alone.

And then I would have to explain last night and there are some things that just aren't meant to be dealt with first thing in the morning. So no Kailash. Is there no one I can talk to? Of course there is!

'Hi, princess!'

I'm already smiling. I don't usually get a brainwave, but this call will definitely be counted as one. 'Xenia! How are you?'

'Still the same in the last twenty-four hours. Gunther is in touch,' she says with a touch of haughtiness in her voice.

'I bet you are treating him right.' I can apply the oil as well as the best of them.

It works. The haughtiness gives way to enthusiasm. 'Yeah, you bet! He is now giving us suggestions about our future. When are you returning? This place is kind of lost without you.'

I can recognise flattery with a fair amount of accuracy, and I decide to enjoy it for some time. It is unusual for Xenia to try and soften me. Her usual attitude is that her birth was a huge favour to the world.

'You can't be missing me, Xenia.'

'Of course I miss you. We all do. You've got to return asap.'

I decide to cut the chatter now. I'm in a hurry to do my own talking, in any case.

'Okay, Xenia, what do you want? Out with it!'

'Hey, how's the ex?'

'Listen, that's why I called, but you go first.'

'Now I'm really curious. But fine, I'll go first. I was

just thinking, it might be a good idea to give Gunther something. And if you say you got it from India, I bet he'll be thrilled. So if you go shopping....'

That's twice that 'Gunther' has been mentioned. Should I smell a rat? Gunther and Xenia? Well, why ever not? But I shall not go into all that now. Xenia's suggestion is great on its own merit.

'Done! I shall get something that will knock his eyes out. Now about Jaggu.'

'The ex? I'm all ears, princess.'

It is a relief to unburden myself of the events of the last one day, ending with Rats's threat.

'Wow! That's a lot to pack into one day. So what're you going to do?'

'Any suggestions?' I ask.

Xenia chuckles. 'Tell Rats to fuck off, give the ex a kiss and put Lash in the cooler for some time. Do his big head some good.'

'Xenia! Talk sense, please. I'm in a spot. You need to help.'

'All right. Why don't you speak to the wife? You've already met her, right?'

'And tell her what?'

'That her husband loves her?'

'That's a lie! He doesn't give a damn, as far as I can see.'

There's a pause at the other end and then Xenia says, 'Get the ex to speak to her. Keep your hands clean of blood.'

'But I don't think he even knows her.'

'So? Introduce them, and then step back. Let things move without you. Be a woman, for chrissakes!'

'Thanks a lot. You've been a big help.'

'Anytime, Tee. And hurry back. This place needs you.'

'I think I'll stay on for some more time, Xenia. Allow you to look after Gunther, and so on.' And on that note I hang up.

What Xenia says makes sense. Let Jaggu do the dirty work. It is partially his fault that I'm in this soup in the first place. Why should he have tried to revive old times? As anyone who has been to a college reunion knows, it never pays to go back. Nothing is the same. Except Rats, perhaps.

During my talk with Xenia, I have been gradually strolling towards Shanthi Hotel. When I enter the shack I see the two women again, chopping a mountain of onions. They grin at me, and their smiles seem to light up the dim shack, and my mood as well. This morning there are a couple of young men seated at a table; they seem to be students and look like they've been up all night. I wonder if they have exams going on. But I'm too shy to go up to them. They pay no attention to me. They are talking softly, and as I sit at another table, I can only hear the odd word from their table. The women obviously recall my preferred brew from yesterday, and within moments a steaming glass of tea is placed in front of me.

I'm taken aback when one of the men walks up to me and says, 'You're the batch of '88, right? I'm Akshay, and this is Prashant. PGP '09.'

'I'm Ruts.'

'You must find everything changed here,' says Akshay.

The thought of Rats springs to mind and I smile. 'Not everything.'

'Sasi taught you, didn't he? He was telling us about it. Said you were a great bunch.'

'Oh, thanks. I suppose he says that about every batch.'

'Priya is also your batch, right?'

Now I'm curious. 'How do you know Priya?' I ask him.

'She has lectured here a couple of times. Sasi says she was his best student.'

Now this I can't believe. We chat for some more time. I ask the two students about their future plans. Marketing or finance, I ask. Prashant, to my surprise, is emphatic that it is neither for him.

'I'm planning to start a chain of elementary schools in Belgaum, in the deep rural areas. I've already started looking for funding.' Prashant goes into a detailed explanation of how he plans to make his project successful. I am stunned. I have no doubt that this young man will achieve his goal. But what surprises me is his choice of profession. To forgo a multimillion rupee salary in favour of such a humble project is a remarkable sacrifice and I tell him that.

'It isn't a sacrifice, believe me. I'm just anticipating the future. Tomorrow's India is going to be all about skill development. I'm just starting on the raw material early on.'

'What about Priya?' says Akshay. 'She has also found a career in the poverty sector.'

Poverty sector? What a funny term! But he does have a

point. 'In fact, one of her lectures in the eco class probably helped me to take my decision. I've already spoken to Priya. She's going to help me in this. She might even come on board.' Prashant is smiling as he says this.

'We have to go now,' says Akshay. 'It was a pleasure meeting you.'

'Likewise,' I reply with complete sincerity.

This time I pay for my tea before returning to the guesthouse. I'm not sure I appreciate Shridhar's logic about benefiting from free land. These women, for all their viciously neat appearance, don't look as though they are flush with funds. To deprive them of their income seems unfair. Ah well, when all is said and done, I'm glad I'm not Shridhar. I wouldn't like to be remembered for my acerbity though I'm not quite sure what I would like to be remembered for.

Before I can ponder this existential point, I have come face to face with Jaggu. He is sitting in the lobby with, of all people, Shaina. This can't be a coincidence. It isn't.

'Ruts,' says Jaggu, getting up from his chair in the dining hall. 'Mrs Saluja was looking for her husband. Have you seen him?'

Jaggu's face is innocent, and I don't know what to make of this query. I decide to simply tell her that he has gone to his office. Shaina looks distressed. I don't think any woman expects her husband to walk out on her so callously in the middle of a huge crisis. Jaggu, on the other hand, is twiddling the index finger and thumb of his left hand, and I know he is suppressing a smile.

'These banker types really earn their salaries. The man can't have slept for more than five hours last night. Give me engineering any time. I can't work these insane hours, and on a Sunday, of all days!'

That's right. It has escaped me that today is a holiday. Then how come Rats is working? Shaina laughs. 'That's Ravi. No day is sacrosanct for him. I suppose it's a good thing. But at times I can't help wondering if not having any kind of leisure time with one's family is really a price worth paying for all the fame and money. I pity his subordinates. He drags them out on holidays, and one of them complained to me, I believe he was drunk at that time, that his boss frequently upset his holiday plans. He was even thinking of quitting his job. I don't know what he did finally. It's easy for employees to quit, but where do families go? How do wives quit?'

Jaggu looks appalled at this change of tone, and I almost giggle at his expression. He has no clue what's going on, that much is obvious. I think regretfully of the leisurely morning I was planning to spend with Rohan and Isha and Kailash, but Rats has put a spoke in my family wheel fairly effectively.

'Shaina, would you like some tea?' I interrupt.

'Sure, but I couldn't find a bearer anywhere,' she replied.

I get up to hunt for a bearer in the dining room, and drag Jaggu along and tell him about Rats and Shaina, and what we are expected to do.

'The prick!' says Jaggu. 'Was that piece of scum actually our classmate? Shit, no wonder Shaina wants to get rid of him. I hope she does it today. I think that's what I'll tell her.'

'Jaggu, no, wait. Let's decide what to say to her. I mean, for all you know, she could be making a mistake.'

'Ruts, you know what, you need a therapist. You're so goddamn hopeful about people. That woman wants to throw her husband overboard. Anyone can see that. We just need to help her, that's all.' Help. Is that what they call conspiring to end a marriage? I look at Shaina's tear-stained face. There is anguish there. No, I don't think I can 'help'.

'Jaggu, I think we need to stay out of this.'

'I would have loved to stay out of it, Ruts. Shit, until five minutes ago I wasn't even in it. But Rats hasn't left us with any choice.'

'I'm sorry. I seem to have started something. I didn't mean to.' I turn to look at Shaina who has just walked up to us.

'It's not you,' I reassure her. 'You should go back to bed. You look tired.'

'I didn't get much sleep last night. There were some crickets outside my room, I think.'

'And a rat inside,' says Jaggu sotto voce.

I don't find my former classmate at all amusing. Hopefully glaring at him will shut him up. It doesn't.

'Your husband was a good friend of ours,' he says, tongue firmly in cheek.

'Was he? Funny. Ravi has never mentioned any of you till yesterday,' she says in an expressionless voice. 'I think he thought we weren't worthy of his highbrow friends, the children and I. We were always too dumb for him.'

It is I who am dumb. Dumbstruck, that is. How do I speak after that damning statement? Jaggu comes to my rescue. 'Well, Shaina, obviously you've never been told the inside story about the IIM,' he says easily. 'My wife, who didn't study here, I should add, thinks it produces the weirdest people that were ever born on earth; psychotics, each one of them. And that's being fairly dumb, I should say. The rest of humanity is wise to stay out of this fucking – oops, do pardon my language – this sick place. It brings to the front a number of neurological disorders, believe me.'

Shaina is actually smiling at this bullshit. I gaze in awe at Jaggu. He can really charm the ladies! But then Shaina frowns again.

'I'm sorry, I'm not at my best today,' she says in what I think is a masterpiece of understatement. 'Ravi and I....'

'Please, Shaina – may I call you Shaina? You don't have to explain,' Jaggu jumps in. 'Ravi has already told us about your break up.'

So Jaggu has taken the bull by the horns. I suppose I'll just play along at this stage.

'Perhaps you should reconsider your decision,' he continues, and I hitch my fallen jaw back into place. 'Seriously. I don't want to preach, but this is a really devastating thing you are thinking of doing. Why don't you discuss all this with someone close to you?'

'Why don't I discuss it with you?' she says sitting down at a table. 'You already know what's going on. If you think I need advice, go ahead. Lay it on.'

Not for nothing is Shaina the future head of the Katwal Corporation. She has cornered Jaggu and me neatly. Jaggu pulls out a pack of cigarettes, and then, seeing the distaste on Shaina's face, puts it back again hurriedly. The hypocrite! Even he is not armoured against the lure of a powerful woman. Shaina the heiress is to be respected. Ruts the classmate is to be ignored. I get it.

While Jaggu does his juggling act with the cigarettes, I step into the conversation. 'Shaina, I think you should take a deep breath before taking such a drastic decision.'

'Deep breath! Ruts, I've been practically catatonic for the last sixteen years. The last time I exhaled was when I got married. It's only now that I'm breathing. You guys don't know Ravi, obviously, or you wouldn't be advising me to take a breath. I have to do something to get out of this trap. Dying was another option, but of the two, this seemed better.'

Shaina is getting more and more agitated, and the dining hall staff, who are preparing the breakfast tables, look in her direction curiously. Jaggu must have observed this as well for he says, 'I think we should discuss this some more. But in a more private place. Let's talk after breakfast.'

He walks off, and I'm left alone with Shaina. The cup that contained her tea is long empty now, and she lifts it and puts it back repeatedly, her action quick and steady. Then she tilts it till the dregs are almost about to spill before setting it upright again. I watch her movements, absorbed. Neither of us is prepared to say anything. It strikes me how ridiculous Rats's threat is. Even if I were willing to give in, there is no good reason why Shaina should listen to me. It takes me precisely half a minute to come to this conclusion, and I feel a weight lift off me. I have nothing further to say to Shaina, I decide. Now it only remains for me to tell Jaggu. But before I, too, can walk off, Shaina opens the conversation once again. The dregs have ultimately been spilt, a couple of muddy drops stare at us gloomily from the white table.

'Your friend Priya is really in love,' she declares.

The change of subject takes me by surprise. I was in the process of getting up from my chair, but now I sit back down.

'Oh?' is all I can say. Now is not the time to reveal that I have no idea what Shaina is talking about, or why I should find the thought so distasteful.

'Yeah. I mean, whether she is twenty or forty, you can always tell if a woman is in love. Something in the eyes, I think.' Shaina's voice contains authority, different from the tone she had taken earlier when her marital status was in the spotlight. 'So who is it?'

The dreaded question. 'I don't think you are right. Priya is not in love.' By any stretch of imagination, I add silently.

Shaina is unimpressed. 'Listen, I'm a pro where the love game is concerned. Just because my own love life is a mess doesn't mean I don't know what I'm talking about. Your friend is crazily in love, even if she isn't telling anyone. You can try asking her if you like.'

The last time I asked Priya about love, we stopped

talking for twenty years. I'm not going to take that chance again. Fortunately, Shaina recognizes my disinclination to gossip about Priya and lets go of the subject. She veers back to her own concerns again.

'So you think I'm doing the wrong thing by leaving Ravi.'

'I don't know,' I say honestly.

'Yes. Neither do I. But what else can I do? Nothing I do attracts his attention. I took lovers at one time, several of them. By then I needed to prove to myself that I was still desirable, that I wasn't just a plate hanging on the rack. But even then he didn't pay attention. I don't think I really exist for him. His stained shirt gets more attention than me. The only time he notices me is when I inconvenience him. So I did that for a while, not showing up for parties, falling sick when he had to go out for a "with spouse" dinner, things like that. But the guy is a jellyfish. He sprang back into shape again. If I could, I would put a spoke in his career. But that's one place I don't have any influence. So now I want out.'

'And the children?'

'They'll survive,' she says, and I remain quiet.

Of course they will survive. We all do. It is coded in us, to survive no matter what the situation, no matter how hard the blow.

These thoughts flee my head as soon as I enter my room, where I find Kailash stroking my daughter's head gently. Her face is flushed and her eyes look rheumy, and it's obvious that she has a fever.

'What's up? Why didn't you call me?' I ask my husband. 'I was downstairs having tea. How long has she been like this?' I touch her hot forehead.

'Shh,' whispers Kailash. 'I just found out myself about fifteen minutes ago. Shall we give her a Crocin?'

'I think we should call for a doctor,' I whisper back. The one thing that spooks me out in an alien country is falling ill. And make no mistake, when it comes to illness, India is definitely an alien place.

Isha has heard me for she starts whimpering, 'I don't want a doctor.' My daughter has a pathological dislike of doctors ever since one of them did something nasty and painful to her a few years ago. But I have to stand my ground on this one. Though it is Sunday morning, the campus medical officer is quick to respond, and Isha is given her medication. He assures us that it is nothing serious, and being just a child, my daughter should make a quick recovery.

Kailash and I minister to Isha together. That is how we have always done things. He bathed, I fed. He read to them, I helped them with homework. He played soccer, I played Scrabble. And on occasion, both of us kept awake to nurse our two children through bouts of fever, diarrhoea, sore throats. In such things neither of us is 'father' or 'mother'. We have always been each other's counsellor, not supervisor. Now our movements are economical and practiced. We know what is required. Kailash sits with her while I give her water to drink. He talks to her as I tuck her in properly. Now that I'm assured Isha will be fine, I derive comfort from the functioning of our trio. We form a comprehensive unit.

Eventually, Isha sleeps and I heave a sigh of relief. Being the younger child, my daughter gets more than her fair share of indulgence, and it has not done her much good. Normally an intelligent, quiet child, she is ill-tempered and whimsical when anything untoward takes place. Any illness means the end of all peace and quiet for the entire household for quite a few days.

It is time for breakfast. I offer to stay on with Isha but Kailash is adamant that of the two of us, it is I who should be socializing more. In actual fact, the thought of going to the dining room is faintly unattractive. I have no desire to face Jaggu or Shaina so soon after our previous meeting. At the same time, I'm reluctant to talk about the morning with Kailash. I will have to tell Kailash about Rats, and then about why he expected me to intervene. Someone else in my place would already be sitting at the breakfast table, figuring out how to stay away from her husband for the rest of the day. I have no such game plan in my head. I have no doubt that when the moment is right I shall tell Kailash the whole miserable story. But only when the moment is right.

At present I think I shall just stick to Priya. She can soothe my frayed nerves.

10

At breakfast there is no sign that Shaina has only hours earlier effectively broken off her marriage. But then, she is a good actress. At tea yesterday, I had not the shadow of an inkling that this is what she was going to do. Neither, I'll bet, did Rats. And yet here she is, laughing and chatting with her new acquaintances, and I can see how attractive she can be. Whenever she is asked about Rats, she coolly replies that he has been called away on work, but has asked her and the children to stay on and enjoy the day.

'Ruts! What's the matter?' Priya asks me as we go to the buffet to help ourselves to some more sambhar. At least the food has improved from what I remember it to be all those years ago.

'You've been staring at Mrs Rats all through breakfast,' she says as we settle back into our seats.

'And you've been staring at nothing,' I retort.

Priya blushes, much to my amazement. I didn't know she knew how to do this. The Priya I remember had the franchise on making others blush with her antics and with her coarse language.

'So tell me what's going on. Coz I know something is,' I say.

'Like what?'

'You tell me.'

'I've been thinking this weekend about what an idiot I was back then,' she says.

My hand stops halfway to my mouth, where I was planning to put a spoonful of idli. 'And that makes you blush?' I ask, incredulous.

'Well, it would, wouldn't it? It would make anyone blush.'

'Unhunh,' I shake my head. 'I'm not buying that. The Priya I know doesn't blush about the Priya I knew.'

'Well, I did do some pretty wild things in those days.'

'Yes, you did, didn't you? But I don't think that's it. Priya, what's going on?'

She doesn't answer. Instead, she sighs. 'You must admit that some of the things I did were pretty shameful.'

'What are you talking about?'

'Well, the whole Sen incident. It was so awful. I really wonder at myself. How could I have been so damn irresponsible?'

'Hey! Stop talking like this, a'right? It's over, it was twenty years ago, for heaven's sake!'

'Yes, but don't some things stick forever? I feel like I'm branded. That female, wasn't she the one who did that thing with Sen, that kind of stuff....'

The conversation continues beyond breakfast, and the two of us find ourselves walking into a small playground where a couple of young students are kicking a football and yelling encouragement at each other. Suddenly, the ball comes my way and I kick it hard back towards the boys. To my surprise, the ball finds its way back to where it came from, almost to the exact spot. I used to be fond of soccer, though the last time I played it was as a lone girl in a field full of some dozen boys, all of whom thought that the ball could be propelled to its goal through the power of the worst kind of profanities. Then I remember that it was this very ground where I used to play, and I smile. Priya looks at me curiously.

'What?' she says. I explain.

'See, that's what I mean. So many folks are going to remember that about you. What are they going to associate me with?'

I have never known Priya to be so insecure, but intuition tells me that it would be incorrect to point this out to her at this moment. Priya's behaviour is so out of character that I feel Shaina was correct about her. Maybe she is in love. She doesn't seem inclined to tell me at this stage, and I want to respect that, though I wish she would trust me. Her not telling me can only mean one of two things, that the association is inappropriate, that the man is married, for instance, or that she doesn't trust me.

I can't blame her for that. I haven't exactly proved to be a rock of support for her in the past. When she needed me the most, I let my friend down. That realization is going to cut into me for the rest of my life. It has certainly haunted me in the past. I am amazed that Priya continues to treat me as a friend in the same way. In her place, I would have kicked such friends as myself.

'I'm sorry,' I say, interrupting Priya's narration of a film she saw recently about the IIMs.

'For what?'

'You know what.'

We have reached the far end of the field. There is a dusty bench there, and after a moment's hesitation, I sit down on it, mentally consigning my jeans to a thorough wash. Priya follows suit. I know I should be going back to the room and taking over from Kailash, but this needs to be sorted out now. I feel a sudden sense of urgency. After twenty years the moment has arrived when I can say what I should have said long ago.

'I was a real asshole, and you should have said so then,' I say in a rush. Priya is smiling now. 'What?' I ask. There's nothing funny in what I've said as far as I can see.

'I'm sorry. You sound so funny when you curse. I thought that was my domain,' she replies.

'Yeah, well, I learned a lot from you including this. Anyway, forget that. Why didn't you tell me where I could stick my disapproval at the time? Why did you let me get away with climbing my high horse? I had no business being so snooty. What a wonderful friend I was! Instead of standing by you when you needed me most, I abandoned you. Asshole doesn't even begin to describe it. Traitor, cheat, fair weather friend, I can think of a dozen words for myself.' My voice has risen in agitation, and now it is shaking.

'Stop it, Ruts! Please! It's all right. Please.' Priya is looking at me, and there's a frown between her brows. 'You were always hyper emotional. Some things don't change. Honestly, it never occurred to me that you hadn't buried all that. Look, do you really want to talk about this now?' When I nod, she smiles. 'You want to exhume that corpse? Perhaps it is for the best. We could have cleared the air many years ago. But a long time ago I stopped feeling bad about it. You gave me a lot, Ruts, but the main thing you gave me was acceptance. I had started feeling like a freak before you came along. Well, I guess I was a kind of a freak. And I didn't win any popularity votes with my attitude. Now I know that being judged by one's appearance is normal, but at that time, I resented it when people rejected me without knowing the real me. And then you came along. And you did exactly what I wanted the rest of the world to do. You saw into me, and then extended your hand. Before you came along, I was either super lover or super bitch. The people who befriended me – well, what can I say? They weren't in the business of looking deep, merely looking. You... you were different. At first I didn't like you, you know. You were everything I hated. You were such a square! If you had put on a veil and started cooking chapatis on a coal fire, I wouldn't have been surprised. Your wide-eyed wonder annoyed me, annoyed me like hell.'

'I think I know what you are talking about. I remember feeling that something about me bugged you, and I didn't know what it was. I felt confused around you.'

'As you had every right to feel,' says Priya. 'So I thought I could play some games with you, nothing nasty, just confuse you, teach you a couple of lessons in growing up.'

'Was that why you were always offering me a smoke in the beginning? I thought that was strange.'

Priya laughs. 'I wish you could have seen my brain. It was all churned up. I was going to damn you as a hypocrite if you took a cigarette, and call you a prude if you didn't. Talk about being confused! My brain was so fucked up! Anyway, gradually it dawned on me that behind that butter-won't-melt-in-my-mouth exterior there was a core of steel. And I knew I had to respect that if I wanted to get anywhere with you.'

'Steel? Are we talking about me?'

Priya looks at me with exasperation. 'Ruts, what's wrong with you? Why don't you see yourself properly? You were always fiercely determined to do what you thought was right. Haven't I seen you quarrel even with Jaggu over me?'

I stare at Priya. 'You knew about that?'

'Of course I did. It was Jaggu who told you about Sen and me, didn't he? That was his revenge for you sticking up for me. Didn't you realize that? No, how could you? You had no guile in you, and in your eyes everyone else was equally spotless. I mean, you actually believed Rats liked you when all he was doing was being a snake. Every other girl in the hostel knew what our man was like but not you. You believed in him, just like you believed in everyone around you. While I saw only the filth around me, all you saw was the goodness. I liked that. I felt safe around you. You were like a mother, Ruts, without the lecturing and scolding.'

'Really? But what mother abandons her child?'

'It depends on what the child has done. Sometimes, realization comes only with a shock. I overstepped the boundaries completely with Sen. And I had to get my reckoning. How else would I have understood the gravity of the situation? I haven't said this to anyone before, but your abandoning me was a bigger blow than anything the institute was contemplating. And it is what really brought me to my senses. Until then, I thought that everything was par for the course. It never is, of course. We realize that only when it's too late.'

'You can say what you like, you can forgive me, but I can't forgive myself, ever.'

'I'm damn glad that doesn't happen outside stories. We would never be able to live our lives, do anything positive. All of us have said at some point that we cannot forgive ourselves ever. Think where we would all be if we actually kept that promise. But in this case, there really is nothing to forgive. You wouldn't be the Ruts I knew if you had done any different.'

In the distance I see a young girl waving at us. It is Anya. She comes up to us, breathless. 'I've been searching for you all over. Professor Sasi was looking for you.'

Sasi? This is a thunderbolt indeed! And then the import of Anya's message strikes me. Sasi? Oh my god! Is he THE ONE? I cannot believe it, I simply cannot. Not after what Priya has told me she thinks about him. She hates him, always has.

'I'll talk to him. Thanks, Anya. Come on, Ruts, let's go back.'

I explain that I have to return to my room because of Isha.

'I'll come with you then. If Isha is up, she can play with Anya.'

'But what about Sasi?'

Priya's face clouds over for a brief second. 'Never mind. I'll talk to him later.'

Anya chatters on as we walk back to the guesthouse. I allow my mind to go over everything Priya has said, and it is inevitable that the memory of that terrible time should surface.

━∽∞∽━

It all started with the matter of leaving Jaggu. Priya's advice to me to stop going steady with him was preying on my mind. I could dismiss her words only so much. She was, after all, the expert on the anatomy of a love affair. Yet I could not think of a way to tell Jaggu that I wanted to call it off. It would have a terrible effect on him, and his bitterness about his earlier girlfriend was always at the back of my mind. To top it off, the midterm exams were looming close, and I was finding it difficult to concentrate.

I had been seeing Jaggu for about three months. They were good months, filled with passion and laughter and companionship. Jaggu was first my friend and then my lover. But slowly his involvement had started interfering with my work. It seems unbelievable now. Now, I could never get into a relationship where I wasn't fully involved, but at that time, life's lessons were yet to be learned. It didn't matter that I was not wholly into Jaggu. I was into him partially, wasn't I?

The turning point came one evening when I was in my room, suffering the usual nervous stress that preceded an exam. Dinner was still a couple of hours away. I had skipped tea as well, since the syllabus seemed practically infinite. It was a rural marketing midterm exam that was scaring me so much. The professor was known to be a stickler for bookish language, expecting answers that were lifted almost directly from the various text and reference books that he had prescribed at the beginning of the term. I was convinced that the elusive A grade was this time completely out of my reach. My annoyance with the professor, a dry lecturer at the best of times, along with a sense of my own inadequacy, were making me far more irritable than usual. It was not, therefore, a propitious moment for Jaggu to call me to his room.

'Not now,' I said, as we stood on the landing outside my dorm.

'I was waiting to see you at tea. Why didn't you come?'

'You aren't in rural marketing, so lucky you. But I'm feeling royally buggered okay? And I need to study, Jaggu.'

'Ruts, what's wrong with you? An hour is all I'm asking for. You're not going to fail if you don't study non-stop.

Besides, it'll help you chill. Stress is a bad scene for exams, you know that.'

This from a man who was known to smoke an entire pack before a two-hour exam.

'Sorry, Jaggu. I just can't.'

'You mean we're not going to meet at all tonight?'

'I guess not.'

'Ruts, isn't this going too far?' said Jaggu again, a line of anger creasing his forehead. 'I haven't even spoken to you all day.'

'Sorry. I'm really stressed out about this exam. We'll hang out tomorrow.' It wasn't a promise, just a hope. The next day there was another major exam, macroeconomic theory, our very own Sasi's subject. Though he was a soft-spoken man, and more a friend than a teacher, when it came to grading and assessment, he was hard as nails. That was another exam I couldn't afford to take lightly.

'Tomorrow? That's like a whole twelve hours away.'

Jaggu put his arm around my shoulders but I quickly shrugged it off. Public displays of affection were a strict no-no in the rules I had made for myself. Jaggu looked at me for a moment but fortunately refrained from commenting on my very un-loverlike behaviour.

'So, we'll meet at dinner?' he said, evidently resigned to my refusal to spend any private time with him.

'Sure. Eight o'clock. I'll be there.'

I was a little late getting to the dining hall. The usual din seemed to be at its peak when I entered. Jaggu was already seated with a bunch of his cronies, and I took a seat at another table. I was only set upon eating as quickly as possible and getting back to my books. I'm sure my behaviour was annoying, and Jaggu was ready to be annoyed.

'Can you see me in my room after dinner?' he said, coming up to me as I was finishing my food.

'Not tonight, Jaggu, please.'

There were a couple of interested people listening to this conversation, and I didn't want to make a fuss after Jaggu said, 'This will only take a minute.'

'What's the matter?' asked Jaggu as soon as I entered his room.

'Nothing,' I lied. 'Why?'

'Things are changing between us. I just thought I'd ask.'

This was one confrontation I wasn't prepared for at this moment. I needed time to think up my answer, to ascribe reasons for what I was doing, to let Jaggu down softly. I couldn't do all that without notice. 'Things are just the same, yaar. You're imagining things.'

'You don't meet me any longer.'

'That's not true. The midterms are going on, Jaggu, in case you hadn't noticed. I can't afford to go easy on those.'

Jaggu looked at me closely. 'Are you sure that's all?'

'What else?'

'Has Priya said something about me? You always listen to everything she says. But watch out, Ruts. She's not such a paragon. Superbitch has really done it this time and she might not be able to come out of it.'

'What do you mean?'

'There are rumours doing the rounds about her.'

'What rumours?' I asked curiously.

'You'll find out for yourself. Why should I tell you? You never believe me anyway.'

If anything could have indicated the demise of our relationship, it was this conversation. There was no love in it, only a host of accusations flying thick and fast. In a way I was glad. It was a mean thought but I felt that if Jaggu also started thinking badly of me, he wouldn't take my betrayal so hard. Oh, I was so naïve! But at that time, I was not thinking about that as much as about what he had let on about Priya. I wondered what he meant. I pressed him for more details but he wouldn't say anything more, merely went on abusing Priya, much to my annoyance. It occured to me that Jaggu had called me to his room just to talk about Priya. I had learnt to keep these two friends separate in my life, and never talked about one to the other if I could help it. Jaggu often expressed his frustration about my unwillingness to gossip. I had once told him that it hurt me to hear him being unkind about Priya, but that had had no impact, and after that I simply kept quiet. Perhaps that was why he was letting off steam now. Finally, I left his room seething. But I was glad I had resisted the temptation of telling him to get lost. That wasn't how I wanted to do this.

Fortunately for my curiosity, I found out what Jaggu had been talking about the very next day, happily for me, after the exam.

The office boy came to the class when the exam had

finished, and told me Chinnaswamy wanted to see me in his office. I was now sufficiently senior not to feel scared when such a summons came. Some professors liked to meet students individually to get their opinion on things concerning the institute. Students who were linked to large industrial houses were asked to help with placement issues, this being an all-important activity for the institute. Others were asked for their advice on how to manage the hostel dining room better, or which books to add to the voluminous library. Sometimes professors would call the brighter students to discuss research ideas with them. I, of course, was none of these. And neither, I knew, was Chinni. I couldn't help wondering what lay behind his summons. There was only one way to find out.

When I entered Chinni's office, he was on the phone. 'Yes, I have called her. She is right here, actually. Yes, I know that, you don't have to tell me.'

He looked grim, and for a moment I felt afraid. I knew from his demeanour that he hadn't called me to tell me anything pleasant. Like a child, I mentally took count of all my sins, and except for holding back a couple of library books beyond their due dates, found my life to be fairly blameless.

'Please sit down, Shruti. Make yourself comfortable.'

I sat in the second of three chairs that were placed opposite Chinni's desk, facing his leather upholstered office chair. There were also two armchairs and a round coffee table in one corner of the room, but obviously this was not going to be that type of meeting.

'Thank you, sir,' I said, and waited for him to speak, resisting the urge to fold my hands in my lap like a schoolgirl being reprimanded by the headmaster.

Chinni cleared his throat noisily, and then shuffled the papers on his desk, trying to look busy. In spite of myself, I could not suppress a smile. He looked stern and fussy and completely devoid of any imagination. I had been in one of his classes and the entire term had passed without a single laugh. That was how he was. No doubt he had kindness somewhere in him, but he kept it well hidden.

'Well, let's not beat about the bush then.'

I could never understand why people spoke in metaphors. What bush and why beat it?

'Yes, sir,' I relpied in a neutral tone.

'Good. I'm afraid I have some bad news to give you. It's about one of your friends.'

There was a stone in my chest that seemed to prevent my voice from coming out. I just nodded silently.

'We are planning to conduct a small, err, well, enquiry into something that Priya Pathak has got involved in. You have been called to help with this, umm, process.'

Chinni looked at my face for a moment as if to judge my reaction. I showed none. I felt numb. I couldn't think or speak. Chinni looked down at his desk again and continued speaking. 'We have, umm, discovered, actually, that, err, that the, err, the culp... I mean Priya, that, Priya was umm, was... was....'

He looked up almost helplessly at my face, but there was no help he would be getting from it any time soon. I had no idea what he was talking about. Priya's behaviour had always been questionable, but what she did in her personal time was nobody's business but her own. Her academic performance was beyond reproach, so she could certainly not be hauled up for that. As for consuming drugs, half the campus did that so it wasn't she alone who would be in trouble for it.

Chinni made another attempt to tell me what was going on. 'The thing is, we have found that, umm, that Priya is involved in something rather serious. I was wondering if you could help us to find out what's really going on.'

'Yes, sir.'

'Good,' he said as though I had actually added something valuable to the conversation. 'Well, then, tell me what you know.'

I was getting a little tired of all the mystery, and now I decided to end it. 'Sir, if you could just tell me what you are referring to...?'

'Professor Sen, of course.'

For a moment I had no idea who Chinni was talking about. I vaguely remembered seeing Arnab Sen's nameplate on a door near my classroom, but I didn't recall what he looked like or whether I had even seen him. Sen was one of those shadowy professors who lurked on the margins of academia at the IIM, there to teach a subject that practically no one ever opted for but which made the institute look good to the outside world. I wondered what he had to do with Priya.

'I'm sure you know about the whole, umm, business

between Priya and Professor Sen. A very regrettable thing to have happened. We are trying to hush it up but I'm afraid the institute is going to come under a cloud for this. People frown heavily upon such things. It is scandalous for a professor to get involved with a student. Fortunately, so far it hasn't come to the attention of the press, and I want to keep it that way. My only fear is that your friend might file a case of sexual harassment against the institute. Of course, she doesn't have a leg to stand upon where that is concerned, but people are always quick to believe a woman. From what I know, it was consensual. I have spoken to both of them. Between you and me, we are asking Sen to leave, but I trust you not to reveal this to the other students till it is made official. We are trying to decide what to do about Priya. Her behaviour has been deplorable.'

I deplore the word deplorable, I thought irrelevantly. Chinni's dry voice was grating on my nerves and I was getting a headache. I could feel my eyes closing to avoid the light, and was thankful that the professor hadn't noticed my distress.

'I know you and Priya are... close. Good friends, so to speak. You might know her, umm, her plans....'

So he was asking me to spy on her! But without talking to Priya, there was nothing I could tell Chinni. I mumbled something to the effect and made my escape straight to Venky's. So this was what Jaggu had been referring to! I blamed myself for not noticing what was going on right under my nose. I had been so caught up in my own affairs, or rather affair, that I had not given any thought to Priya's actions. Now when I thought about it, I remembered her prolonged absences from both her room and the dining hall. I hadn't bothered then, merely wondered fleetingly what my friend was so busy doing. Now I knew! I stared at my coffee idly, grateful that there was no one else in the shack. At first, I couldn't recognize the emotion churning my insides, and then I knew. It was rage, pure, unadulterated rage at being conned by Priya. She was in trouble, obviously, and had not confided in me. Having Chinni pour the whole affair into my ear in that dry, pedantic manner of his had been horrible, and made everything seem so *cheap*. He had caught me unawares with his questioning, and made me feel as though I was the one doing something dirty. And what was the need to get involved with a professor, I asked myself indignantly. Wasn't the student population enough to satisfy her? I was fed up of defending Priya and I was beginning to think that perhaps the majority was right in its opinion that my friend was an arrogant nymphomaniac.

I marched up to Priya's room straight from Venky's. I felt a little deflated when I found it empty. Mangala was coming out of her room and I asked her, 'Do you know where Priya is?'

'I think I saw her going towards the bathroom. What's the matter?'

I hesitated. Mangala was a good friend, but it seemed unfair to say anything before talking to Priya. The rumour mill was churning enough without my adding to it. 'Nothing. I just needed to speak to her about something.'

'You lied to me,' I said to the empty washbasin area of the bathroom. I could hear splashes from one of the shower cubicles.

'I'm sorry,' came the muffled reply.

'Well, it isn't all right. If you ever wanted to see me look like an idiot, you should have been in Chinni's cabin today. You would have been happy.'

The cubicle door opened and Priya emerged, fully dressed. She hadn't been doing any bathing inside, that much was clear. 'Chinni spoke to you about this? But why? You have nothing to do with it!'

'He seems to think, and rightly so, in my idiotic opinion, that friends have everything to do with friends. And of course I had not a clue what he was talking about. He must be still laughing at my stupidity with all the other professors. What a prick!' I said, unconsciously repeating Priya's opinion when we first joined.

'I'm sorry,' said Priya again, looking out into the distance, as though we weren't in the same room at that moment. Her indifference made me madder still.

'Did you ever think that I could have helped?'

'How?' asked Priya, snapping back. 'How could you have helped with anything? I knew it was going to be a disaster from the day it started. How could it not? There were so many things wrong. He is married, he is a professor, I'm a student, and your god, Sasikant, is a sneak.'

'Sasi? What did he do?'

'He, my dear Ruts, is the one who went and sneaked on us to the other professors. We were going to end it anyway, or at least I was, and no harm done, but the bugger couldn't keep his damn mouth shut when he crept in on us like that. What business had he in Arnab's room anyway? Ruts, I'm in this mess because of him. God! You should've seen the expression on his face when he entered Arnab's room and saw us together. He looked shocked, like he had never seen two people embracing. And then what could he do but go and tell the whole world about it? By evening, I knew there was something wrong. If he had kept quiet, none of this would've happened. Arnab and I were parting ways permanently. Of late, he had become really jealous,' she added, meditatively.

It was odd to hear her say 'Arnab' like that. It introduced an alien feeling into that bathroom, almost as though Priya and I belonged to different social groups. I felt like asking her to please stop calling him Arnab, he was Professor Sen.

'Wait a minute. Sasi reported you to the authorities? That doesn't sound like him,' I said instead.

'Look, everyone knows you are infatuated with Sasi. You'll never believe anything bad about him. I don't know about the authorities, but the day after Sasi saw us, all hell broke loose. That can't be mere coincidence.'

So Priya was annoyed about being caught, not about doing anything wrong herself. Perhaps she wasn't in the wrong. It could be that Sen had seduced her. Knowing Priya it was unlikely, but possible.

'Why did Sen come on to you?' I asked.

Priya laughed. 'Of course he didn't come on to me. Well, he did, but only in a nice, gentle way. We both hit upon each other. At the time I didn't know he was married. I wouldn't have touched him if I'd known. That's not my style. But there he was, and I thought it would be a nice change from the infantile boys out here. He was clever about hiding his marriage from me. That was a shitty thing to do. But otherwise he and I were in it together.'

'Chinni thinks you might file a sexual harassment case against the institute.'

As soon as the words were out, I wished I hadn't said them. Priya looked frightened. I'm sure she hadn't thought she was going to get embroiled in a major legal issue when she decided to have a fling with a professor.

'I'm meeting him today. I guess he'll tell me what he's going to do,' she said shakily.

Even now Priya wasn't seeking my advice, I noticed. 'What are you planning?'

'Nothing, really. It looks like this is the end for me. I heard they could ask me to leave.'

Privately, I didn't think so. There would be a bigger scandal if Priya were expelled. But I remained quiet. Clearly, Priya was unwilling to involve me, and I didn't intend butting in uninvited.

Other people entered the bathroom, and we became quiet. There were a hundred things I wanted to say but didn't. I was still fuming. Having an affair with a married man was right up there on my list of things a person just didn't do. It didn't matter that Priya hadn't known about it initially. But what about later?

'You should have done something when you found

out he was married,' I said hotly, when we were alone once more.

'Like what?'

'I don't know. Something.'

'Right. I could have told someone from the institute what he was up to. And then he would have told them what I was up to, and so on. And god knows where it would have ended. God knows.'

'But he would have stopped it then.'

'Ruts,' Priya uttered my name on a sigh of pure exasperation. 'There was no force involved in any of this. I started it on my own, and I was ending it on my own, when I saw that he was unwilling to stop it. God!' Her tone changed to one of bitterness. 'I thought he would be leading the way, but ultimately he proved to be absolutely spineless. He was cheating, and he still couldn't let go.'

We were now in my room, where my books covered every available surface. I shoved a few aside and made Priya sit on the bed. 'I'm so tired of this bitch of a place! Everyone is a moralizing bastard. Why should anyone care what I do with my private life?'

'You broke a rule, Priya,' I said. 'Of course people care.'

'Yeah, breaking a rule is the biggest issue, right? You can fucking lie, cheat, plagiarize papers, and no one gives a damn. You can be an idiot in class, drag your ass at work, be mean to friends. It's all accepted as long as no rule is being broken.' I don't think I have ever heard Priya sound so bitter. It shocked me. It made her seem vulnerable, and again I was angry with myself for thinking this about her.

The last thing Priya was was vulnerable. She was hard as nails, she knew all about rules and breaking them, she could take everything that came her way and give as good as she got. She didn't need anyone, and she had proved it by not even telling me, her so-called closest friend on campus, about the whole mess. She deserved to be pulled down a peg or two. My mind dwelt almost pleasurably on such thoughts, the way a child would stir a patch of filthy mud with its fingers and take delight in the act. At that moment the only satisfaction I sought was to see my friend, whom I had put on a pedestal, actually be humbled.

'Oh shut up, Priya! Just listen to yourself! What's so wonderful about you? I mean, what licence do you have to do what you like, huh? You're just a student out here, like the rest of us. The rules aren't any different for you – you break them, you're punished. Didn't you know what you were getting into when you started all this? And why do you *have* to get into every man's pants? What are you trying to prove? Why couldn't you stay away from this man? Just because he was different from the boys? And you're such a woman, aren't you? You make me sick! I'm your friend, but this time you've gone too far, and I... I don't understand how you could do it.'

Priya stared at me, her mouth agape, and then she quietly left my room, leaving me standing at my window, staring at nothing.

A few days after my encounter with Chinni, I noticed that Arnab Sen's nameplate was missing from his office door. Sometimes the wheels of justice moved fast. With a tremor I wondered if the dispensation would be equally swift for Priya.

Apparently not. Chinni called me again to find out about Priya's plans. I told him, with perfect honesty, that I had no idea. It was true. Priya and I hadn't spoken after that day, though, knowing Priya, if asked to leave, she would go without a fight. Filing a sexual harassment case against the institute was not something that Priya Pathak would contemplate, even if it were in her favour.

'Shruti,' said Chinni patiently, 'it would be better for all concerned if you told me what you know. We are only trying to help your friend.'

I saw what Priya had meant about lying being acceptable but not breaking rules. Chinni had no intention of helping her. He was only trying to save his back. He, and the institute, should come out looking clean. That was all that mattered.

'So, is the mistress in or out?' Jaggu asked me as he chewed gum almost maniacally in a bid to ward off non-smoking blues. We had gone to the coffee house on M. G. Road with a few students, Rats being one of them. I thought it was his presence that was making Jaggu so irritable and nasty. Fortunately, he couldn't hear us since we were sitting two to a table.

'I don't want to talk about it,' I replied.

'Why not?'

'This place is a tad too public, don't you think?'

There was nothing to talk about anyway, since I didn't know much myself.

Jaggu wasn't going to let go that easily. When he was being stubborn, his mouth had a way of closing tightly, his lips clenched so much that they stretched and you felt he was smiling. At such times, his expression was at war with his face. One of the things I liked about Jaggu was his face. It wasn't handsome, the way Rats's was, and it wasn't very distinctive either. One could very easily forget what Jaggu looked like. But it was a face that exuded a sense of balance. Everything about it was smooth and neat, the eyes were just rightly placed below the slim brows, the nose was sharp but not overly so, the mouth was a natural progression from cheeks that were neither fleshy nor gaunt, and the chin formed a nice pedestal for the mouth. Put together, these organs proclaimed to the world that their owner was a calm man. The ears were placed just right to receive confidences and the mouth was shaped to always be polite. This ensemble was placed at the pinnacle of a body that was neither short nor tall, neither fat nor slim, but perfectly proportioned, so that neither with tall people like Rats, nor short ones like Shridhar, did Jaggu appear either tall or short. His stature, it had always seemed to me, was independent of his physique. That was why it always amazed me when some profanity emerged from that tranquil visage. But I allowed Jaggu this. He was, after all, still my lover.

Now he said, 'I'm going to wait, madam.'

'Hey, you two, stop mooning over each other,' called out Rats from the next table.

Jaggu looked at him with utter dislike and muttered under his breath, 'Asshole.' I suppressed a giggle.

Rats continued, 'Ruts has a certain glow about her these days, what do you say, Paxi?' addressing the fourth member of our group.

'That's a very personal remark,' said Jaggu angrily.

'Come on, we're all friends here,' said Rats, winking.

'They say in the last term, there'll be two visiting faculty, and everyone will get an A for those subjects,' Jaggu said, trying to change the subject.

'Yes,' said Rats. 'They are replacing Shanthi Mani, the Eco prof. She's going on maternity leave. And of course, Arnab Sen has gone, been asked to go, I'm told.'

I held my body very still and felt I had succeeded in showing no reaction until Rats looked at me and sneered, 'Ruts would know all about that, right? Big things your friend is involved in.'

'If we are done with our coffee, let's go,' I replied.

'What's the hurry? There's still an hour to go before the bus. Let's chill here,' said Paxi, and I contemplated dropping a steaming cup of filter coffee on his stupid lap.

'Yeah, man, no fuss.'

'I guess I'll go to Higgin Botham's then,' I said, standing up.

'Sit down, Ruts. Let's have a chat,' said Rats. 'Don't run away. We're not monsters, are we, Jaggu?'

Jaggu didn't reply to this. I sat down, and listened to Rats tear Priya to shreds. 'Whore' and 'bitch' were two of the milder words he used for her. I knew Rats was trying to see if I could be provoked into saying anything that he could then add to his hoard of gossip. I decided to stay silent, a fact not unobserved by Jaggu.

'When will you give up on your friend?' he asked me on the terrace that night after dinner. It had been my suggestion to meet him there instead of in his room. I had finally prepared the all-important break up speech.

'Does one give up on one's friends? Do you?'

'Depends on the friend, doesn't it? If she is a misguided whore, then perhaps....'

'You and abuses don't suit each other, Jaggu,' I interrupted the flow of vitriol.

'Never mind that. You should let go of Priya's coat-tails now. You're a big girl, or aren't you?'

'What's that supposed to mean?'

'You're doing everything that she does. Sometimes you even talk like her. You use four letter words freely now, and you didn't used to, did you?'

Guilty. 'Does that mean you see me as Priya?' I asked.

'No! I wouldn't be able to come near you if I did. But you are no longer the Ruts I knew.'

What you mean is I'm no longer a sweet pushover, I thought to myself uncharitably. 'I suppose you're right. But you're wrong about it being Priya's influence. She is a friend, and of course, friends learn stuff from each other. But are you saying I have no judgment of my own?'

'You're misunderstanding me.'

'How?' I demanded. 'Everything I say or do that

you don't like is ascribed to Priya as though I have no independent will. Well, you're wrong. I can separate right from wrong as well as the next person, if not better. I hold no brief for Priya for what she has gone and done this time, but she is still my friend.'

Why was I sticking up for Priya even now, even when I had had a flaming row with her and was no longer talking to her? I was disgusted with her, and in my present frame of mind, I didn't care if I never spoke to her again. But that didn't give Jaggu any licence to abuse her.

How had the discussion strayed to Priya? I had called Jaggu for something else entirely, and instead of talking about that, we were discussing a subject that had far less significance for me at that point of time.

The kind of mood I was in, there should have been thunderclouds looming overhead and a dirty breeze blowing about us. Instead, it was a balmy December night, chilly but not overly so. A crescent moon shone in the cloudless sky, and the stars seemed close enough to touch. It was the kind of night that could easily inspire romantic poetry. But all I felt was a mild irritation. A breeze sprang up, and I shivered and gathered my shawl around me more snugly. I didn't know how to say what I wanted to without sounding either heartless or childish. The speech I had prepared in my mind seemed totally inappropriate now, and I could feel a blanket of exhaustion creep over me. But the deed had to be done, and it had to be done now.

Jaggu was sitting against the wall, and I could sense his discomfort. His fist was clenching and unclenching in a sign that I had come to recognize as being one of nervousness. The perennial gum was being chewed to a pulp in his mouth. Jaggu had indulged in the occasional joint, but nothing heavier than that in the drug department. Now, though, he showed all the signs of cold turkey, with his twitching eyes and nervous hands and tapping feet. Obviously, the weather wasn't having any effect on him either.

'I want to say something,' I said.

'I know what it is and I don't want to hear it. So please don't say it.'

I almost smiled at this childish request. I had been standing near the opposite wall, close to the exit, trying to put physical as well as mental distance between the two of us, but now I went and sat next to him, and took his hand. We were facing the parapet, and I could see the darkness beyond, both sky and earth merging into one element.

'It's off, right?' said Jaggu in a soft voice.

I nodded though Jaggu couldn't see me. Words seemed to have run off somewhere.

'May I ask why?' asked Jaggu, guessing my answer.

'I don't know. Honestly. I mean, you are one of the best people in my life....'

'But?'

'There's no but.'

'That is not true. If there's no but, then why are we here instead of in my room?'

'Don't you like it here?'

'I do, but I like my room even better. Come there, Ruts, we can talk there.'

I knew what Jaggu was angling for. He thought we would get carried away in his room, and this discussion would end. I didn't want to tell him that he was wrong. I liked Jaggu, and I wasn't flattering him when I said he was the best person in my life. At that point, it was true. He was a true friend. But he was never going to be more than that. I knew that. As for the sex, surely one could do that even without love.

'I like it here, Jaggu,' I said. 'This was where it all started, remember?'

'Hmm. I didn't know why I loved coming up here so much. Do you remember that evening when you came up here, ridiculously late at night I think it was, maybe past one, and you were so surprised to see me?'

'Yeah, I thought I was doing something stupid, but I felt I just had to come.'

'Same here. There was a party in Shakti's room. We were celebrating his sister's engagement. The fellow had got a dozen bottles of beer and the six of us were bent on making short work of it. I was having such a good time. Someone was singing and someone else was telling lousy jokes, perhaps Curry, I don't remember now, and halfway through my first bottle, I started feeling restless, like I needed to be somewhere else. I had an urge to carry the party off with me, bundle them all onto a magic carpet and make them witness my own delight, though I didn't know where that was. And I kept my bottle on the window ledge and walked out to look for the source of my enthusiasm. I walked around, and then I walked all the way up to the terrace, completing forgetting my beer, and when I was here, I found it so peaceful. You weren't here, perhaps because I had told you about Shakti's party, but that didn't matter. I just sat here, right in this spot. And it felt absolutely right. I must have sat here for ages. Maybe I was waiting for you. Maybe not. I was completely relaxed, which is not how it is when one waits. And then you actually came! For a moment, I thought I had fallen asleep and was dreaming. I don't know about you, but it felt so right to me. And we weren't up here for too long after that either. But it was enough for me. The restlessness had gone.' Jaggu paused for a moment. I noticed all his restless movements had stopped. His hand was still lying loosely in my hand. Then he covered it with his other hand and turned to face me. 'I should have known then what was going on. But even if I had what would have been the use? I wasn't going to try to stop it. My god! I would probably have tried to make some move, and that would have been the end!'

So many shoulds and woulds! I had my own share of them, though they chiefly consisted of shouldn'ts and wouldn'ts. Shouldn't have developed this relationship, wouldn't have done it like this given another chance.

'We had some good times,' I said and cursed the inadequacy of this statement. Fortunately, Jaggu didn't notice.

'Don't talk of them as being in the past, Ruts. These are good times all the way. Why should they end?'

'You're right,' I said trying to sound convinced. 'They're

not ending, just changing. We are friends, the best of friends. Nothing can change that.'

I don't know which is better, to expect a bombshell and see it land on you, or to be completely unprepared and suffer a shock forever. The violence is the same in both, just presented differently. I was never less prepared in my life than now when Jaggu dropped his bombshell. 'Forget that stuff. I was going to ask you to marry me. Not right now. But I was clear. You are it, Ruts. For me. I mean, forever. Shit! This sounds terrible. What I mean is, you and me, we're meant to be together. Please say you'll marry me. If you like,' continued Jaggu, his tone changing from despair to eagerness, 'if you like, we won't announce it yet. We'll keep it between us. I know you must be wondering why I haven't brought this up before. To be honest, I was scared. I mean, I was certain that this is what I want but I didn't know how to tell you. I'm glad we are here. You're right, this is the right place to talk. I think this is the most important thing I've ever said in my life. And this is the most important spot in my life. I thought I would make this something special. But nothing can be more special than this. At least we can promise ourselves to each other tonight. The rest can come later. We can tell our parents in the Christmas break, and have some sort of formal thing after we pass out. My parents are quite conservative, I'm warning you, so they may act a bit pricey, but ultimately they'll come round. My dad is not too bad. He'll talk to mum. They'll want to do things the traditional way, you know, a thousand guests, Kanjivaram silks by the mile, tons of gold jewellery, all that stuff, but I can make them tone that down as well. Of course, you'll have to convince your parents that I'm not such a bad chap....'

'You're not bad at all,' I said warmly. 'You're priceless, and you'll be a gem for the right woman, but I think, my friend, that woman isn't me.'

It wasn't so hard to say it after all. In fact, the words seemed to emerge from my mouth quite smoothly. If it hadn't been for Jaggu's eloquence about the technical details of marriage perhaps I would have remained tongue-tied. But his ridiculous speech had made me conscious more than anything else of the need to end this at once. Wedding guests and trousseaus! It sounded like a fairy tale, a particularly bad one. And I felt like a witch for turning down Jaggu.

It was dawn before I could finally convince him that I meant what I'd said. The moon was stubbornly staying on in the sky, but eventually, of course, it would be vanquished by the sun. The grey light turned the moon into a lustrous pearl, worshipped by the starry diamonds that respectfully maintained their distance from it. Jaggu and I hadn't budged from where we were sitting, and the dew had settled on us quietly. It had grown very cold, and in one corner of my mind I wondered if Jaggu wasn't feeling the chill in his thin cotton shirt. But he didn't seem to mind and I didn't draw his attention to it. The time when I could say such things, I knew, was past.

11

The thought of that night still gives me a shiver. Jaggu and I argued, or rather he argued and I listened, for more than six hours. There was more than one instance when I thought of capitulating, more, I fear, out of getting out of the argument than because of a change in my true feelings. But ultimately, my own conviction that I had to end this now, prevailed. Funnily enough, it isn't the memory of that night that has dogged me all these years. I think about it once in a while, and am amazed by our stamina then to pursue things with so much vigour. Now I would merely be fatigued and possibly, I am ashamed to confess, bored by so much talk. Now arguments are won through a cold statement of facts. But when did I last feel so strongly about anything or anyone? No, what I am still haunted by is the manner in which I let go of Priya, despite knowing that there was every possibility that she might get thrown out of the institute. Even the knowledge that this would offer no small satisfaction to many students, especially those who had had to suffer that acutely poisonous tongue whenever they displayed even a hint of hypocrisy, had not influenced me into holding out a helping hand to my beleaguered friend. After that I had often looked in the mirror and asked my reflection what this said about me.

I never spoke to Priya after that day. At first, it was because she didn't speak to me. I felt bad about berating her like that, but she had behaved badly, and the least I expected was an apology from her. It would mollify me, not totally, but just a little. Then maybe, just maybe, I would condescend to speak to her. Perhaps I should be forgiven for such prudery. I was twenty-one. My ego wanted a massage, even a gentle one, perhaps just a feel good one, and Priya didn't give it to me. Why didn't you, Priya? Why did you let me go?

I pretended it didn't hurt that I was one friend less, or rather two, for it was but natural that after that night on the terrace, Jaggu should cool off towards me. I allowed him that. In fact I was glad of it. I felt awkward around him now. In my mind he was a friend. But for him, I was a jilt. If he hated me, I couldn't blame him. I remembered Priya's advice to call it off right at the beginning. I wished I had listened to her then, and saved myself so much bother. I had pretended that I was in command of the situation. Perhaps my ego didn't really need a massage after all. It seemed to be doing very well on its own then.

Of course, I was curious to find out what had transpired with Priya. Every day I expected to see her room lying vacant, and her chair in the classroom unoccupied. And everyday she was there, almost as though nothing had happened. I was too miffed to ask her what had happened, but too curious not to think about it. I could not come up with any way of finding out what the outcome of Chinni's enquiry had been, but ultimately I got my chance when I least expected it and from a very surprising quarter.

There was a time after every exam that I privately called the Vacuum. It was when classes were laidback, attendance was thin and the library was empty. Usually the Vacuum lasted about a week. But with the end of the programme drawing near, it dragged into the second week. It was understood that the senior students would now be focusing on getting a good job and could be excused from doing any rigorous academic work for the rest of the year. There were only about ten of us who had opted for Sasi's subject, macroeconomics, and on that day only two turned up for class, I and another student. Even Sasi's diligence wasn't proof against such a small class, and after about half an hour of lecture he gave up and told us he was letting us out early.

'Shruti, can you stay back for a moment?' he said as I was gathering my books.

He waited for the other student to leave before saying, 'Care to join me for a cup of coffee? We can go to the cafeteria.'

I nodded, too surprised to refuse. Why would Sasi invite me for coffee?

'Tell me about your summer placement,' he said once we had settled down and placed our order.

Summer placement? From my perspective that was almost ancient history. 'I was with a market research organization in Delhi,' I said, and went on to describe my area of study.

'I glanced through your project report,' he said, again surprising me. 'Good job.'

'Thanks,' I said, gratified.

We kept up the small talk for a while. Though it was always a pleasure to chat with Sasi, I couldn't help wondering what the purpose of this tête-à-tête was. Finally, he said, 'How's your friend doing?'

'Friend?'

'Priya. I hope she's okay.'

'I think so,' I replied, not too untruthfully.

'I'm glad. I think this place is wonderful but sometimes it's hard to agree with some of the things that are done here.'

I couldn't believe my ears. Was Sasi actually criticizing the institute?

'I couldn't agree with you more, sir.'

'I mean, what was the need to haul up Priya before a committee? Good lord! We can't turn ourselves into a bureaucratic set up! We are the IIM, not a Government of India office. If anything, the poor girl needs counselling, not censure!'

'Yes, sir.'

He ignored this interruption. 'I was appalled when I heard she had been called to answer an enquiry. What's the point of holding an enquiry? She hasn't committed any crime? And Sen....' Sasi suddenly recalled who he was talking to, and shut his mouth momentarily. His face was flushed and his eyes had widened slightly in anger.

'Well, anyway, thank god sense prevailed. Just imagine, if she had actually been sent off! What a waste of a fine career! She made a mistake, and I'm sure she is regretting it. I hope this doesn't turn her totally against this institute, though I wouldn't blame her if it did.'

'So she wasn't expelled?'

Fortunately, Sasi didn't find it curious that I didn't know the facts of the case. 'No. There was some apprehension that her expulsion might not be legal. I guess people felt it wasn't a big enough issue to get into a tangle for.'

'I'm glad it has worked out for Priya,' I said, and I meant it. I couldn't have beared to see her expelled. I was angry, but I couldn't hate her.

'She is lucky to have you,' said Sasi, giving me another jolt. 'It means a lot to have a true friend to depend upon. She must be really shaken right now. She shall need support.'

Just for a moment I wondered why Sasi should be so concerned for Priya. But there were other, more important things to be reflected upon. Like who was going to support Priya now, and whether she needed any help at all.

'She is annoyed with the institute,' I said cautiously.

'She is entitled to be,' said Sasi warmly. 'She has been treated abominably. Any other country in the world, she would be seeking compensation for sexually harassment. But of course, in India we don't believe in such things.' He sighed. 'Anyway, take care of her.' We sat there silently for some more time and then I took my leave. Sasi continued to sit there, an abstract frown on his face.

—◊—

When I finally make my way back to Isha, she is sitting up and chattering with another girl whom I recognize as Jaggu's daughter. Kailash, it seems, has gone off somewhere with Jaggu. My antennae are up. Rats's threat suddenly seems very real, and I curse myself for putting off telling Kailash about the kiss. I have always trusted Jaggu in the past, but people change. Why should he have any loyalty to me? On the other hand, what happened two decades ago could hardly have any impact on our lives today. Perhaps memories can hurt, but they can be kept aside. Last night's kiss has proved once and for all that what is past is past, that what I feel for Kailash isn't moonshine, and that ultimately, I have stuck to the truth. There can be no bigger sense of release than that. But that still doesn't make the uneasiness I feel about seeing Kailash and Jaggu in conversation together go away.

Why did I bring my family along for this do? It seems so silly now. How would I react if I were confronted with Kailash's ex-girlfriend? The answer is immediate and obvious – *badly*! So why subject Kailash to the same test? He isn't made of stone, though it has suited me till now to think he is. I haven't given him much thought this weekend, I can see that. My mind has been preoccupied with other people. And yet, who could be more important than my husband? Is this what love does – make one blind to all the bylanes of temptation, rumours, gossip? How much does Kailash love me? Enough not to bother about my past? How much love does that require?

'How's the evil fever?' I ask Isha, brushing some hair off her forehead gently.

Isha shrugs and says, 'We are going for a picnic, all of us.'

'Who's all?'

'Anya, and Tanushka, and me and Rohan, if he wants to come, and a few others.'

'Where?'

'There's a nice pond behind the last building,' says Tanushka, her tone dripping excitement. 'We can play there, and have our lunch.'

I remember that pond. I can't believe it still exists, that someone hasn't built a six-storey building on top of it. Of course, then it was a source of water for the neighbouring villages. Buffaloes, I recall, used to swim in it, and the women would wash their clothes by the side of the small water body. 'Can I come along?' I ask, only half in jest.

'Adults not allowed,' says Isha gleefully.

'Well, don't go in the water then. It's bound to be filthy,' I say. 'But wait. What about your fever? Let me call the doc and take his permission.'

Dr Bhaskar is amused when I make my anxious enquiry. 'There's nothing the matter with your daughter, Mrs Narayan. Just tell her not to go into the water. She'll be fine. India isn't such a bad country for illness now.'

He is teasing me, this man ten years my junior, but I

remain unprovoked. I thank him. He is a nice man, and can be trusted, I feel. 'All right,' I tell Isha. 'You are cleared.'

I ignore the celebrations that ensue. Kailash is still not back. What are he and Jaggu up to? It is almost time for the mini-seminar that has been scheduled for the day, the last event before people return to their homes. By the time I'm ready to go to the auditorium, the children have already left for their picnic. Anya is the natural leader, I notice, and doesn't seem to mind that Priya isn't there with the rest of the parents. Kailash is still missing, and I head for the auditorium alone. I could call him on his cellphone, but I resist. He should be calling me to tell me where he is, not the other way round.

I wonder where they could have gone. I have my answer when I arrive at the auditorium. Kailash is sitting alone at the rear and there's a beatific smile on his face when I join him. 'Where were you?' I hiss just as the director launches into his inaugural speech. Much to my annoyance, Kailash puts a finger to his lips. There are four panellists on the dais – Captain, another of my former batch mates whose name I don't recall now, and two professors. The entire student community has turned up for this event, and the auditorium is reasonably crowded. A student has a question for one of the panellists, Captain to be precise, but it is Shridhar who jumps up from his seat and says, 'I want to answer that,' heedless of the curious glances that come his way. Shridhar's answer is convoluted by any yardstick. I wonder how cogent he actually was even as a student. My brief interaction with him, as I recall, wasn't at all pleasant.

It was during Placement Fortnight that Shridhar and I were actually introduced to each other. It was such a bizarre encounter that I wonder at myself for having almost forgotten it. Placement Fortnight was the event for which the IIM student community agreed to go through the grind of those two years. This was when hordes of large corporations from India and abroad descended upon the campus to get their pick of young managers from amongst the students. The process was a combination of luck, ability and sheer nerve. It created euphoria and despair at the same time, and if one wanted to feel like a really despised human, placement fortnight was the place to be.

The promise of jobs led to euphoria, euphoria led to partying, partying led to drinking and drinking led to my encountering Shridhar Acharya in the open space between two hostel blocks one Saturday evening over a glass of beer.

'So, I saw your name wasn't on the list of placed guys today,' was his opening salvo.

'Neither was yours,' I replied with my own volley.

'That's true,' he acknowledged. 'But don't worry about me. I'm trying for a consultancy. Should be getting it soon. They aren't coming to campus, incidentally.'

'I'm not – worried, I mean,' I said coldly, adding in my mind 'you bumptious prick'. But it wouldn't have been polite to say so.

'Well, you should be. Placement isn't all that easy this

year. And companies are looking at academics pretty closely.'

Shridhar turned to look at the antics of some very drunk guys who were trying to dance the conga and falling upon each other in the process. He didn't notice the look of utter dislike that I threw in his direction. Then he turned back at me.

'Just look at these jokers. Making such asses of themselves. How much beer have you drunk, by the way? Hope you won't get drunk. There are interviews tomorrow morning as well.'

Right. This conversation had gone far enough in my opinion. I wouldn't have minded someone like Jaggu peppering me with such advice, but I barely knew Shridhar. I was certainly not going to take it from him.

'Do you have a problem?' I asked him.

'Problem? No, why?'

'Well, it sounded like you are a little uptight about my drinking, that's all.'

He laughed. 'Listen, fuck your drinking. What do I care? I just thought I should warn you. I thought you'd be grateful.'

'Well, thanks for the concern. Next time show it when you mean it.'

'What makes you think I don't mean it?'

'The fact that we've never exchanged a word before tonight, perhaps?' I answered sweetly. And then I said something that I never had before to anyone. 'The fact that I don't like you, and you can shove your so-called concern you know where?' The moment I said it, I was appalled at myself. Shridhar didn't say anything, just moved away and left me to drink my beer in utter misery.

I thought about what I had said for a few days. Or was it weeks? My own insensitivity worried me. What on earth had come over me? I wondered how I would have reacted if someone had said the same to me. It required a particular brand of meanness to put down another individual so badly. Was I really like that? The whole thing bothered me constantly for a while. Then other events intervened. Finally, I forgot about it. Though not entirely, judging by the way the memory has surfaced now, as I see Shridhar drone through his answer. Some people turn making themselves unpleasant almost into an art.

⟶⟶

Some more questions follow. The students appear really keen to get the most out of their time with the alumni. The questions are challenging, and the panellists, I notice, are extending themselves to give acceptable answers. In order to accommodate all the students, the allotted time for the seminar that is concerned with emerging marketing possibilities in the twenty-first century in India is extended by half an hour. Nobody is in a hurry to leave. Ideas and controversies flow back and forth, and we leave the auditorium talking amongst ourselves, the excitement palpable.

I find myself walking next to Shridhar and I turn to him.

'So, what do you think?' I ask him.

'About what?'

'About the seminar. About the issues raised in it.'

'Everyone seems to be really optimistic. But I'm concerned about how we never talk about how this country treats its minorities.'

'I know....'

He doesn't let me finish. 'I mean, you live in the US. See how they treat the minorities there. Everyone is free to practice their own faith and live with their own convictions. Shouldn't that be the case whenever there's progress?'

'Well, I don't know,' I reply cautiously. 'I think the blacks have a pretty hard time out there.' I'm not sure I want to enter into such a serious debate right now.

'Oh, the blacks! That's a separate issue altogether. That's a practically insoluble problem. They were brought over as slaves, as a different community altogether. So, of course they are treated differently. But otherwise, I mean, look at the Jews and the Asians and the Native Americans. Look at the gays and lesbians and transsexuals. Look how much freedom all these people have in that country. Whereas out here they are treated like shit. Now I don't call that progress.'

I wasn't willing to concede that point, not yet. 'Yes, there is discrimination, but people are allowed to speak up for their rights, and that's the starting point for any discrimination.'

'Shit, Ruts, you speak like such an ignoramus,' said Shridhar, much to my amazement. It seemed as though he was indulging in a personal attack just to deflect my argument. 'How long will it be before people call themselves tolerant? Even in this community, which is supposed to be educated, enlightened, blah, blah, blah, there is so much intolerance towards those who are different.'

It occurs to me that there is an almost personal note to Shridhar's diatribe, as though he himself has been the victim of some slight. I wonder what it was.

As we walk back towards the cafeteria, Jaggu joins us. I try to ignore his presence, just as I have ignored Kailash, who is now walking towards the cafeteria with a professor. I will not yield to my curiosity, I will not. Jaggu has heard the last part of Shridhar's speech, and he looks at me interrogatively. My shrug communicates nothing yet everything, or so I hope.

'You two look ready to kill each other,' he comments jokingly.

Indeed, Shridhar does look beside himself with anger. His face is flushed, his chest is heaving, there is sweat on his brow, and before I know it, he has fallen on the ground, hand clutching his chest, face twisted with pain. I know what's going on even before I can switch to analysis. This is a heart attack that's happening before my very eyes.

For a moment I am paralyzed. But not Jaggu. He quickly gets into CPR mode, and I snap back into action. I know who to call for assistance, fortunately. Within minutes, Dr Bhaskar, my new acquaintance, comes rushing up to us. Not far behind him follows an ambulance, and Jaggu, I and the doctor jump into it along with Shridhar. Only then do I realise that Kailash probably has no idea about what has happened. He was entering the cafeteria, I recall, when Shridhar collapsed. Within moments I have called my husband and filled him in on my whereabouts.

'Don't worry about it, Shruti,' he says. 'Stay there as long as it takes. Who else is with you?'

I hesitate for a fraction before replying, 'The doctor, and Jaggu. Jaggu, Shridhar and I were talking when it happened.'

Kailash hasn't noticed my hesitation. 'Well, I'll manage things here. Give my best to this Shridhar. And you take care.' The last is said with a caress that fills me with warmth. I smile and that's how Jaggu finds me when he turns away from the window towards me.

Shridhar is one of the people who have no family accompanying them to this get-together. Jaggu, Dr Bhaskar and I discuss this fact afterwards when the hospital staff has wheeled the patient into the ICU, a maze of tubes snaking around his head. Dr Bhaskar says, 'Looks like you people are his family now. I've been called out a couple of times by your other friends over the weekend. All of you are amazingly close. I don't mind saying it, but with friends like these, who needs family?'

Jaggu and I merely exchange a conspiratorial smile when we hear this verdict. Looks always do lie, don't they? 'You're right,' says Jaggu, amazing me. 'Some bonds just never break. Thanks for all the help, by the way.'

'You guys were really prompt,' the doctor says. 'That CPR probably made things much simpler for Mr Acharya.'

'It's doctor,' I find myself saying. 'Dr Acharya.'

'Really? I didn't know that,' says Jaggu. Like much else, I say silently. 'How do you know these things?'

'I get around.' My reply is deliberately vague. There's an undercurrent of something between us, and the doctor looks at us curiously.

'If you don't mind, I have to get back now. Dr Acharya is in good hands, so don't worry.'

'Your friend is going to be fine,' says the doctor on duty to Jaggu and me a couple of hours later. 'He suffered a minor heart attack. He should be back on his feet in a few weeks, and then of course, the regular care. If you see me during the OPD hours, I'll give you all the details.'

Jaggu and I mirror the question in each other's eyes. How do we handle this responsibility now? And what do we tell the doctor? Jaggu answers the question.

'I'm sorry, doctor. We aren't Shridhar's relatives. We are just his friends, and we'll be leaving by tomorrow morning, both of us. We'll try to get hold of his parents. Perhaps they can come down to take care of him.'

The doctor, a young man of thirty or thereabouts, clearly unused to non-medical conundrums, is distressed and looks not completely in charge. He looks at his watch. There are never any moments to think and ponder in a hospital. The next case is due.

'Please have someone speak to me at the earliest,' he calls out as he rushes off into the white netherworld of illness.

We walk across to the ICU to look in on Shridhar. The tubes and monitors that surround Shridhar have dwarfed

him. His eyes are open and they seem to fill with gratitude
when he sees us. We sit in silence, unsure of our next move.
Jaggu speaks up.

'Hey man, how are you doing?' he says gently. 'You
gave us a scare back then. The doctor says there's nothing
to worry about. You're going to be fine.'

'I don't know how to thank you. I thought I was going
to die.'

So did I, I say to myself.

'Well, take care, Shridhar,' is what I say. 'Don't worry
about anything right now. Just get better.'

Shridhar is already looking tired. I motion to Jaggu that
we should leave, but he asks me to keep sitting. 'Boss, we
need to get someone to be with you. Give me your parents'
number. I'll call them. They can come down for a few days.'

'No,' says Shridhar, suddenly energetic. 'No, please
don't do that. I haven't told them I'm in India. I don't want
them to visit me. Please.'

I do not comment on the strangeness of this request.
But we can't leave him like this without anyone to look
after him.

Shridhar sees me frown. 'You people have been hassled
enough on my account,' he says, the old Shridhar surfacing
just a little bit. I can hear it in his voice. 'You can carry on
now. I'll think of something.'

This is as much discussion as we should be having with
the patient now. The last thing he needs at this stage is
anxiety. Jaggu is reluctant to let go of the topic but I get
up and walk towards the door. He has no choice but to

follow me. Shridhar has already closed his eyes and we bid him a soft farewell.

I am still shocked by what has happened. I've just seen death being held at bay, almost literally. A tremor runs up my spine, shaking my entire body violently.

'Relax, Ruts. Are you okay?' asks Jaggu when we are in the taxi.

'I'm fine. Delayed reaction, I think.'

'Yeah, that was pretty scary. Thank god you had the doc's number. You probably saved the guy's life.'

'I think that's an exaggeration. It was a minor heart attack.'

'But grim.'

'Yes, pretty grim,' I agree wholeheartedly.

Jaggu raises the subject again. 'We should have insisted on finding someone to take care of him.'

'I don't think he was in any condition to be pushed. I wonder what his peeve with his parents is. Not that it's any of my business.'

'Rescuing him from this mess, taking him to the hospital, handling the trauma, makes it our business, Ruts,' points out Jaggu, not unreasonably. 'The man needs help, and he is in no state to get it for himself.'

'Yes, but we can't call his parents,' I say. 'He was clear on that score.'

'So, we'll find someone else. I'm sure he has someone apart from family who would want to be with him in this crisis. No person lives absolutely alone.'

It occurs to me that until a few hours ago, Shridhar was

smaller than a blip on my horizon. And now, I almost feel
as though I am his saviour.

'I really don't know all that much about Shridhar,' I tell
Jaggu.

'Except that he has a Ph.D.'

'I didn't know that was a state secret,' I reply. 'I met him
for a brief while yesterday, and he told me about himself.
I thought that's why we were here. To catch up with each
other.'

'You seem to have caught up more than most,' says
Jaggu somewhat accusingly.

'I don't know what you mean by that.'

'I don't know. One moment you are with Priya, and
then Rats is claiming you for his own, then....'

'Okay, stop. Nobody's claiming me for their own, okay?
I thought we had sorted all that. Anyway, Shridhar did tell
me he isn't married.'

'I can understand that,' says Jaggu to my surprise.

'You can? How?'

'What do you mean, how? How could he marry?'

I'm missing a few steps here. 'Huh?'

'You really don't know, do you?'

'Know what?'

'Shridhar – *Doctor* Shridhar Acharya – cannot, or will
not, marry because he is gay.'

'How do you know?' is my first reaction to this bit of
information about my former classmate.

'I should be asking instead, how do you not? Shridhar's

sexual preference was common knowledge. Didn't Priya tell you?'

'Forget Priya. Why didn't you tell me?' I demand.

'Because I probably had other, more important things to talk about. Shridhar wasn't exactly a great pal.'

'Was this the reason?'

'That he was no friend of mine? I don't know, to be honest,' says Jaggu. 'It could have been. I think it had more to do with his attitude, though. I never thought about it, frankly. I mean, hey, there were tons of people who weren't my friends, right?'

'And was that all there was to it?'

'Ruts, you are one touchy person. Does it matter why? And let's not do a post-mortem, okay? I'm not here to be judged by your exacting standards of what is morally right.'

'You're right, I shouldn't be doing this. I have no right.'

'That's not what I meant. You do have every right to question me. Heck, for nothing else but our past friendship, you have a right. But don't try to simplify matters. Please. Shridhar means nothing to me, now or then. Let's just leave it at that. There's no point delving into why I didn't get along with him. I guess ninety per cent of the class didn't get along with him. And for god's sake, it's all in the past now. But for this get together, I might never have met the man. And wouldn't even have cared. So he's in hospital. I'm sorry. That's all.'

He looks out of the taxi window. For some reason I am moved to hold his hand. Perhaps not the most appropriate of gestures, but there we are. Appropriateness is singularly irrelevant where we are concerned, it seems. 'Thank you,' I say.

'For what?'

'For being you. For spending all this time tending to a man you don't like.'

'And you do?' he asks, a strange expression in his eyes.

'Not particularly, no,' I admit.

'Then if you can help out, why can't I? Why should you be the only one up for sainthood?' asks Jaggu with a faint smile.

'There's that. Well, anyway, now what? I mean, about Shridhar. We can't just leave him there. Who'll look after him?'

Jaggu shrugs. 'He is bound to have someone, a friend, relative, cousin, someone who can take charge. No man is completely alone.'

'You know, I don't think there is anyone. At least that's the impression I got. He might have someone in the US. How do we find out?'

My eyes go to the bag on the seat between Jaggu and me. It contains Shridhar's personal belongings, his watch, a gold chain he was wearing around his neck, a signet ring, his belt and his wallet. I take out the wallet and look through it. Apart from the money, both rupees and dollars, there are two credit cards, a driver's licence, a tiny phonebook, the identity card of the university where he works and a picture of a young, white man. To some extent I can empathize with Shridhar's bitterness now.

Unemployed, unattached, unliked. A triple whammy if there ever was one. The picture in the wallet gives me a little hope, though.

'Who is this?'

'I don't know, Detective Ruts,' says Jaggu, mimicking an American accent. 'The lover, perhaps?'

'I know that. I'm just wondering if we can find out his name.'

'Look, it's none of our business who this is. Leave well alone.'

'I would if I could. But Shridhar isn't well, so we can't leave him alone. Come on, Jaggu. You've done so much for this guy. Now don't draw back.'

Jaggu gives an exaggerated sigh. 'Same old bleeding heart Ruts. Old people and injured animals, watch out. Florence Ruts is on the rampage. All right. How do we find out the name of this very good-looking young man?'

Jaggu is right. The face in the picture is extremely handsome. The expression is a little bemused as though he doesn't understand why anyone should want to take his picture. From the unshaven chin and the backdrop of unsavoury looking apartment blocks, it is obvious that this is a spur-of-the-moment picture, taken perhaps when he had just woken up. I would not keep someone's picture in my wallet if I weren't deeply attached to that person. As a matter of fact, I have four pictures in my wallet, one each of my children and Kailash, and one of Xenia and me standing in front of an oak tree at one end of the Big Creek.

'Xenia!' I exclaim.

Jaggu looks at me curiously, and I'm not surprised. He has no idea about that part of my life. He never asked and I never told him. 'Who's Xenia?' he asks. When I explain, he asks, 'How does she come into all this?'

'Don't you see? I can ask her to do the investigating for me.' I am now quite excited with my brainwave. 'I'll just send her a mail explaining all the facts, and then wait for her reply. Let me see, it would be six-thirty a.m. there. She should be up by now. Come on, let's send that email right now.'

'Now, just a minute,' says Jaggu authoritatively. We are back on campus, the taxi having just driven off after depositing us at the entrance to the guesthouse. 'I haven't had any lunch, and barely any breakfast, thanks to your friends, Rats and Mrs Rats, and I don't know about you, but I don't think well on an empty stomach. So we shall first go and eat something.'

'You make a lot of a sense sometimes, amigo,' I say, as I follow him to the dining room. Jaggu is prone to linger over his sandwich but I rush him.

'What's your problem?' asks Jaggu finally, in total exasperation. 'A few minutes can't make all that much of a difference. Relax, Ruts.'

I realize I am acting hyper, but I can't help it. From the moment the plane took off from Delhi exactly forty-eight hours ago, I don't think I have relaxed for a single moment. Even my dreams seem vague and threatening. 'I'm sorry,' I say, forbearing to voice my thoughts. 'I just want to get this over with. Look, you carry on. I'll just walk across to Kailash and enlist his help.' Which brings me to something else. 'By the way, where did the two of you disappear to this morning?'

Jaggu grins. 'Wouldn't you like to know! We were just, umm, exchanging – shall we say – notes on our mutually favourite person.'

'I'm not sure I like the sound of that.'

'Scared, Ruts?'

'No,' I lie. 'Why should I be?'

Jaggu laughs. 'I can think of a very good reason. But I won't tease you. Your husband is a great guy.'

'I know, but thanks anyway.'

'You don't ask why I think so.'

'My mistake. Just because I think he is great, I assume everyone else agrees.'

'Okay, let me tell you. First, I admire him for getting my girl, and managing to keep her, something I couldn't do. Wait,' he says, when I try to interrupt. 'Let me finish. Then he knows that there was something between us, but he's okay with that. In his place I would probably kill my wife. And he trusts you enough not to ask either of us what we were up to last night.'

'You make Kailash sound like a saint. He isn't. I would behave the same way if it came to that.'

'Don't fool yourself, Ruts. He's a man. Take it from me, men are far more jealous than women. We aren't so trusting. He is extraordinary, and you should appreciate him.'

'I do. You don't have to tell me.' I wonder why Jaggu should encourage my sentiments towards Kailash, going by what we were in the past.

'You're wondering what's in it for me, right?' When I nod, Jaggu laughs. 'All that is in the past, Ruts. We weren't meant to be together. That's it. I know it. And I'm truly glad to see you so happy. You've got it all.'

'And you don't?'

Jaggu smiles, and this time his eyes light up, making him look about twenty-five. 'I think the answer to that is obvious,' he says as he walks off.

I run Kailash to ground in the library, the very same basement where Rats had once tried to play his nasty games with me. There's no one else there, and we sneak a kiss. We switch on the computer after I have explained the situation to Kailash.

'Where's Jaggu?' asks Kailash eventually, after I have sent off the fairly detailed email to Xenia.

'Gone off to his wife,' I say. 'Why?'

Kailash looks at me for a moment and then says, 'No reason. Just asking.'

'Oh, by the way, Jaggu asked me to give you a message.' I tell my husband about the impression he has created on my classmate. 'He thinks I undervalue you.'

'No problem. You can always do a re-evaluation.'

'Don't worry,' I say with a smile. 'I already have.'

'And?'

Is that really uncertainty I see in his eyes? Not much about Kailash is uncertain where I'm concerned. From the first day we met, I don't think I've ever been shy about telling him how I feel about him. There are people who always hold something back from their partners. They think this is the way to remain on top in a relationship. I don't think I have ever used this route to derive security in my marriage. Nor, I can say honestly, has Kailash ever made me feel lost. We think the world of each other. He is my best friend. I have friends who gossip about their husbands, laugh at their quirks whenever they get together, sadly recall the good times they had when they were single, and wish an end to their marital slavery. I have never indulged in this sport.

So why, my dear, do I see that strange look in your eyes, as though the oak tree in your front yard has suddenly disappeared, making your garden barren? I haven't given you cause for that look, cross my heart I haven't.

'What do you think?' I ask. The answer has to come from him, I tell myself. Yes, I am unreasonable. I'm not going to give my husband anything he doesn't already have. He has me. But he has to know it without my saying so. It has always been that way.

'I think you need to talk to Xenia.'

I sigh in frustration at this wriggling out. 'You're right. I'll get to it.'

I'm lucky. Xenia is awake and has been for some time. Things start early at the writers' colony. We serve breakfast by seven, and the kitchen staff is up at four in the morning. That means Xenia and Carlita. I plan to get one more person in the kitchen, funds permitting.

Gunther's stay, in all likelihood, is going to get me the required money.

'Hi, princess.'

Xenia's sunny voice succeeds in bringing the smile back to my face. I tell her the reason for my call. 'Are you all right?' I ask politely.

'Forget me. How's the ex?' Her voice booms over the cell phone. Kailash is staring at his book, and I wonder if he has heard this badinage.

'How's Gunther?' I counter.

Xenia laughs. 'Touché. I'm getting my novel work-shopped from him.'

'Sounds interesting.'

'You bet! Okay, this call is costing you a fortune, I guess. So, I'll send you the info stat.'

'I hope she gets somewhere. It's all so vague. And where will Shridhar stay once he's discharged from hospital? He can't travel right away, can he?' I voice my doubts to Kailash.

He closes his book and stands up. 'Time for some tea. I guess you haven't had time to meet Priya.'

'Not since this morning. Why, what's up?'

'You should know. She was looking for you earlier today.'

'I wonder where she disappeared to. I'm sure she wasn't there at the seminar. Do you have any idea where she went?'

Kailash shakes his head. When he does that his ponytail swings a bit. About two years ago, Kailash decided to grow his hair. I was ambivalent about this. Nobody I knew wore their hair so long, which was surprising considering I was in the company of writers constantly. But most writers I knew were quite conservative in their attire. Women writers, I noticed, tended to be especially well-dressed and groomed, as though they expected to give a performance any time. Male writers, too, were quite inconspicuous when it came to their appearance. Though long hair is no longer considered unusual amongst men, my conservative Punjabi background forbade me from taking it in my stride at first. But we each need our own space, and I didn't give voice to my discomfort. Now, I confess, I rather like the curly tail hanging down halfway to Kailash's nape.

'I saw Priya blush today,' I tell him.

'So?'

'If you really knew Priya you'd know that blushing is against everything my friend holds most dear,' I say, smiling a little.

'You know, you should be careful about being judgemental,' replies Kailash, closing the book in front of him with a snap and looking at me.

'What does that mean?'

'Like why shouldn't Priya blush if she wants to? I've seen you blush, several times, in fact. Remember when you addressed Richard Lowe as Mr Hayworth at the writers' dinner, or when you discovered that A. S. Byatt is a woman, or when....'

'All right, I get the message. But blushing is a sign of

embarrassment, and the last person to feel embarrassed about anything is Priya. She is the epitome of brazenness.'

'Correction. She *used* to be the epitome of brazenness. Now you don't know what she is. You haven't spoken to her for twenty years.'

'Priya can't change,' I say, shaking my head. 'She just can't. She is Priya Pathak.'

'You mean, she is *your* Priya Pathak. Well, write a story and make her a character in it, and then do what you like with her. But, Shruti, the real Priya isn't Shruti's puppet. She has a life now, a daughter. For all you know she might be learning yoga and practicing ayurveda. Or going to religious gatherings, and covering her head when she visits a temple. How do you know the real Priya? She's no longer your childhood, Shruti, and you might as well come to terms with that.'

I feel unaccountably sad when I hear Kailash's words. Of course I recognize the truth of what he is saying. That cussing, smoking, brooding Priya has almost become a figment of my imagination, so different is the present version from her. But that was the Priya I loved, that was the woman to whom I apologised a million times in my mind for letting her down, that was the person, though she never knew it, whom I referred to whenever I took a major decision. *What would Priya say or do?* How many times in the past have I asked myself this? Now who do I go to for advice? If I think of the young Priya, won't the image of the 'new' Priya intrude upon my thoughts? Come to think of it, this one is almost a stranger. For once someone other than myself actually looks up to her. Anya's adoring glances in her direction aren't lost on me. And then I remember the two students I met in the tea stall. I am, of course, happy that Priya now has the one thing that was missing from her life before, i.e. recognition. She deserves it more than anyone else I know.

I was ten when my best friend relocated to Australia. She might as well have gone to the moon. I knew she would never return, and I would never see her again. She came to our place on the eve of her departure to bid farewell to my parents. I didn't cry when I stood at my gate and saw her little, upright, slightly concave back for the last time. She didn't look back. For me the sadness was too overwhelming for tears. My body, I remember, turned into a giant hole into which all happiness, all hope disappeared. I knew I would never have a friend like Shaila again.

Something similar is happening to me now. Just like that, my friend, who had become for me, over the years, a place, a refuge, an icon of wisdom and calm and peace, has vanished. I no longer, I discover, have a Priya.

In that library, with its austere chairs and hard, laminate-topped tables, I want a place to lie down, or if not that, at least a corner where I can sit and cry out my despair of twenty years. I want to quietly squeeze my heart dry of all the tears that it has stored up for so long, until there's not a particle of moisture left. There's no such place. The discovery makes me cry harder until I find my head nestling on a shoulder. I've found my refuge.

'There, there, Shruti, there, there,' says Kailash, repeating these words again and again, his voice reflecting what I long for – stability. My face is buried in his shirt, which is getting increasingly damp. I don't know when I last cried. My shoulders heave, my nose is getting wet, and my cheeks feel hot to the touch. I hear a soft sob, and I don't understand who could be sobbing like that, until Kailash says, 'Relax, Shruti. What's wrong? Tell me what's wrong.'

His tenderness makes me cry even more, a blanket of despair enshrouds me, and I say, 'I... I... I d... d... don't know.' And then for a long time I don't say anything at all. I've squeezed my heart dry of words and tears, both.

The sobs subside after a while, and I find Kailash stroking my head, a bemused expression on his face. 'Do you want some water?' is the first thing he says.

We leave the library, Kailash's arm around my shoulder, almost as though he is supporting me. I'm not sure why I'm so sad. The memory of days past is haunting me beyond belief. All my mistakes, my cruelty and foolishness, every wrong move I ever made, have come to the surface like the dirt that is released by boiling sugar. I hate the way I can't recognize my friends any longer. It's as though all of them have moved on while I have remained the same, silly, gullible Ruts. They all seem like strangers, and I'm amazed that I was on such terms of intimacy with them once upon a time.

The evening breeze is beginning to pick up, though the sun is still strong and hot. The campus is quiet and almost remote in its silence. I can hear a voice from the hostel block and as we walk towards the guesthouse, the sounds of an old Kishore Kumar song come wafting through the air. Closer home, the trees seem to rustle to a rhythmic tone. The sounds seem completely isolated and we could be the only people in the world.

'Let's go for a walk,' I suggest. 'We should look up the children. I know where the pond is.'

'No, we won't go for that walk, at least not now. I will go to the children, and you, my dear procrastinator, will go to Priya and see what she wants. Perhaps she'll tell you why she blushes.'

'Shaina thinks she is in love.'

'And who is Shaina?'

'Mrs Rats.'

'Clever woman. She seems to know more about your friend than you do.'

I sniff away the remnants of the tears. 'That's not true. I'm sure she has misread the situation. She doesn't know Priya at all. Priya swore off marriage a long time ago. The only reason she wanted to marry was for Anya's sake. She doesn't trust men, any man.'

'Then there can be no harm in finding out what she wants. So go on. I'll bring the kids back. I can probably take a swim in the pond while I'm at it.' And my husband laughs at the genuine look of horror on my face as he strides off.

I wish I could explain to Kailash why I broke down earlier. But it would mean too much history and too much emotion. I'm not ready for any kind of catharsis yet. Perhaps later, when all this is behind us, when we are back home in Philadelphia and once again arguing over the relative merits of different playwrights and novelists, perhaps then, on a winter's evening, when the children are asleep and we are sipping hot rum toddies, I shall tell him about my past. Or rather, I shall fill in the gaps. Perhaps we shall laugh about Priya's rudeness, and Rats's cleverness, and the whole Jaggu affair. But all that's in the future, when I'm eighty years old, I think.

My cellphone rings just as I'm about to enter the guesthouse. 'Is Shridhar all right?' asks Priya. 'I know you're back. Kailash told me. I'll wait in my room for you.'

I catch a glimpse of the old Priya in this rapid-fire delivery, and recognize Kailash's hand in making me go to Priya. He need not have bothered. I'm curious about what she has to say myself.

Tea is being served in the dining hall as I enter. I decide to carry a tray up and have my tea while Priya unburdens herself. She won't take a cup amiss herself, I'm sure. At least this has not changed. She gives me a quick hug when she sees what I have brought for her.

'Thanks. You're a lifesaver. I've been busy. But you have to tell me all about Shridhar.'

As I'm narrating the day's incidents, my phone buzzes.

'Hi, Xenia.'

'Hey, babe. Okay. The guy's name is Josh, and this is his number.'

When I've finally disconnected after exchanging gossip and getting the latest news about everything work related, I find Priya looking at me, a mystified look on her face.

'I've unearthed Shridhar's gay lover. I'm going to call

him, and ask if he's interested in coming over to take care of his boyfriend.'

Priya pats me on the back. 'Still Miss Busybody Ruts, managing others' lives for them.'

'Do you think I shouldn't be doing it? You're right. Shridhar might not like it. I mean nothing to him, after all, so why should I poke my nose in his affairs?'

'Ruts, look at it this way. He has just had a life threatening experience, he has no family or friends, and I bet he is insecure as hell in this country. Would he or would he not appreciate a friendly face to nurse him back to health? Ruts, he is damn lucky to have you care so much for him. Nobody else in the class would.'

'Are you sure?'

'Yes. So go ahead and call this lover.'

'What if he doesn't care enough to come?'

'Hey, where's all the optimism? When did you start thinking of things not working out, huh? Come on, Ruts, make that call. Only you can do it.'

'But you wanted to tell me something,' I remind Priya.

'That can wait. I'm right here. You call this man first, and then we'll talk about me.'

Josh. The name seems to suit the smiling face somehow. But who knows what lies behind the face? I decide that in my most clinical voice, the one I use with customer care executives who don't understand my problem and don't care either, I shall tell him about the mishap that has befallen his friend and leave it at that.

It is eight in the morning in the US. Will Josh be

awake? 'You have reached Josh,' says a voice in a cultured accent. 'Leave a message and I'll get back to you asap.'

I turn on my clinical voice to reply to the machine, but halfway through there's a click and a breathless voice yells into my ear, 'What's wrong with Shri?'

'I'm sorry, umm, I'm Shruti, actually...,' my clinical voice has mysteriously abandoned me.

'Yes, yes, please just tell me where Shri is.' Josh brushes aside my introduction.

'He, he's not well....'

'It's his dickey heart right? Damn! I bet he's forgotten his medication again. Is he all right? Does the hospital have the machines and stuff?'

I skip getting offended by the assumption that we are living in a jungle here in favour of being impressed by the man's concern. Before I can answer the volley of questions, Josh says, 'Who's taking care of him?'

'Actually, nobody,' I confess.

'Jesus! I need to talk to him, I really do. The poor guy! What a mess! Do they have a phone where I can call him?'

'He is in intensive care at the moment. But I'll make sure he gets the message that you asked after him.'

'No, no, that's not the message.'

My heart sinks. Being an optimist isn't all it's cracked up to be. The man is going to duck. 'All right then.'

'Ma'am....'

'Call me Ruts.'

'Ruts? All right, Ruts, can you get the message across

to Shri that he is not to worry. I'm coming right over. Tomorrow, if possible. He is not to worry,' repeats Josh.

'Are you sure? I mean, can you get leave? From work, I mean?' I feel foolish asking this.

'I don't think I really care right now. Just tell him I'll be right over, and he is to take it easy. Otherwise give me the phone number. I'll tell him myself.' Josh sounds a little curt. I don't care. He can be as miffed with me as he likes. It doesn't matter.

When I disconnect the phone, I do a high five with Priya. 'Thanks. You pushed me into doing the right thing. As always. I must learn to listen to you all the time, my conscience keeper.'

Priya laughs until the tears stream from her eyes. She sees my bewilderment and laughs even more, until I too am laughing with her, albeit uncertainly. Then she gasps, 'That's the first time anyone has called me their conscience keeper. I'm supposed to be fucking up people's lives.'

'Don't be insane,' I protest. 'That's a lie.'

'Why? Tell you what. Let's do a survey with everyone assembled here and find out what they think. You'll know you are wrong then.'

'Priya, look around you. These are happily married men – well, most of them,' I amend, thinking of Rats. 'They have successful careers, nice kids. So they did some stuff in the past, and you did some stuff in the past. But all that's history.'

'And history is irrelevant? I'm not so sure. Oh, Ruts, things are such a mess.'

Things were never a mess with Priya. Even when she was going to get rusticated for fornication, she was calm. So who is this woman? I'll have to tread cautiously around her.

'That's not true,' I say stoutly, promptly forgetting my resolve to be cautious. 'Everything can be sorted out, Priya, everything. Look at yourself, look at us and think about all that we did, all the crises we've come through. Where is the mess?'

Twenty years ago I wore my hair short, so that I wouldn't have to bother grooming it. Over the years, I have acquired a more mature approach to this as well. Now my hair falls almost to my waist. Most times I gather it in a barrette, but today it hangs loose, and in an old gesture, Priya sets about ruffling it. 'You're such an optimist,' she says. 'You always were. But some things just can't be sorted out.'

'That's what we believe about every situation,' I tell her. 'I'm sorry to bring it up, but didn't you think you would never come out of the Sen scandal? And you did. And not much can get worse than that.'

'You think so? Listen, we didn't know it then, but the stuff we did when we were that young could hardly have any impact on our lives. But now, now it's different. Now we have reached the mid point of our lives, Ruts. Now whatever we do is going to stay with us forever, good or bad.'

Now I am really curious. What crisis is Priya facing? If she is in love, she is entitled to it. Priya's love will last forever, I know. I honestly do not see any obstacle in her

path of true love. So why this squeamishness on her part?
And where do I come into it?

'You're in love,' I blurt out.

Priya's room is neat as a pin, a far cry from the almighty
mess that was the norm in the hostel. There is only one
armchair in the room, and I am occupying it. Priya is curled
up against the headboard of the bed, a couple of pillows
supporting her back, her favourite pose. Now she gets up
to come to me. She takes me by the hand, and makes me
sit on the bed, all the while looking at me.

'Yes,' she says.

'That's wonderful!' I cry. 'Wow! Who is it? Is it Sasi?'
I've been dying to ask this question since this morning.

'Yes.'

'And does he... Is he...?'

'Yes. He proposed today.'

'Priya, congratulations! This is utterly fantastic. I'm
thrilled! We *have* to celebrate. This is the best news I've
heard in years!' The exclamations spill out of my mouth
in quick succession, and all the while I pump Priya's hand,
ignoring the fact that there's no corresponding delight on
her face. 'When's the wedding?'

Priya brings her other hand round to cover mine
and still its movement. She is smiling, or rather, she is
grimacing. There is a blankness in her eyes, and it is this
that makes me shut up finally.

'I've said no.'

'You're kidding. This is a joke, right?'

'I wish it was.'

'No, you don't. You don't wish it was. You will absolutely not say no, Priya. This is Sasi we're talking about. One never says no to Sasi.'

This time Priya's smile is genuine. 'You always were in love with him.'

'And he is in love with you. And ditto for you. And that's the recipe for happiness. I'm not sure what the problem is.'

'You're not? You're blind then, Ruts. There is a truckload of problems. There's the problem of Anya, and how she'll take to sharing me. There's the problem of my age. I mean, even I can see my wrinkles now.'

'Bah! He will love Anya. She is an adorable kid. And she is old enough to take this in her stride. And what's age got to do with love?' I have no hesitation in decimating Priya's objections. She is finally getting the chance to find a man who will love her. She can't scorn it!

'Ruts, you'll never change. I knew you'd say all this. I think the same myself.'

'I'm confused. Are you saying then that you're okay?'

'No. I'm saying these are problems that can be sorted out....'

'But?'

'I don't think I can trust Sasi.'

'Tell me you're insane.'

'Seriously.'

'Why? Why can't you trust him? Listen, how long have you known about Sasi and all this?'

'A couple of years, maybe.'

'And you still don't trust him? What's he done?'

'Nothing, actually.'

'Then what?'

'Ruts, you can't have forgotten. If it hadn't been for Sasi, there might not have been all that trouble over Arnab.'

'Arnab?'

'Sen.'

'Dammit, Priya, you can't hold that against Sasi. He must have had his reasons for that.'

'I don't see what they are. Because of him, I almost lost everything. Why did he do it, if he didn't wish me ill? Look at me. I'm so pathetic. I'm in love with a man who hated me enough to want to ruin my life.'

'I can't believe that's true.'

'The facts are there. I can still see his expression. He was horrified when he saw the two of us together. And why didn't he knock before entering Arnab's room?' she asks irrelevantly.

My phone rings just then. It is an unknown number. I'm tempted to ignore it, but Priya waves to me to take the call. She herself dials someone on her phone and I leave the room to take the call in the corridor.

'Mrs Narayan?' says the caller, a male whose rolling accent sounds slightly familiar. 'Is this Mrs Narayan?'

'It is.'

'Madam, hello, how are you? This is Ramamurthy.'

I still can't place the name or the voice, and wonder if there's some mistake. 'Who's this?' I ask.

'You don't remember me.' Ramamurthy sounds

disappointed. 'We met, madam, on the plane. I sat next to you.'

Of course. 'How are you, Mr Ramamurthy.'

'How's the visit, madam? Your children, do they like IIM? And your husband?'

'Yes, they do.' I don't know what this is leading up to. When I had casually written my number on the back of a visiting card supplied by my neighbour on the plane, I had no idea he would actually use it. But then, this is India. People claim a right over each other. 'Can I help you?' I ask.

The man laughs at the other end. 'Madam, I hope you are enjoying yourself. Bangalore is a fantastic city, no? Madam, I'm very sorry.'

'Sorry? For what?'

'I should have offered to help you. You are our guests here. If there's anything I can do for you... please let me know. I should have asked earlier.'

For a moment I'm unable to speak. Then I clear my throat. 'Thank you so much, Mr Ramamurthy. Thanks.'

'When do you return?'

'Tomorrow morning,' I reply, mystified by the query.

'Then, madam, I will take you to the airport in my car.'

'No, no, I'm sure we'll organize something. There's really no need.'

'It will be my pleasure. Please let me know what time your flight is. I'll pick you up. Don't bother with taxis. They are anyway not reliable. I know. You should let me do this.'

'That's very kind of you. Are you sure?'

'Of course. I insist. You are our guests,' he says again.

He calls off after exchanging a few more pleasantries, leaving me completely bemused. I enter Priya's room to find she's still talking on the phone, and from her manner I guess its Anya at the other end.

'Who was that?' she asks me once she hangs up.

I laugh as I explain about Ramamurthy. 'Wow!' says Priya at the end of my recital. 'You're still busy impressing people, Ruts. This is something!'

'I honestly don't know what impressed the man. I don't think I said more than a couple of words to him. You can ask Rohan if you don't believe me. He was there. I have no idea why he is being so friendly.'

'Maybe it's the IIM name.'

'Maybe.'

'Anyway it's damn kind of him. After all, you are a total stranger. And you didn't even remember him, did you?'

'Frankly, no. Why should I? I've met dozens of people on journeys before. I don't remember any of them.'

'Except when they are admirers of the IIM,' laughs Priya.

I shake my head. 'Not even then.' We both burst into a gale of laughter at that. It does me good to see my friend loosen up. She is beautiful, this Priya, not because of her aquiline nose, sharp chin, almond eyes, and perfect dusky complexion, but because there's a strength that emanates from her to anyone who is open to receive it, a strength that isn't domineering or overbearing, but refreshing.

Whenever I'm with Priya, I feel... emboldened. Though she wouldn't thank me for saying so. She always hated any form of flattery. And anything said in her praise she always considered a lie.

'Forget Ramamurthy. We were talking about you,' I remind her.

'Why should we?' she says tartly. 'There is nothing to talk about, is there? Why should we talk about love and all that crap? Look at us, Ruts. Our children have or are going to have boyfriends and girlfriends very soon. It is ridiculous for us to feel love anxiety at our age. Shit! I thought I had more sense than this. As for Sasi, he's practically in his dotage. What's he thinking, proposing to a middle-aged woman?' Priya's voice rises on a note of indignation.

I can't help smiling at her words. Dotage indeed! 'Sasi's one of the most eligible bachelors I know. Do you want me to explain why? He is tolerably good-looking, reasonably healthy, I presume, has got all his teeth, and earns a good living. The fact that he is an internationally recognized economist and will soon become the director of this place is probably a good thing too. And oh yes, I forgot a small thing. He loves you!'

'That still doesn't take away from the fact that he's a sneak.'

'Priya, I'm not sure you're right about that.'

'Ruts, you know what he did, and you still believe in him? It's all right to say that one act does not mark a man. But you're not marrying him. And I can't live with him in the knowledge that he almost ruined my life.'

I have always been puzzled by this act of Sasi. I can't say that I've known him intimately, but it seemed to me that it wasn't in his character to go behind someone's back. To add to that, I remember his concern and anger on Priya's behalf. Those didn't seem the sentiments of a man who was a stickler for law at any cost. What was the truth, really, and how would I find out?

12

'Look, Ruts, forget about all this, okay?' says Priya in a bid to get me out of her room. I can hear children's voices out in the corridor so I know they've returned from their picnic, and I should probably go to my own children and assure myself that Isha has no lingering after effects of her morning fever. But that's easier said than done.

'Can *you* forget it, Priya?' I ask her, looking at her face, trying to decipher the expression that I see on it.

'What I think doesn't matter. You'd better carry on. Your children will be waiting for you. You can't go on fighting other people's battles. I'll sort this out, I promise. It'll just... take a little time, that's all. And that shouldn't be a problem. I can ask Sasi to... to wait. We're not teenagers giving in to hot passion, are we? We... we...' she stops when she sees my expression. 'What?'

'Nothing. You ran out of reasons yourself. I didn't say a thing.'

'Oh, go away, Ruts! I don't like you when you're being clever. I don't want you to be clever.'

'Then what?'

'Just be Ruts, for my sake. Listen to me, and don't argue.'

I laugh, and Priya is confused, rightly so. I leave her with a small frown on her face, as I go to my room. Perhaps I should just nod my head and let her be happy. Except that she isn't. Happy.

When I enter the room I find Isha and Rohan having a scuffle on the bed while Anya is sitting in the chair, going through one of Rohan's books. The scuffle halts temporarily as Rohan informs me that he has now formed the intention of studying at the IIM when he grows up. Yeah, you and about half a million others, I say in my mind. He is only twelve so the facts of life can stay hidden from him for a few more years yet. It is easier to enter the vault of the Bellagio Casino than to become a student at the IIM. No wonder Ramamurthy offered me a ride. In his eyes I must be one special dude.

Isha has more important things to tell me, like what they did at the pond, who fell into the water, who rode a buffalo, and so on. There is nothing more soothing than her childish chatter until my daughter declares, 'Khushi's parents are getting a divorce.'

Apparently, only I am affected by this announcement. Having given me this news, Isha continues to play, now teasing Anya into playing Dragonball Z with her. I, on the other hand, feel the earth folding up on me. Children gossip as much as adults, and I suppose Rats's children have let out this information during the picnic. There's no sense in asking Isha for more details. She would only wonder about my curiosity and think there's more to her announcement than I want her to think. It doesn't matter how Isha knows, only that Shaina has made a final decision.

Any hope I had of Shaina postponing her decision to after this weekend is now summarily destroyed. The mean streak in Rats is a mile wide. He is not likely not to follow up on his threat to me. Perhaps he is too busy at work to think about these things. It's been known to happen, though knowing Rats, his intellect is fully capable of handling multitasking of this kind.

It is already past seven, and there's an hour left to go for dinner. I can meet Kailash, explain the situation, and sort out everything the way I've been promising myself since morning. I know my Kailash. Things will be fine. They always are.

Kailash is not in the room when I go there looking for him. I wonder where he could have got to. It seems foolish to be hunting for him all over the campus, and I call him on his phone. Strangely enough, he disconnects and my unease increases exponentially. What is he up to now? He has been behaving a little strangely since we've come here. On more than one occasion I have felt that he's got something up his sleeve, something I don't know. I don't like it when he has secrets.

The guesthouse has a beautiful terrace located just over a vast lawn. Beyond the lawn are the faculty residences, and the terrace offers a view of both. In my bid to find Kailash, I have climbed up to this place. It is barely three levels above the ground and one can get a clear view of the lawn, which is dotted with flowerbeds interspersed with wrought iron benches. It is still light enough for me to see the two people sitting on one of the benches, though their backs are towards me. But the ponytail is unmistakable. One of the men is Kailash, and the other, as I can discern in the faint light, is Rats.

I halt in my tracks. Shit. Kailash and Rats! I wish I had a magic wand that could separate these two by seven oceans and all the mountains in the world. I wish there was an earthquake that would shatter the earth right now. I would give all the world for the sight of these two separating from each other at this very instant.

A flash of hot anger courses through me. What business does Kailash have meeting people like Rats behind my back? Why should he be sneaking around? I would have told him everything, I really would. If I could I would punch him right now for betraying me!

And then it happens! The punch, I mean. It's as if my thoughts have been divined. Only, and this is the most shocking thing, it's not me who's doing the punching. And it isn't Kailash getting punched.

If I was angry before, I'm horror-struck now. The sight in front of me will haunt me for the next hundred years at least, or as long as I live. My quiet, good-natured husband, my lamb has, even as I see him, grown claws and teeth. Before I can blink or say 'baa' the grandmother-turned-wolf has hit my former classmate in the stomach. The whole scene seems so surreal that I am sure that I am imagining it, that this weekend has made me lose my balance. I've become delusional. But then how, in my deluded state, can I see Kailash stand up from the bench, dust his hands, put them in his pockets and walk back towards the guesthouse?

Shivering with shock and rage and sheer disbelief, I finally manage to move from my spot on the terrace and then I do something utterly unreasonable. Instead of rushing to Kailash to find out what's going on, I run down the three flights of stairs out to the lawn, to the far side where Rats is still sitting immobile on the bench.

'Are you all right? Are you hurt?' I gasp.

Rats looks up at me as though I'm a stranger. 'It's you. What do you want?'

'I, er, I... I saw... did Kailash...?'

'Yeah, Godzilla there laid into me. Oooh!'

'But why? What happened? Kailash – why would he...?'

'Why don't you ask him, huh, ask your angry young man, or not so young man.'

Rats stands up slowly, grimacing as he straightens up.

'Does it hurt? Can I...? Can you walk? Shall I call a doctor?'

'Ruts, fuck off,' says Rats as he limps off. 'You make me sick, all of you.'

Well! Talk about ingratitude! As always when I'm worried,I bite my lower lip furiously as I wonder what madness I have dropped into. When did Rats return to campus? And why? Can he bring action against Kailash for assault? What if his injuries are serious? This could become an ugly scandal. What could he possibly have said to Kailash to enrage him so? My steps are moving rapidly as these questions race through my head, and I reach my room in thirty seconds. I'm glad it's open. The mood I'm in, I would have battered it open had it been locked. When I enter, I can hear splashes of water from the bathroom. I sit on the bed. Kailash's phone is lying there, and I wonder why he didn't take my call. I scroll through the call register, and Rats's number with its multitudinous zeroes stares at me. Presumably then, my former classmate asked for this meeting. Kailash emerges from the bathroom before I can investigate further. He has discarded all his clothes in favour of only a pair of briefs. Before I can say anything, the doorbell rings, and I take a tray of tea from a liveried man. When I turn back Kailash is lying on his back, staring up at the ceiling. The television has been switched on to a news channel at a volume that provides a background without actually intruding.

'Are the children all right?' he asks in an absolutely normal tone. 'I don't think Isha's fever is going to recur. They enjoyed themselves at the picnic, thank god. Anya and Tanushka took care of them pretty well. When I got there, they were all throwing mud balls at each other, egged on by a couple of goatherds who obviously thought these kids were some crazy foreigners. The pond didn't look clean enough for a swim, though. I could have done with some exercise.'

'Why did you hit Rats?' I ask, doing what I do best, coming to the point straight away.

'Oh, you saw that, did you? Interesting.'

'Lucky for you that only I saw it, though I'm not sure. Perhaps someone else also noticed. *Kailash!*' I scream, as my husband deliberately pours himself a cup of tea, slowly stirring the sugar and measuring out the milk almost to the drop.

'Shh. Don't shout. Someone could hear you.'

'What were you *doing*?'

'Something you people should have done a long time ago. I don't like bullies.'

'*That's it?* You don't like bullies? So you *beat* them? You a... a....' A menopausal professor. For some reason I can't say the words aloud though I dearly want to. 'And I don't like street brawls, especially when it is a professor of a university who's involved. It looks ridiculous, if you must know.'

'Well, too bad. Drastic cases need drastic remedies. If your friend had received some punishment when it mattered, he wouldn't be such a prick now.'

'He's not my friend.'

'Whatever.' Kailash sips his tea, and then suddenly starts laughing so violently that his tea spills onto his saucer. 'I'm s... s... sorry. I just remembered the look on his face when he got my fist in his belly. Oh... oh...!' And he goes off into peals again.

Reluctantly, I smile. There *is* something funny about the scene. Rats would have reflected a ton of injured dignity. And surprise. Kailash is right. Rats should have got it a long time ago. My good humour is restored only partially. I still need to know what was going on there.

'It seems that once upon a time, you and Rats were more than, shall we say, friends? And then he decided he couldn't go on with it. And then you got in touch with him after several years, desperate to get back with him, only his wife found out and now she's threatening to divorce him. So he wants me to tell you to "get off his back", Kailash makes quote marks with his fingers, 'and let him and his wife live in peace. Or rather, he wants me to convince Shaina, even if falsely, that you love me so that she doesn't divorce him since he loves his wife to hell and back.'

'And that made you beat him?'

'No. It was because of a reference to some sexual prowess he claimed you had that only he knew about!'

'Thanks. For preserving my honour.'

'What's the matter? Why the anger? Would you rather I had let him go on talk that nonsense?'

'No,' I say hotly. 'I would rather you had come to me first to check the facts before flying off the handle like that. What the hell came over you, Kailash? Rats is just the kind of man who would sue for damages at the snap of a finger. Did you think of that? And anyway, he's told you a load of shit.'

'You mean his wife isn't divorcing him?'

'That's the only part that's true. The rest of it is rubbish. And you beat up a man for telling you a bunch of lies. He must be thrilled.'

'Well, lies or not, I'm glad I did it, even if you're not,' says Kailash mutinously. 'And what's the truth?'

This is not the way I wanted it, Kailash looking like a

particularly belligerent boar, his lower lip sticking out, his brow furrowed in three parallel lines between his eyes, his body coiled into a million units of tension. I can't speak to him when he's looking like this. I know this look. He has it when Rohan gets a bad mark in school for not doing his homework, or when I accidentally damage his best pair of trousers while ironing them. It does not bode well for the recipient.

'Shruti, I said, what's the truth?'

'The truth? Like the truth, the whole truth, nothing but the truth, so help me god?'

'No, I don't. You don't believe in god, and neither do I. Just the plain, unvarnished variety will do for now, thanks.'

There is nothing remotely ridiculous about Kailash sitting by the side of the bed in his underwear sipping a cup of tea. I would be foolish to underestimate his ability to lay me low with one verbal blow, clothes or no clothes. Kailash's command to tell him the whole truth seems to imply that that isn't what I have been doing so far. I should resent that, I really should. But there's a measure of justification in what he says. And then I have to trust him enough to tell him about Jaggu. I can feel Kailash's steady gaze upon me as I stare out of the window onto the lawn, the very same lawn where he and Rats gave each other a little bit of themselves moments ago. Now the lawn is empty and only some birds whose names I don't know have returned to frolic on it.

'I'll tell you the truth,' I say to Kailash, still looking out of the window. 'And it will have no varnish on it, not even the hint of a veneer. But on one condition.'

'Ah! Conditions! I wondered when we were coming to those. And can I guess what the condition will be?'

'No, you can't. It is my condition. You have no right to guess it. My condition is that we wait till we return to Philadelphia.'

'May I ask why?'

'No, I don't think so. If you trust me, please wait.'

'Of course I trust you, of course I do.'

'Then let's talk about all this after we are back at home.'

'All right. Only tell me this, did you have the hots for Mr Rats ever?'

'That is so crude,' I say with a touch of hauteur. 'I might get carried away but I'm not completely insane. Those are the only kinds who would have anything to do with that man. Though Priya....' Oh dear! What impression will get Kailash get about Priya now!

'So he and Priya did....'

'Look, it was all a hundred years ago, okay? We had no sense then. And that includes Priya. In fact....'

'No, no, let's not talk about that paragon, please. Ever since we've landed here, we've done nothing else. I know she's a wonderful person, god's gift and all of that, but I guess she's human, and maybe, just maybe we can talk about something or someone else.'

'You're exaggerating. And she is human. And she is in trouble.'

'There! I knew there was something. How could we ever forget Priya!'

'Please, Kailash, don't be flippant. This is serious.'

'Then I need to put on some clothes, don't you think? Serious things have to be treated seriously.'

'Well, hurry up. We have to go for dinner. It's almost eight.'

I am now sitting in the crook of Kailash's elbow, my pulse rate only moderately stabilising. Let's talk normal, let's *be* normal, let's forget the drama of the last half hour. Let us pretend that the next big crisis is deciding where to have dinner. Perhaps that's the best way forward.

'Hey, we're no longer students here, remember? What I mean is, you're no longer a student here. Dinner can wait. Or we can eat out. You can show me some eatery where you went with your boyfriend in days of yore, young blood gobbling young food and all that.'

'That's not a bad idea at all. In fact, let's do a foursome tonight. Let's call Priya and Sasi as well.'

Kailash groans. 'Oh no, not her!'

'Come on! She's wonderful. You'll enjoy her company. She does some wicked imitations of the profs here. Anyway, I need to talk to Sasi. And you forget. This might be my last night with her.'

'So *she* was the lover. *Now* I get it.'

'I think your sense of humour is warped. And has become more so since we came here. So here's the plan,' I say, ignoring Kailash's demented chuckles. 'You tog yourself up, I'll attend to the children, and then we'll call for a cab. Should we do casual or formal?'

'Depends on the occasion. Is there one?'

'I'm not sure. Casual, I think, as things stand.'

'Mystery Shruti! All right, I leave it to you!'

It is easy to say that I'll attend to the kids. I'm not sure how I'll attain this objective. They are still in their room, now joined by Khushi, much to my surprise.

'Oh, hi! I thought you'd left,' I tell her.

'No. Dad went but Mom wants us to stay another night. I didn't want to go.'

'Oh. Why not?'

'Coz I like it here. I want to play with Isha.'

'And your mom agreed to that?'

'Course she did,' chimes in Isha. 'You would too, wouldn't you?'

'Hmm, young lady. I'm not so sure about that.' Isha is about to argue when Shaina walks in.

'Oh, great. I came looking for my daughter. We're supposed to go for dinner.'

'I didn't know you were staying on. Weren't you supposed to leave tonight?'

Shaina drags me outside into the corridor. 'I chose to let Ravi leave alone though he wasn't feeling too good. I don't know what's the matter with him.'

I could have enlightened her on that. 'So Rats, I mean Ravi, has gone?'

'Yeah. I didn't want him here anyway. Ruts, I'm having such a good time here! I'm a bit like Khushi. I don't feel like going ever.'

'Well, that might not be feasible,' I smile.

'I know. But we're leaving some time tomorrow. Or not. I might just stay on in Bangalore for a few more days.

I want to. Just be here, have some time with the children, explore this city.'

'Well, I can introduce you to one person who can help you do that.' I tell her about Ramamurthy. Then I get an idea. 'Look, would you mind keeping an eye on my children tonight? Kailash and I are stepping out for dinner.'

'You don't have to ask. It'll be a pleasure. Isha seems to be Khushi's most favourite person at the moment. Though that tends to change every month. But no problem. I'd love it.'

'You don't regret it at all, do you?' The words spill out before I can stop them.

Shaina knows what I'm referring to. 'Ruts, I've been sure about this for more than six months. Don't ask me why but this place seemed the most appropriate to announce my decision to Ravi, that's all. If you knew what it's like to have a hundredweight lifted from your shoulders, then you'd know what I'm feeling at present. I feel like flying, literally.'

By my reckoning, Shaina must be on the wrong side of forty. Cosmetics and grooming have reduced her age considerably. But now she looks positively girlish. I wouldn't be surprised if she started giggling. She doesn't disappoint me. 'I shall play Scrabble with them,' she giggles. 'I used to be good at it.'

Well, good for you. I go back to my room then, aware now that while Shaina looks like she has just stepped out of *Vogue*, I would disgrace any self-respecting urchin. The

lack is easily repaired, though how I'm going to invite Sasi
along is a more intractable problem. He is still a professor
where I'm concerned, though he might be the man my
friend is going to marry, if all goes well. In my mind I still
think of him as 'sir', though when we met yesterday he did
exhort me to call him by his first name.

I know the general direction of the faculty residences
or quarters as they are called, a term that is a throwback
to the Raj, when the army lived in quarters. I saw them
from the terrace of the guesthouse. For some reason it is
important that Priya, who has consented to go out with
us, not know who the person completing the foursome is.
I have a feeling she won't take kindly to this socializing.

There are people who believe that the world spins
because of everyone in it except themselves. And they have
a responsibility to make the world spin. Priya was born to
make the world spin by making everyone around her a
good, sound person, someone who was bold and positive
and strong. And having done that, she just sat back, and
forgot that she too is contributing. Priya Pathak believes
that the world needs everyone but her. Well, I beg to differ.
There is at least one person who needs her, and I shall
prove it to her.

I sprint across the lawn to Sasi's residence. It is only
when I see his front door, a small wooden plate declaring
his name with his qualifications in brackets affixed to it
that it occurs to me that for all I know, he may not even
be at home. And for such a small, such an infinitesimal
reason, perhaps my friend will stop spinning. It is a

thought that halts me in my tracks. And a sense of my own vanity is brought home sharply. The world, I tell myself, doesn't stop and wait for me just because I believe I am right. Why on earth should Sasi be sitting at home on a Sunday evening just because I want him to? He could be in a meeting, he could be in the library, he could be mentoring some student, he could be out with friends.... I should have called and checked first.

The door opens as all this goes through my head, and Sasi's small body is framed in it, the light from the house behind him giving him a halo. He can't see me properly and asks, 'Yes?'

Now that I'm actually standing in front of him, my voice and my thoughts, both desert me. 'Yes? Can I help you?'

There's a fluorescent light just by the side of the one-storey bungalow, one of several along that street. As I move a little, its light falls on me and Sasi exclaims, 'Oh, Shruti! Hello! Please! This is a big surprise, though a pleasant one.'

As he's talking he ushers me inside. His house is the typical bachelor's pad, furnished simply, with mismatched furniture and wall hangings and rugs scattered here and there. The effect, though, is not displeasing. This is not the house of a man with any aspirations to grandeur. The scores of books lying on every conceivable surface make me amend my statement. If there's grandeur of intellect, then perhaps this man has it. When I manage to unlock my tongue I say, 'You must be busy.'

'I was trying to prepare some notes for tomorrow's class.'

'Class,' I say blankly. I'm suddenly reminded that there are students here, that they attend classes, and that Sasi probably teaches some of them. Priya is right. Love, this man-woman thing, should be an insignificant part of our lives. It isn't, though. 'What class is that?'

'Oh, the same that you took once, macroeconomics. Just like in your time, there are some bright students now.'

'Yeah, today's crop looks really brilliant.'

'Don't sell yourself short. Every batch of students has a few stars, every batch. And I've been here for more than twenty years now. Sometimes that feels like an eternity. I'm an old man now.' He smiles.

It is hard to accuse a man who is so *nice,* of treachery. I still can't believe he would have brought Priya on the brink of crisis. But the facts speak for themselves. For some reason known only to himself, Professor Sasikant chose to tell his colleagues that one of the professors was having an affair with a student. Perhaps he felt remorse once the deed was done and he came face to face with the implications of his action. At the time of doing what he thought was the right thing, he didn't realize what it could lead to, but once he saw the gravity of the situation, his innate decency and sense of responsibility resurfaced, and that's why he was so concerned about Priya. That is the only explanation that fits all of Sasi's actions. I believe that a single action must not be the yardstick by which a man is judged for the rest of his life but then, I'm not marrying the man. In all fairness, I cannot blame my friend for not committing herself to Sasi. In her place, I would probably do the same. And then I wonder what the solution to this devil's dilemma is. On the one hand, Priya cannot marry the man because of a doubt in her mind, on the other, she is probably losing the last chance at happiness she is ever going to get if she doesn't. While these thoughts are going through my mind, Sasi has brought in two glasses of lemonade on a tray. The glasses are mismatched and this sign of imperfect domesticity warms me to him further.

I invite him to join us for dinner without revealing that Priya is also going to be there. I give no reason for inviting him and he asks for none, merely looks at me with a curious expression on his face.

'It's a pleasure,' he says. 'I'll be delighted.'

'There's one more thing,' I say, having decided that there's no point in so much hesitation where my friend's happiness is concerned. 'I'm sorry if you think I'm being presumptuous but there's one thing that's bothered me for a long time. Ordinarily, I wouldn't have asked you. I mean I live ten thousand miles away now, so what happened when I was a student here can hardly be of relevance today, but now Priya is involved, and she isn't happy.'

Sasi has a grave expression on his face, and is making no effort to be polite, much to my relief. His politeness might threaten to make my own overtures seem trivial. 'I suppose Priya has told you that I wish to marry her. I'm glad.'

'You are?' I'm surprised.

'I believe your friend keeps too much to herself. If she

learned to share things with someone, her burdens would ease. That much is obvious. But more importantly, she has chosen you to talk to. We have spoken of the old days frequently. It is hard not to. And in all our conversations, your name crops up all the time. You are one of the few people Priya trusts, perhaps the only one. Has she told you about the episode that made her so bitter?'

'Yes, she did, a long time ago. But there's something else bothering her, and if I'm not mistaken, it is bothering her even more than her ill-conceived marriage. And just like that silly marriage twisted her for a long time, this time round also she will be unhappy, perhaps for the rest of her life.'

'Oh?'

I hesitate before speaking further. 'Actually, this has something to do with you.'

He looks confused. 'With me? What are you talking about?'

Sasi's bewilderment is what pushes me over the edge. The man must know what he has done to Priya. How can he act so innocent after all that? Though it's getting late, and both Kailash and Priya are looking for me desperately, judging by the frantic text messages I'm receiving on my phone, I must have this conversation now while the subject is ripe and I have Sasi's undivided attention. 'You shouldn't have told on Priya and Sen.'

'I'm sorry?'

'When you found them together in Sen's room, why did you have to go and tell someone about it? Priya was at that moment telling Sen it was off. But for you, everything would have gone off peacefully. She suffered so much humiliation, and all because you decided to complain about her. I saw her at that time. She was genuinely scared. It was the first time I saw her scared. She tried to hide it, of course, but I knew what she was going through.' I see the look of confusion on Sasi's face at this incoherent outburst but I go on. 'It hurt me to see her so disturbed, and I, like a complete jerk, sat in judgment over her along with the rest of the world and abandoned her as well. I'll never forgive myself for that. Never. But more than that, I can't forgive you for triggering the whole thing.'

There! I've said what I've been meaning to say for two decades. I'm aware of a curious sensation in my chest, and finally discover it is relief. In a narrow sense, Sasi has no hold over me. I'm no longer a student, and nothing in our lives intersects. I can now freely express my views, not only to him but to the rest of the institute faculty, and if I choose to air my grievances to them, well, the worst they can do is ignore me. 'Priya won't marry you because she believes you sneaked on her. If you ask me, she is right in taking this decision. One can't live with a man whom one doesn't trust even if that means a lifetime of loneliness and doubt. Actually, forget about the dinner. It was more of a ruse to bring you and Priya together, but what's the point? She can't live with you knowing what she knows. She loves you, you know.'

'Does she? I thought she did but what you are saying proves she doesn't,' says Sasi, smiling rather sadly.

'Why not?'

'If she really felt for me, genuinely, she would know I'm not what she thinks I am.'

'Look, she knows you are a good man. That's why she loves you.'

'And yet she is so ready to condemn me for just one act.'

'But not a small act. It could have destroyed her life. If she had been expelled, it would have finished her. Nobody can recover from a blow like that. And all for what? A small error of judgment? Yes, she made a mistake. I'm willing to concede that. But don't you see, that's all it was – a mistake. So what was the need to haul her up for it? Anyway, it was a purely personal matter, between her and that man. Why did the institute turn so damn officious?' I feel like going on in this vein forever, now that I've started. In excoriating Sasi, I'm punishing myself as well, for my callousness, my hypocrisy, my pig-headedness. It seems surprising that Priya could forgive me but not Sasi. After all, both of us abandoned her, didn't we?

As I'm running out of breath, Sasi gets up, and for a moment I think he is walking out on me. But he merely walks up to his writing table and takes out a notebook from a drawer and starts turning its pages.

'Here,' he says, handing me the book. 'I want to show you something that I've never shared with anyone else. Read and then decide for yourself. And you should know me. You should know I don't tell lies.' It's such a childishly simple way of speaking, but so direct. No, Sasi doesn't tell lies.

The pages of the diary are yellow but firm, and the handwriting is clear, though the date on top is December 14, 1987. 'There is trouble brewing,' it says in a neat hand. 'Sen's indiscretion is causing all sorts of problems. It is ironical that we can be so priggish about sex while all the time proclaiming to the world that we are the foremost academy of learning. I am disappointed that the professors are willing to hang and quarter a young girl for a minor indiscretion. Instead of cushioning our bright stars from the filth of the world we are actually throwing them into it, to no good end. I wish Sen had had the decency to keep his personal matters to himself. I wonder he wasn't ashamed to talk about it to Gopal. Doesn't he realize the implications of his loose talk? How could he involve Priya like this? He has indulged in adultery and illegal behaviour. He should be punished. But my fear is that Priya too will be dragged through ignominy. What a waste! There is hardly any unity amongst the faculty, otherwise I could try to persuade people to forswear any proceedings against Priya. That is the way internationally. Sen, of course, must leave. For the first time, I wonder if I made the right decision in joining this place. I hardly expected to see such levels of hypocrisy.'

For some time, my mind refuses to accept what it has just read. Then Sasi's voice penetrates the haziness surrounding me. 'I never knew Priya blamed me for being found out. It did give me a shock when I walked in on them that day. But then I decided that though it was wrong, what Sen was doing, it was none of my business. They were responsible adults capable of looking after themselves.

It wasn't as though Sen was seducing a minor. I did feel alarm, though I couldn't understand why. If anyone could take care of herself, it was Priya. Hostel rumours always carried over to the faculty, and Priya's reputation preceded her. And now you're telling me she blames me for what happened? Why should she? What could I possibly gain from ratting on her?'

The incongruously British phrase jars in my ears. Sasi has always been a mild-mannered man, but now he paces the floor of his living room in an almost maniacal way, and I wouldn't be surprised if he 'tore his hair', the way people in Victorian novels did.

'So, it wasn't you?'

'How could it be?' he retorts. 'It was Sen himself. He was squarely responsible for his own downfall, for which I'm glad, quite frankly. Professors have to have a higher sense of what's right than the rest of the world. They have young minds in their hands.'

'I... I....'

'I know. You're sorry.'

'But you don't care what I think. Why should you? It's Priya who's important. I understand. Tell me this, is it too late?'

Sasi knows what I mean. The wrinkles on his face are standing out, and combined with the streaks of grey in his hair, they give an impression of ageing that is unpleasant. I have never known Sasi not to smile, not even when he was setting us some of the most difficult quizzes that I encountered during my stint at the IIM, but now when

I see him looking so sombre, I wonder if the smile was just a figment of my imagination. But no, it wasn't. I can bet Priya fell in love with the smile first. Anyone would. I almost can't bear to look at Sasi's face, at his dark eyes that seem to have hazed over now so that it is almost impossible to read their expression. I make a decision then.

'Sir,' I say, and Sasi looks up, startled, 'I mean, Sasi, let's go. Kailash, my husband, is waiting for us. You'll love meeting him. Come on, let us have this night to remember for the rest of our lives.' I make no mention of Priya. I shall cross that bridge when I come to it. There is a blockage in my mind that prevents me from thinking too intensely about Sasi's disclosure. If I did it now, I would probably not be able to function. It is hard to believe that one has wilfully made a mistake, that one has misjudged a person so badly. It is easier to think a person is good, and then find the opposite to be the case than to needlessly castigate someone for something he didn't do. And in Sasi's case, there isn't even the consolation of a trial. We were the judge, the jury and the prosecuting counsel. Oh, Priya! How could we have been so wrong?

By now, we are so late that there doesn't seem to be any point in going to a restaurant. It is close to ten o'clock. The sounds of campus life have slowly dwindled to nil, and the total silence in a way complements my own reaction. The weather over the entire weekend has blessed us, as though to tell us to take away only the best memories from Bangalore. As I sit in Sasi's living room, staring at nothing in particular, I feel a gush of affection for this city, for its residents, for the institute. It is the affection one feels for the dress in which one gets married. There will always be memories attached to it, even if the dress is old-fashioned and worn. I could never wear it again, but I'll still love it. And of course, I'll never let it go. Much the same feeling pervades me where Bangalore is concerned. I don't see myself living in it, or even in the institute, but there is one spot in my heart that is permanently reserved for this place. Tomorrow I shall be going away, and this time, just like the last one, who knows how long it will be before I return. But if anyone asks me, I'll always say, 'Oh yes, Bangalore. That's where I grew up.'

Sasi has gone into the interior of the house, presumably to change. When he emerges I say, 'Umm, Sasi?'

'Yes?' he asks warily.

'Umm, I'm not sure if a restaurant will be open at this hour. It's pretty late. So what do we do?'

A smile of relief spreads over Sasi's face. 'If you give me half an hour, I can rustle up some food. I'm a mean cook of dal chawal.'

I laugh, and agree to return with the rest of the party after some time. I wonder if it's appropriate to hug him but decide against it. He might not like it. Instead, I hold out my hand. 'I'm glad I came,' is all I say before I flee from his presence.

I'm in no hurry to return to the guesthouse in spite of the frantic calls I'm getting on my cellphone. There's no danger of a search party being sent out for me. There's a wonderful calm in the air, as though the entire world exists only for me, and will stop spinning when I say so. If I turn, the world will turn with me, and I will get to choose the direction. I feel arrogant, and I feel the right to be so. Isn't the world turning because of me? If I call out to the stars, will they bend their ears to listen? They already seem to be doing so, hanging as low as they are. There is a power there, and it has transferred itself to me. The very trees seem to be bending to my will. I can do no wrong now, not while I live in this world.

But such musings cannot last forever, and regretfully I answer the madly blinking light on my phone. 'Shruti, where are you? Why aren't you taking my calls?'

'I'll tell you later. Are you all dressed?'

'For the last three hours, yes.'

'There's a wine store half a kilometre down this road. Can you get a bottle of champagne from there? Please. We might have something to celebrate.'

'And what about dinner?'

'Oh, eat something, biscuits or something,' I say vaguely. 'Look, just get the champagne. I need to do something important.'

Fortunately for me, Kailash does not protest. Perhaps he has understood the urgency in my voice. I make one more call. 'I'm sorry,' I say to Priya. 'You must be famished.'

'Have you eaten?'

'Of course not. We're supposed to be together. Did you forget I invited you for dinner?'

'Ruts! I thought you had forgotten, you being such a busy woman and all. In fact, I checked with Kailash and even he didn't know where you had disappeared to.'

'I was on a very important mission, actually.'

'More important than dinner?'

'Much more important than dinner. I almost forgot I was hungry, as a matter of fact. But now I'm sooooo hungry.'

'You know, I hate people who talk in riddles. So just tell me straight out what's going on.'

'All right, straight out is that the world has righted itself on its axis, and you're soon going to find out why.'

'And that's being straight?'

'Yes, my dear. And if you want any more answers, I'm afraid you'll have to go to one address that I'm about to give. You'll also get some food to eat there.' And I tell Priya Sasi's address.

'But that's....'

'Yeah, I know. But just go, Priya. Please. For my sake.'

'Ruts....'

'I said please. One last favour for your poor old friend.'

'I don't....'

'Priya, *go*.'

'Oh all right.'

Kailash, when I reach our room, is still missing. I lie down on the bed, completely exhausted but in no way sleepy. I'm quite prepared to stay up all night. In fact, I would like to. I would have liked to go up to the terrace to my favourite spot, but it is now out of bounds for the rest of my life. Let some other student make that her place of relief, and romance. I make do with my bed, where Kailash's body's indentation where he lay earlier on is still visible. The Bernard Shaw book is still lying open, face down, on a page from *Arms and the Man*, and I pick it up to start reading it. Nothing in the play registers though my eyes go through the words systematically. Finally I get up to go and check on the children. There's no need, of course. They are fast asleep. I adjust the sheets over them. The night breeze, as usual, is cool. I wonder if I should call Shaina to thank her for babysitting, but it's late. She would think it odd to hear from me this late at night. I sit in the chair in the room, and allow the children's innocent aura to wash over me. With their tiny snores and snuffles, they soothe the turbulence in me, and before I know it, I have fallen asleep.

Someone's kissing me on my forehead, and it feels like a benediction. I wonder who could be blessing me in this manner, though I feel incredibly grateful for it, as though I have been rescued from the deepest seas. The lips move away, and I stir in protest. The kiss must go on for me to feel secure. My protest must be audible for I hear Kailash's voice in my ear, 'Shruti, wake up. Wake up, darling.'

'You kissed me.'

'Yes.'

'Why did you stop? That was a beautiful kiss.'

Kailash smiles and says, 'Come on, get up, my sleeping beauty. I've brought the champagne.'

'Champagne? What for?'

'I don't know. You asked me to.'

'That's right, I did. Umm, I think we might be celebrating something.'

'What?'

'Come on,' I say briskly. 'Let's not waste time here. I'm starving. Let's go and eat.'

'Something has turned your brain,' says Kailash with a hint of resignation.

'Yes, in the right direction.'

'All right, don't tell me. Be like that.'

Kailash follows me out of the guesthouse, and towards Sasi's house silently. Halfway there, he clasps my elbow and we stop. 'This is where I want to kiss you. Actually,' he says in a conversational tone, 'this is where I want to make love to you. With your permission, of course.'

'Well, you don't have it. This is the IIM, not a country barn.'

'Same difference,' he says with a shrug, deliberately riling me into a crushing retort about the merits of the Indian Institute of Management. Nonetheless, before I know it, I have been enveloped in a tight hug, and Kailash is giving me a proper kiss, one that can still, even after so many years of getting it, turn my stomach to mush.

'What...' I gasp finally.

'That's just to tell you how much I love you.'

Yes, the stars are definitely bending to my command.

Epilogue

'Are you sure?' asks the man at the desk sternly. He has a sour face, as though his task is repulsive, even unnatural.

'Of course I'm sure! *We* are sure,' says the bride, looking at her husband-to-be with a smile that spreads all the way across the room. The groom smiles back, and the rest of the bridal party seems to take a step back, as though it doesn't wish to intrude upon so much love.

A few words, a couple of signatures, a small form filled by the registrar and it's over. The newly weds look dazed. I can't blame them. To enter a new life with the stroke of a pen is a shattering experience. The lack of ceremony only enhances the sense of unreality. In that noisy, shabby place, with its mixture of stinking paper and dust, nobody is given the right to feel married, to feel loved and wanted. The registrar's office of Bangalore, like all registrar offices all over the country, registers everything, lease agreements, property sale agreements, marriages, whatever. Of course, the registrar can't favour marriage. Why should he? It has nothing to do with him, two people affirming their vows. He's just there to ensure that the mandatory forms are filled in, the necessary witnesses are present and, of course, the required fees are paid. If it were two trees getting married, there wouldn't be a problem in that place if all these conditions were met.

We almost stampede out of the ten by ten foot room, glad to breathe some air, even if it is the carbon monoxide laden fumes of Bangalore city that we're breathing. There's traffic everywhere on M. G. Road, on the road, and on the sidewalk, but everyone seems to know that we belong to a marriage party and the traffic automatically skirts around us. We step away from the newly-weds, but they want none of it. The bride links her arm through mine while her husband is instantly surrounded by friends and family, and I know that in some ways this is still a conventional Indian wedding.

If I could live a dream, this would be it. My friend's face, radiant with love and happiness, looking at me. She comes up to me. 'Ruts....'

'Not now. We'll talk later,' I say hurriedly. ' I think Sasi wants to say something to you. You'd better not annoy him today of all days,' I add wickedly, and am once more amazed by the blush that creeps up on Priya's cheeks.

There is a slightly stunned look on everyone's faces at the speed with which things have happened. Priya, more than anyone else, looks dazed, as though she can't understand what she is doing there. Of course she has come completely unprepared for a wedding, especially her own, so her only nod to anything ceremonial is an extra layer of lipstick. Nonetheless, nobody could mistake her for anything other than the bride. Her face radiates excitement.

There's still lots to be done, as Shaina is quick to remind me. 'Ramamurthy is waiting for us at the hotel with the flowers. I've checked with Jaggu. The arrangements are all in place.'

I have barely slept a wink last night and yet my senses are all on high alert. I am going to ensure that Priya doesn't forget this day, ever. It's the least I can do. Of course, I'm aided by Shaina and Jaggu and dozens of others including, surprisingly, Mr Ramamurthy who, as a local man in the know, can get things done quickly and efficiently, and if required, as in the case of getting hold of the registrar, illegally.

There is a party now, one that Priya doesn't know about. Jaggu is waiting with all the arrangements. He has ensured that there is a full guest list, particularly all the professors. Classes have been cancelled for the day, and there's satisfaction in knowing that Chinni will be there to witness the union of the two people who have probably challenged him the most.

I have already said my goodbyes to the institute. We shall not be returning there. From the wedding reception, we shall head straight for the airport, making a brief halt at the hospital where Shridhar is admitted, on the way. There is nothing more to be done. Except, perhaps, sleep, and look back on this time for the next twenty years. It is wrong to say that I met my old friends. I believe those friends are gone forever. Instead, I have made some new friends, and this time, this time, I'm never going to lose them.

You Were There

The most friendless situation is that of the first-time writer who is yet unpublished. The first input she receives is humiliation, at the hands of the publishers, the agents, the other links in the publishing industry whose only job appears to be to reject anyone who dares to put pen to paper for the first time. The fact that I mostly escaped this humiliation I ascribe solely to my MFA Committee at the University of Pittsburgh. Lucy Fischer read my manuscript and painstakingly marked out errors, but at the end told me that she loved my book. Fiona Cheong looked me in the eye and told me that I would see my dream of being published fulfilled very soon. She said the same thing to the audience that came out to listen to me read at the end of my masters' programme. The legendary Chuck Kinder merely smiled when I asked him what he thought of my book. That smile has remained with me in all my waking and sleeping hours, for accompanying it were suggestions that have turned this book from a non-starter to a full-fledged production.

Not only did V. K. Karthika give me a warm and spontaneous welcome in her office, she allowed me the space to unleash all my ideas, all the time flashing that wide-eyed smile that says that though she knows it, she wants to hear it from you. What more could a novice ask for?

The meticulous attention to grammar and articulation that readers will see are Neelini Sarkar's contribution.

Mr Prabir Bhambal's generosity in putting opportunity my way can be forgotten only in hell.

Three years after I wrote the first word, I think of *Cloud 9 Minus One* as a cake. I put together the ingredients. Then my committee helped me bake it. But the gourmet delight that I placed on Karthika's table, covered in icing and cream, was the outcome of the suggestions from many friends.

Piyul and Anjan Mukherjee, Sonia Sharma, Jyoti Sood, Mala Rajraman, Preeti Vyas, Radhika Nayak, Sonu Sahani, Hema Kannan, all stood by me steadfastly and put a supporting hand on my back when I thought I was going to collapse.

As with all births, I stopped getting excited when this particular baby was born, and I was done writing it. Tejaswini Adhikari, Dali Agarwal, Rishabh Arora, Omendu Prakash, Ashni Biyani all put the sparkle back in my eye with their own excitement.

If babies come can mothers be far behind? None of the above would have happened if my mother-in-law Savitri and sister-in-law Asha hadn't patiently defended the Mall fortress against chaos and destruction while I struggled in the US to get my degree.

My mother Madhuri and sister Ilina will always be the two biggest women in my life. Their respect and belief have boosted my self-esteem no end. They believed, therefore I believed.

Yash's delight at being the son of a published author can have no equal in boosting my ego. Harsh, my older son, and now my guide, did everything that I couldn't to get this book in the public eye. They are my fellow travellers on this journey, and to them I owe my deepest gratitude.

This page would be incomplete without Natwar who gave me so much food for thought.

To you, and all the others who so keenly awaited the publication of this book, my heartfelt thanks.